SHELBY Cameron's hands lingered on the collar of Hansi's cloak, softly caressing her neck.

"And how happy my little slave will be to pour chocolate for the famous Captain Jess Taga!"

Hansi shivered under his touch. She said, tartly, "I wish you would not think of me as your slave. I am your wife."

"So that's it?" He went on, "Is that why you have been behaving so badly this past week? Why should you not wish me to speak of you as you are, my love?"

Shelby pulled her toward the long mirror. "Consider. I created that enchanting creature you see before you. Do you actually believe you are the same female I found at Fort Blaine? . . . That bedraggled little flower I plucked out of the mud? Don't you see . . . I molded you with infinite care. Any man would envy me the prize I hold between my hands."

Hansi shuddered and said nothing.

FIRE
DAWN

Virginia Coffman

FAWCETT CREST • NEW YORK

FIRE DAWN

THIS BOOK CONTAINS THE COMPLETE TEXT OF THE ORIGINAL HARDCOVER EDITION.

Published by Fawcett Crest Books, a unit of CBS Publications, the Consumer Publishing Division of CBS Inc., by arrangement with Arbor House.

ISBN: 0-449-23640-4

Printed in the United States of America

10 9 8 7 6 5 4 3 2 1

This book is for
Donnie and Johnny Micciche
with all my love

Book
One

1

HANSI Verin was a child of the sunrise. Ever since childhood, she would perch on her sacred rock, facing the Virginia mountains on the eastern horizon, and wait for the instant when light pierced the Ohio River forest. A few minutes later, as she knew very well, the night watch changed along the fort's high stockade walls, and if she was lucky, she might catch a glimpse of the commander, Lieutenant Colonel Shelby Cameron.

Newly arrived from the British command post at Fort Detroit, Shelby Cameron was the first true gentleman that she had ever seen.

Across the clearing, in front of the heavy, palisaded gates, Hansi moved in the direction of the river to get a better view of the soldiers manning the towers and patrolling the corner lookouts.

On this lovely spring morning in 1775, Hansi had to wait ten long minutes before the morning gun went off, signaling the changing of the guard. Around her the sun rose above the thick growth of the forest, burning off the night frost. She huddled against the cold mist in her mother's long, worn brown camlet cloak, intending to throw back the hood to reveal her face and hair when she glimpsed Shelby Cameron. Her thick, lustrous red hair was one of her chief claims to beauty. The Englishman laughingly called her "Fire-Dawn," the childhood name given to her by her father's Cayuga tribe, much to her Dutch mother's violent disapproval.

Inside Fort Blaine an English boy began his rapid, steady drumbeat. The waves of sound echoing through the great Ohio River forest probably aroused every Shawnee for a hundred leagues, Hansi thought. It was a perpetual reminder of the white presence. Neither Hansi nor her father, Nick Verin, a half-blood Cayuga Indian who served as scout for the army, understood the strange military rituals of the British. Quite different were the campaigns of the Virginia colonials under the command of Captain Jess Taga. Though they served alongside the Redcoats, their tactics were like those of any Shawnee brave. It was commonly said that Jess Taga thought like any full-blooded Indian. The name "Long Knives," which had become synonymous with the Virginia militia, was the compliment of the Shawnees to a respected—although hated—enemy.

Hansi and Captain Taga had been the best and the worst of friends. Her sometime dislike for him was partly due to her mother's constant warnings against his well-known charms. Legend said he always got his way with females. Thus far, he only pulled Hansi's hair, laughed kindly at her when she was dressed in her best, and teased her with talk of "taking her to his bed when she grew up." She did not know which was the more offensive—the idea that she would be happy to go to his bed, or that she was not yet old enough to do so.

Her mother, Eva, having married a half-breed herself, strangely had an absolute terror of Hansi marrying a rugged frontiersman.

Backing farther away from the fort's walls, Hansi tripped over a coil of tree roots. Before she could scramble up, she was seized under the arms and set back on her feet like a clumsy toddler. After a momentary stab of alarm, she recognized that rough overpowering grip. Craning her neck to scowl up at Jess Taga, she tried to lie elegantly. "I happen to be looking for something I lost. I'll thank you to attend to your own affairs."

The captain's teeth flashed in his wind-burned face. "Why bless you, infant, I have no affairs of my own today. How about running away with me? But no—you are still too young!" Gently he brushed off her homespun gown and smoothed back her hair. She could not help but grin up at him. Old Jess, her friend and protector ever since she could remember. He used to toss her high in the air, laughingly calling out her pet name, "Fire-Dawn," as she landed in his outstretched arms. Yet she was not a little girl anymore. She was already seventeen and knew Jess was not just playing with her. But she knew she could never come to love him the way she dreamed of loving Shelby Cameron.

"Jess, stop fooling and tell me the truth about the Shawnees. Will Chief Cornstalk talk peace with you? Do you think there will be trouble? Do you want papa at the parley?"

Jess Taga's high-boned, eagle features with their aquiline nose and weathered eyes softened as he looked at her. He knew he need not mince words.

"If Nick isn't too drunk to make the march. God knows, I need him."

Her mouth twisted, stung by his criticism of Nick. "Papa will be ready," she assured him. "Count on him."

He tilted her chin up with his bent forefinger. "I'll count on *you*, infant. It's a safer bet. Have him at the river door by sunup. And he'd better be sober."

"Ay, sir."

She watched him stride away toward the fort. He moved very lightly, making an attractive figure all in gold, as his worn buckskins caught the morning light.

From the northeast tower overlooking the river a male

voice called down, "Good morning, mistress. How is Miss Fire-Dawn today?"

Out of the corner of her eye Hansi saw Captain Taga stop and glance up at Colonel Cameron's tall figure, black against the rising sun. For her own feminine reasons Hansi was pleased at Jess' interest, then turned her attentions to Colonel Cameron.

"I'm well, sir. Very well indeed." She fancied she saw the kindness in his brown eyes. Already she knew the gentle yet firm way he had of treating women. She knew she loved him when he treated her that way. The colonel was a gentleman, as her mother had said time and time again— brave as well as elegant. Even Jess Taga had been overheard saying, "Whatever this London popinjay may be, he is not a coward." Hansi waved to the soldier and turned toward her parents' cabin.

It had taken Hansi all of her seventeen years to face the truth about her own life. She was a half-breed, neither white nor Indian. Her life was so strikingly different from the lives of the Shawnee and Piankashaw girls her age. She envied the young girls of Fort Blaine. Girls without mixed blood were treated like ladies, treasures to be won with gallantry and respect.

Hansi had seen her own reflection often enough in the still pools of the Ohio, and in the mirrors of the military wives she served at the fort, to know her looks were superior to theirs. She had her Dutch mother's fine complexion and delicate features, her Indian father's lithe grace and physical strength. She did not envy those fort girls their dull, drab, washed-out looks and silly manners. What she longed to know was the warmth and affection between their parents. Hansi had never seen Nick and Eva act like them.

An old settler's cabin had been assigned to Nick Verin's family while he scouted for the British Army. The cabin was even older than the fort, although several times in the last twenty years it had nearly been burned to the ground to retrieve the valuable nails used in its construction.

As usual at this hour, Hansi's mother had come out with a water pail and rags to scrub the stoop, a flat rock laboriously dragged to this spot by Nick Verin in the hope of pleasing his Dutch wife. Eva Verin gestured to her daughter without looking up and fell to her knees to scrub the flat stone. She still looked beautiful from a slight distance. Her pale blonde, fine-spun hair retained its luster and her dainty features haunted many a frontiersman's dreams, but the bitterness of her life was in her eyes and in the angry, bitter twist to her once tender mouth.

Hansi came over to her, trying to communicate some of the pleasure of life that she felt, especially after inhaling the spring air and being greeted by Shelby Cameron.

"Mama, I cleaned that stoop last night. I made it spotless. I scrubbed and scrubbed. Truly, I did!"

Eva Verin glanced up for a moment, then returned to the rock. Her eyes told Hansi she had scarcely heard a word her daughter had said. Her hand continued moving in vigorous circular motions but she was looking toward the fort's palisaded gates. "I saw you talking to someone."

"Captain Taga wanted to know if papa would be ready to guide them tomorrow. The captain wants a meeting with Cornstalk."

"No! No! I'm not talking about that frontier savage. The other. The commander. Hendrickje, listen to me. Shelby Cameron is a real gentleman—"

"Hansi, Mama. Call me Hansi."

"You even scorn your good Dutch name. Are you an animal like your father? Haven't you any ambition to live like a human being? Anywhere but here in this forsaken wilderness? Colonel Cameron is interested in you. I've seen the way he watches you."

Hansi too, in her more self-indulgent moments, allowed herself to imagine Shelby Cameron's love, and life as Mistress Hansi Cameron. But she had the sense to squelch the notion. "Mama, how silly you are! Do you think Colonel Cameron could ever take me as his wife? It's impossible—I am not his kind. And Master Shelby Cameron isn't a man to take a mistress. Everyone says so."

"Hansi, has Colonel Cameron made any suggestion to

you? I mean, do you think he might want you if you indicated that you would accompany him when he leaves the frontier?"

"He isn't going to leave the frontier. He's only just arrived."

"You know what I mean."

"I know exactly what you mean, mama. Let's not talk about it."

Eva Verin stood up. She hurled the soggy rag into the pail, sending a spray of water over the stone stoop and the muddy ground beyond. Hansi was startled, and scared. She had never before heard the harsh note in her mother's soft voice.

"Despise me if you like. But never, never allow yourself to be taken and degraded as I have been. I should have killed myself. Or made them kill me. I thought of it often, but in the end I was too weak. I was foolish enough to think living was better than death." Her hard, choking laughter lashed out at Hansi, who stared at her, seeing a stranger who looked like the terrible stone goddess drawn in one of Eva's old books.

Her mother had never spoken of the beginnings of her relationship with Nick Verin. Hansi had always imagined it was a romantic meeting between dark Nick and blonde Eva, an attraction of opposites. She pictured them when they were in love, although somewhere she doubted it was ever so.

"Mama, don't!" she pleaded. As she reached out to comfort her mother, she saw her father in the cabin doorway. His smoothly braided hair had come loose from its confining leather thong while he slept. His buckskin breeches were stained from last night's rum bout at the fort. He had slept in them and in a homespun shirt that smelled of the rancid bear's grease he used on his hair. These were things about Nick that Hansi had come to expect and love—and which Eva resented anew each day. Hansi saw the pain in his eyes. For the one thing Nick Verin worshiped more than his honor was his wife, and after more than eighteen years was still incapable of earning her love.

Torn by her sympathy for both her parents, Hansi felt that her father needed her more at this moment.

"You will not speak of me like that. I will have respect from my woman. It is my right."

"Respect! Oh, yes. Respect!" Before Eva Verin could blurt out any more of her bitter accusations, Hansi grabbed her father's arm and tugged him into the dark, chilly interior of the cabin.

"She is cross with me, papa, not you. Come and sit down. I'll have breakfast on the table in no time."

Slowly he began to brighten, placing himself carefully in the delicate, ladder-back chair he had made for Eva long ago. It was an absurd, impractical piece of furniture for a meager cabin on the Ohio frontier. Nick happily remembered how, after accepting it, she had stopped dreaming about the streets of New York City which she remembered from her childhood. The peace had only lasted a short while, but Nick always sought new ways to make her forget her misery and love him just a little.

Nick Verin watched his daughter's brisk movement as she set the rickety table with big, imperfect pottery. Nick spooned up his breakfast of pounded corn, honey, butter and milk silently. Eva came inside the cabin, thrusting aside the big square of deerskin that served as a night curtain over the window embrasure. Morning air poured in, ventilating the stuffy room with its pervasive smell of bear's grease. Nick shivered but said nothing.

Eva pulled up a three-legged stool to the table, ignoring Hansi's gesture toward the one faded armchair. To break the silence that she knew could last for hours and sometimes days, Hansi turned to Nick and said with false cheer, "Captain Taga marches to Chief Cornstalk's camp tomorrow. He believes they will parley with him."

Nick grunted. "Parley! The Shawnees hate the Long Knives. They will kill my friend Jess Taga. And then the Puans will have Cornstalk's ear and will whisper their poison. Never trust a Puan."

Eva raised her eyes heavenward, eloquently expressing her own cynicism.

"Well, someone must do something," Hansi said. "The

Shawnees are afraid of the Long Knives, afraid they will bring settlers who take their lands. But Cornstalk trusts you. There isn't a tribe on the frontier who won't take your word.

Eva spoke for the first time. "We are still under civilized English rule, no matter what those troublemakers in Massachusetts say."

Looking up from his breakfast, Nick said matter-of-factly, "The Shawnee Confederacy prefers English rule. The English do not take their lands away. If the English and the rebels go to war, the Shawnees will be most happy. The Shawnees will have the English to help kill Long Knife enemies." He looked around. Hansi and Eva were both listening carefully. They could sense the too-real horrors of a pending battle. Hansi was torn by conflicting loyalties.

"The English will never raise the tribes against us!" Colonel Cameron was her idol; yet Hansi was frontier-born. No child knew better the sufferings of war. The French had used their Indian allies against the English and colonials. Would the English now do the same to their colonies? "Papa! A man like you could prevent war. You must lead Captain Jess tomorrow, please!"

Nick's pride rose to the challenge. His shoulders straightened. His indifferent shrug did not fool Hansi.

"I go. It is understood," Nick said solemnly.

"Thank you, papa."

She almost ran from the cabin, frantic to escape.

2

SHE crossed the quadrangle inside the fort, passing the noisy schoolroom where the children recited aloud under Mrs. Abernathy's stern eye. Hansi heard one group repeat "A Discourse upon Virtue," and "The Whole Duty of Women." Mrs. Abernathy threw Hansi a disapproving look out the window as she flew past. She smiled, glad to have escaped a face-to-face encounter with the ever-scolding Mrs. Abernathy.

A young English sentry called out to her as she walked along. He was climbing a roughly built ladder to reach his post and grinned down at her between the rungs. "If I was going off duty I'd carry your load, Mistress Hansi."

How good to be addressed by a title, like the other girls. She flashed her best smile and pretended to bob a curtsy.

"You are gallant, sir. Many thanks."

"A pleasure, ma'am."

Whatever one might say about innocent redcoat babes in the woods, she thought, their manners were certainly beautiful.

She hurried over to Mrs. Abernathy's to pick up the laundry. Inside sat her yellow-haired daughter, Dolly, who

Hansi always thought was the silliest of all the fort girls, with her airs and gowns! Hansi also knew Dolly had her eye on Colonel Cameron. Dolly reached behind the big storage bin next to the hearth and drew out an exquisite pattern doll.

"Isn't that the dearest, most elegant gown you ever saw?" she asked, pushing it at Hansi. "I must have a gown just like that for the next assembly at the fort. That's what Shelby Cameron calls them, assemblies, just like they do back home in Williamsburg. Oh, Hansi, will you make it for me?"

Hansi tried to be noble about it. She touched the doll's panniered skirts, the very low-cut square neck. She wanted to throw it at Dolly.

"Oh, silly me!" Dolly chirped. "I hope I didn't offend you. I wouldn't dream of saying the horrid things mother says. She has no tact! Please, I must have this gown . . ."

Hansi went into the Abernathy bedchamber and began gathering up the pile of shifts, petticoats and sheets. Dolly came pattering in after her.

"I'll do it for a full guinea," Hansi said slowly. But to herself she thought, guinea or no guinea, the idea of making a gown for Dolly to attract Shelby Cameron with is horrible. "One guinea," she repeated evenly, gathering up the wash and tying it inside the sheet. She slung the bundle over her shoulder and started out. In her own bitter mood she felt amused by Dolly's desperation. Meanwhile, Dolly had climbed up into her parents' big alcove bed, pushed the heavy, dusty curtains aside and started pounding the mattress.

"You must do it. That gown is mine. I just know it was meant for me." The beginnings of a tantrum had always served their purpose with her parents, but they only provoked a laugh from Hansi, who continued on her way.

Dolly jumped off the bed and raced after her.

"Hansi, please! Listen to me. I think mama might be willing to pay if she was sure Colonel Cameron would come courting me." She considered this romantic picture. "I know she would. He likes me already. I'll wear my flowered dimity this afternoon, if only the weather is warm enough. And I'll put myself in his way at dinner. We are dining with him tonight, you know."

Hansi went out the door with Dolly's voice trailing after her. "You know, Hansi?"

Feeling wicked and implacable, Hansi said over her shoulder, "Yes, I know. And it will cost you one guinea."

Hansi smiled to herself as she walked out of the Abernathy quarters into the early morning sunlight. She put Dolly out of her mind and concentrated on smiling as soldiers called out to her, knowing her hair glowed in the light and that they treated her like a very special lady. Feeling happy again, she wondered if she'd be lucky enough to see the colonel.

She hurried along the trail, through the greenery interlaced overhead, dripping as the last of the night frost steamed away under the sunlight. The willows and delicate birches were alive with chattering birds.

The cove she headed for was out of sight of the fort, lying at the bottom of a footpath. It proceeded westward toward a turn in the river where Shawnee hunting parties crossed after forays into the new settlements in the Kentucky country. She looked around and set to work.

As she was spreading the shifts and petticoats over the bushes to dry in the sun, she sensed a strange movement through the dogwood bushes that hid her cove from the main course of the river. A canoe passed slowly downstream moving in toward shore, an unlikely move so close to the fort. The Indian with the paddle did not have the traditional shaven head and scalp lock of the enemy Shawnee. His blood-red single feather, stuck haphazardly into the braid at the nape of his neck, was limp and soiled. It was a combination rarely found among the great tribes of the Ohio.

She hurried up the path with the soaking laundry in both hands for a better view of the river's edge. The Indian in the canoe looked like a Puan, a tribe long ago decimated by disease and war. The few who remained had attached themselves to other tribes. Hansi, sharing her father's tribal prejudices, mistrusted them completely.

As Hansi ducked behind a clump of dogwood, the Indian looked up, then settled against a tree to wait. It was a tiresome wait for Hansi, who did not know what she herself was waiting for or hiding from. After a while, she gave up and began to hang the sheet across two bushes. At that moment, she heard more movements from the Puan's direction, and turned to watch. This time she caught a glimpse of a second man, half hidden but taller than the Puan and wearing buckskin breeches and jacket. What intrigued Hansi even more than the Puan's presence was the furtiveness of the meeting. Something about it felt wrong. Remembering what she knew of Jess' plans for a peace parley, she knew it might be serious.

Meanwhile, it would be well to make certain neither of the conspirators knew she had seen them. She grabbed the sheet and crept down to the cove. As she collected the garments, she was shaken by a sudden spurt of angry words.

"I'm English, damn you! No French, you understand?" The white man spoke with a French accent. "The French take the side of the settlers. They are the enemy. Remember that."

They were moving closer to the cove. What had the French language to do with an affair between a Long Knife scout and a Puan brave, Hansi wondered. The Indian might be expected to speak the language common to the Six Nations, or the Shawnee Confederacy, though some of them knew French and English tolerably well.

Hansi scrambled to the path with her hands full. Close behind her the Indian asked something which the buckskin man answered in accented English: "Why? It is simple. These settlers will aid the colonials in the rebellion. Soon the whole frontier will be at war. And if you Indians take the side of the colonials against the king, you side with the very people who steal your lands. The British Redcoats are your only friends. You understand me now?"

The voice of the man in buckskins was vaguely familiar. Hansi tried to place him.

"You think I am stupid," the Indian said. "I am not. I know there is a Hairbuyer who promises to pay for scalps of settlers and colonials. I must be paid as the Hairbuyer would pay me."

The rumble of anger in the voice of the Puan named Yellow Painter reminded Hansi of her father's slow, terrible anger when his pride was wounded. But the Puan seemed interested only in money.

The men had reached the cove. Hansi managed to scramble to the top of the path out of their range. It was impossible to see them without being seen. She hurried toward the fort, stopped once more on a high cliff above the river and looked back. This time she was able to see the Puan moving downstream again in his canoe.

But where was his white buckskin-clad accomplice?

The attack came so suddenly her first thought was of a gigantic snake coiled around her neck. Intolerable pressure squeezed her throat, cutting off all breath. Her arms went limp, scattering the laundry over the ground. She clawed at the hand applying the deadly pressure to her throat.

The muscular arm was covered to the wrist by buckskin. It relaxed its pressure slightly, as if her attacker wanted to examine her to see if she was unconscious. She gathered her waning energy and screamed until her attacker's other hand cuffed her so hard across the side of the head her ears rang with the blow.

Half-conscious, she heard a crackling noise, like branches and twigs breaking. The pressure around her throat was gone as quickly as it had come. Her body dropped to the ground.

Her attacker scrambled away, his feet showering her with dirt, which blinded her momentarily when she tried to open her eyes.

A minute later, another male voice above her demanded, "What in damnation are you doing on the ground?"

By the time she recovered enough to open her eyes and croak out, " . . . tried choke me," Jess Taga had her on her feet and was dusting her off. She burst into sobs.

"There, there, infant, slowly!"

Her throat ached, and there was a terrific pounding in her head. She could scarcely believe it had happened.

"A man in buckskin tried to kill me."

Captain Taga was gathering up her scattered wash. He straightened to his formidable height and stared at her.

"An Indian? You must have surprised one of Cornstalk's men, trying to spy on the fort's defenses. He's gone now. That scream of yours is pretty effective."

"No. I think it was a white man. I felt the sleeve . . . the fringe . . ." He put the soiled laundry in her arms, and she added, "Thank you."

Jess Taga saw the terror in her face and he quickly moved through the reeds and vines to investigate.

She smoothed the laundry in her arms and tried to calm down. She forced herself to swallow. No irreparable damage had been done. But she did not believe Captain Jess' explanation was right. She was certain her attacker was the same as the companion of the Puan she'd overheard. Obviously, the two men were responsible for the footprints she saw. Perhaps the white man, finding one of the shifts she had dropped, decided to wait for her return.

With the grace of a Shawnee, Jess Taga materialized again out of the woods and onto the path before her. She was stunned by the sight of him in those old fringed buckskins. From her memory of the assailant's sleeve, Jess might well be that man! She was not sure about the voice. She remembered it as strained and angry, but she could not believe Captain Taga could have been plotting anything with the sinister Puan, Yellow Painter. He might annoy her when he teased her, but he was not likely to sell out to the Indian tribes, who had been his bitter enemies since the French and Indian Wars.

"I saw your Redskin friend," Jess reported. "He's a good way down river now. His hair wouldn't be Shawnee." He held up the two shifts she had dropped. "But I did find your pretties."

"Not mine," she said indignantly, forgetting in her feminine vanity that this man *might* be the same one who had just tried to kill her.

"The wind must have blown them into the bushes," he suggested. Smiling, he went on in his teasing way, "They do seem a trifle large. Do you wrap them around you?"

He matched his words with action, reaching around her body with playful hands, but she continued to wonder if she hadn't already known the power of that muscular arm that day, and wrenched out of his hold. And even if he were not the man who had attacked her . . . well, too many other girls on the frontier had let him have his way, as Eva reminded her time and time again. They had found themselves with child and abandoned to the half-blood trappers, traders and hangers-on of the forts.

She did not want to fall in love with Jess Taga, but *please,* she thought, do not let it be Captain Jess who had tried to . . . she would not allow herself to complete the thought.

Jess Taga dropped the shifts on top of her laundry, put one hand on either side of her slender waist, and whirled her around in the air.

"Stop! My head! The clothes! You will make me have to wash them again. I must go and tell them what I overheard . . . what happened to me." Almost too late, she remembered that she should keep her knowledge and suspicions from him. He wasn't, after all, *beyond* suspicion, she reminded herself.

He only laughed and promised, "I will help you wash them. Come, don't tease, infant. You are as warm and full of spring juices as I am."

He pulled her to him. Obviously, he did not believe in her protests. She reverted to kicking him as close to the groin as possible. But he was ready for her, and weakened the backs of her legs by imprisoning them with one of his. When he kissed her, he fooled her again. She had been sure he would aim at her lips and she forced her head away. Instead, he kissed her exposed throat and showed signs of moving farther down. His touch aroused thrilling sensations, totally new to her body. It took her several seconds to work up the resolve to break away from him before he succeeded in uncovering her rich, full breasts.

She kept telling herself that if he were the attacker, he would have finished the task by now. On the other hand, if he were the man she loved, she would not also be thinking of Shelby Cameron. . . . But at the moment she could not think of anything shocking enough to say, as she shyly pulled up the collar of her gown and stepped back.

"You see?" He laughed. "It scarcely hurts at all."

She snatched the undergarments off the ground where they had fallen. "Tell me the truth. Did you hide the shifts in those bushes?"

"Why the devil would I do that?" He walked beside her to the fort. "Don't you know that little girls shouldn't wander out alone in Shawnee country? Not that you wouldn't add something special to any Shawnee long house."

She was still thinking about how those shifts had gotten into the bushes. Obviously, when the Puan's white friend found them he had tossed them into the bushes and laid in wait for her. Then Captain Jess could not possibly be guilty, she thought with relief.

Returning to the conversation, she laughed sarcastically. "You Virginians imagine you are the only ones who know anything of the frontier. I was born out here."

"So was I. We are the same kind, Fire-Dawn. Never forget that."

She glanced at him. He had spoken in such a flat, calm voice it seemed to give the simple statement more weight.

He asked her suddenly, "Is that true about the Indian who tried to strangle you?"

Was he trying to find out whether she really had seen the two men? She wanted to ask him about the Hairbuyer, but was afraid to mention it.

"I stumbled and lost the laundry when a man tried to

choke me. I don't know whether he was Indian or white. If you saw an Indian, then that's who it must have been." She decided to play a game to test him. "I did see a ferocious-looking bobcat this morning. One of those the Indians call 'panthers'."

"Painters," he corrected her.

"That's right. Golden painters. No. Yellow painters."

Jess did not respond.

3

INSIDE the fort her attention was caught by the big stout second-in-command, Major Geoffrey Hay. She waved, causing him to stare across the quadrangle at her with one eyebrow raised unpleasantly in his pudding face.

"Sir? I must see Colonel Cameron, please."

"Eh? Shouldn't wonder," the fat major remarked lazily. He paid no more attention to her but addressed himself to Jess. "You, there, captain, see that this laundress delivers her—ah—merchandise, and leaves. We can't have these females hanging about our men on duty."

Hansi was so angry she hardly knew how to reply.

At that moment a shy young militiaman, openly infatuated with Hansi, started across the grounds.

"Master Albion—please!" she called out to him.

Her plea had hardly been necessary. The boy was already running toward her.

"Miss Hansi," the boy gushed, "are you in trouble? Captain, excusing your presence, Miss Hansi's a friend of mine. I'll oblige her."

Jess looked at Hansi with an amused gleam in his eye.

Haughtily, she said, "Thank you, captain. Master Albion will help me now. I must see the commander."

Albion beamed at this surprising turn of good luck and gallantly offered his arm. Taga yielded ground with an exaggerated bow and strolled away.

"If you've a mind to, we'll get shut of this first," Albion suggested. Under his escort they deposited the clothing, wrinkled and badly in need of ironing, at the Abernathy's and went toward the commander's quarters, leaving a dumbfounded Mrs. Abernathy complaining to her daughter before Hansi was out of hearing:

"Now that Indian hussy is wheedling her way in to see Shelby Cameron. On business. Ha! Likely! Maybe you've been too forward with Shelby Cameron. If you have, I swear I'll—"

Feeling much put upon from all quarters, Dolly insisted, "I never did a thing, mama. I was very cool, very careful—"

"Just as I thought. Too cool. Too careful. Giving yourself airs. Well, Dolly, you will never win him that way. That redheaded half-breed knows all the tricks."

Hansi and Albion exchanged glances. Seeing that Hansi was amused, the boy grinned. "Captain Jess—he calls you Fire-Dawn, Miss Hansi. Fire-Dawn. That's real pretty. Ol' Jess says you're the most beautiful woman on the frontier. And he ought to know."

Much as she could like Jess Taga at moments, it annoyed her that his Long Knives behaved as if he were the great spirit Manitou, or, at the very least, the King of England! She said tartly, "I suppose if he called me the ugliest creature on the Ohio River, you'd say 'he ought to know.' "

"If you could follow Captain Jess in battle, or through Shawnee country, you'd see why we feel the way we do. He even saved the colonel. Them Puans are mighty treacherous."

"It wasn't the colonel's fault that he didn't know Puans are outlaws," she retorted, feeling the need to defend the colonel's ability. "He hired them in good faith to lead him to Fort Blaine. After all, the British and the Shawnees used to get on well, and he couldn't tell the difference, I expect."

"All the same," Albion insisted, "it took Jess only two men to send them Púans high-tailing it off to the forest."

Hansi ignored this. "I've heard Jess flirts with every female west of Fort Pitt."

He gave her a boyish side glance. "He pretends to, anyway. We Long Knives have our suspicions. He's awful taken with a certain fire-haired young lady, don't forget. We joked him about it one night last winter, up near Shawnee Town. He said ask him again when you was a grown-up lady."

"What!"

"He said you didn't know your own mind yet. But he was only joking us right back. You could tell."

Her own pleasure over this news confused her. She tried to assure herself that it was only his daredevil courage which attracted her.

"Colonel Cameron is brave, too," Hansi countered. "They say when he commanded Fort Detroit he made treaties with all the tribes that weren't under the French thumb. That's better than making war."

Albion shook his head. "Beg pardon, Miss Fire-Dawn, but any English fop can make peace. Jess is the kind you can count on in a bad hole. Ask Lieutenant Hibbert. Jess got his wife and twin babies out of the settlement at Point Pleasant a month ago. Near thing that was. A raiding party led by Cornstalk himself had the house surrounded. Jess got the family out through the root cellar."

"I heard about it."

She had thrilled to hear the details from Mistress Hibbert when the family reached Fort Blaine, but every word of praise for Jess now seemed a backhanded slap at Colonel Cameron. Jess might be the frontier's hero but he never made Hansi feel like a lady.

The huge figure of Major Geoffrey Hay suddenly

loomed up, barring their way into the southeast blockhouse where Shelby Cameron had his quarters.

"If the wench insists on seeing the colonel, I will take charge, boy. No need keeping you from your duties." His insulting manner did not fool Hansi. Through the touch of his fat fingers on her wrist she felt the hard bone.

Albion looked at the major uneasily. "Reckon I best get along."

Hansi smiled, giving him her free hand, and said, "Thank you, Albion. You have been very kind."

He stiffened proudly. "It was nothing, mistress." Then he strutted across the quadrangle like a young peacock.

Major Hay rapped on the long door of Lieutenant Colonel Cameron's quarters. A young Redcoat soldier greeted Hansi with a grin that froze to an officially blank expression at the sight of Major Hay.

Lieutenant Colonel Cameron sat behind a long mahogany desk that appeared absurdly out of place on the frontier. He had been studying a map of the Ohio River forest from Fort Pitt to the Mississippi. In the center of this region was Fort Sacklin. Sacklin's importance lay in its strategic position. Whoever controlled Fort Sacklin commanded all trade and communication with the inland Indian confederacies.

Hansi was certain Colonel Cameron had not noticed her until he said quietly, "Major, I think you may trust Miss Verin. It is highly unlikely that she will scalp me in your absence."

Major Hay drawled, "As you say, sir. But may I remind you, this laundress is hardly the most reliable witness. Her father is a known drunk. We've no reason to believe any preposterous tale she tells."

Hansi caught her breath. Did the major fear her story? How else would he know about her "preposterous" tale? But why would Colonel Cameron believe her over his own officer? She had no proof. She felt frightened and sorry she had come. In spite of the commander's attractive features, Hansi suspected they could freeze into a forbidding mask.

The colonel turned to Major Hay. After an uncomfortable silence he said sternly, "You may go."

"But if I may suggest—"

"You may go, major. Now."

The major left the room with great reluctance. Hansi was sure he hoped to overhear what she had to tell Colonel Cameron. But the colonel said nothing until the rough-hewn door was closed behind Major Hay's back. Cameron's brown eyes washed over Hansi warmly. She felt so relieved she almost stammered.

"Thank you, sir. He seems to hate me, but I don't know what it is I've done to him."

Cameron laughed, got up and drew a chair over to the side of the desk opposite him.

"I think we may assume the major dislikes you for no other reason than that he has heard too much praise of you. I have frequently compared you to the other young ladies at the fort—to your advantage. Now, tell me what you want to say, because Major Hay is right about one thing—I do have a great many decisions to make, and not enough time."

"Ay, sir. You see, we are in danger." Nervously, she sat on the edge of her chair. He put a hand out and touched her reassuringly.

"Well, then, take what time you need. I trust you, Fire-Dawn."

She was thrilled that he had used her Indian name. Did he return at least a little of the feeling she had for him? He had noticed her, singled her out. That was a start.

He helped her. "I gather that you spotted some danger. It may have been a few Shawnees spying upon our fortifications." As always, his smile softened what might have sounded like indifference.

"It was not what I saw, but what I heard, sir," she put in, hardly daring to make any correction for fear of losing the gentle understanding he showed her. "I saw a Puan in a canoe. He came ashore, though the fort has no dealings with Puans. My father and others do not trust them."

"Yet we treat with the Shawnees, who are the avowed enemy of the whites."

"Pardon, sir. Not the enemy of the English Regulars. Their real enemies are the colonials, the Long Knives and American settlers. And the Shawnee word is good. Not like the Puan. But the strange thing was the person this Puan met. And their conversation."

She suspected she had lost his attention. He continued to look at her but she could have sworn his singular, motionless quiet indicated that his thoughts were wandering. When the silence became uncomfortable he came back to the subject.

"Excuse me. Yes. Their conversation. Who was this other man?"

"The Puan was called Yellow Painter. The white man spoke of someone he called a hairbuyer."

Cameron looked puzzled. "Hairbuyers? Didn't some of that occur among the French during the last hostilities? Paying savages for the scalps of enemy whites?" He considered for a moment, then asked, "Have you seen this fellow dressed in buckskin around the fort? What about his voice?"

She began to be frightened. She had hoped he would convince her that the Hairbuyer business meant a different matter altogether. Perhaps an affair between tribes. But in the innermost recesses of her mind she had known what it meant—a white paying Indians for white scalps.

"I can't say exactly, sir. A deep voice. French accent. It might have been anyone trying to disguise his voice, perhaps to disguise his identity from the Puan, though I think they knew each other. And so many men wear buckskin. The sutlers bringing in goods. The scouts. Some of the Kentucky settlers. And nearly all of the Long Knives."

Colonel Cameron took a deep breath. His relief was evident. Obviously, he did not want to think one of his own British regulars was guilty. "That is it, of course. Either a trapper from the fort or any of a score of men. Perhaps even one of the Long Knives." He added with a whimsical shrug, "We must admit the Virginians behave as if they owned the territory."

"In a sense, they do, sir," she reminded him. "This land is part of Kentucky County, and Kentucky belongs to Virginia."

"The Cherokees and Miamis—and certainly the Shawnees—would give you an argument on that."

"True, sir."

He considered the matter, studying his fingers spread flat on the desk. Then he thought of something and looked up. "If what you tell me has any significance, you may be in serious danger. Have you told anyone about this?"

"No one. Except . . ." She touched her throat. Even the touch was a painful reminder of the attack. "I think the man in buckskin knows. Someone tried to attack me less than an hour ago. I saw only his arms. He was frightened off."

"Thank God for that. One thing is clear—you need protection. I will have a man assigned to guard you until we are certain of this buckskin fellow's identity. Meanwhile . . ." He took her hands and spread his own under them; she tried to keep her fingers from curling up with nervousness and excitement as her hands lay in his. "These fingers are too careworn for one so young," he said.

She tried to withdraw her hands but he would not let them go. "You mistake me, Hansi. I find them beautiful. I hope some day your life will free those exquisitely shaped fingers for something more pleasant than scrubbing the clothes of wretched harpies."

That made her smile. She was not too surprised when he brought her fingers lightly to his lips, but even that slight touch triggered in her all kinds of delicious notions.

They were interrupted by Jess Taga, who strode into the room hard upon his brisk knock. "My lieutenant, Kentuck Helm, has just returned with a report you should know about, colonel."

Cameron's lips tightened at the interruption, but he

gave no other sign of his irritation. "Certainly, captain," he said. "Miss Verin was just leaving. She came to report on her father's observations."

Jess nodded to Hansi and stepped closer to the desk. "Hansi can hear this. She knows as much as her father does about this country."

He scowled at the map spread out on the desk. "Sir, if you intend to rely upon that map for a campaign, we will all be in serious trouble."

Unruffled by the Long Knife's abrupt manner, Cameron asked mildly, "May I ask why? It was furnished by Geoffrey Hay after considerable work and negotiations with map makers."

"Because, sir, it is a map used by the French twenty years ago. The positions of most of the tribes have radically shifted. The Six Nations—"

"The Six Nations hold no authority along the Ohio. They are far to the north, as this map indicates. They would be intruding upon the Shawnee Confederation if they threatened us."

"I do not wish to contradict you, sir. Merely to point out that my scouts report seeing Cayugas, Mingoes, and even Piankashaws in the Shawnee towns across the Ohio. You and I, sir, have both encountered Puans. Isn't it possible that Chief Cornstalk called to unite the tribes against all whites on the frontier? It would be the ideal time for them, knowing that civil war is threatened in every colony on the coast."

"The Long Knives would like us to believe that. We British have always gotten on well with the redskins. It is you colonials with whom the Shawnees are at war. . . . And, captain, don't forget, if civil war does break out the redskins will be on the British side." He paused, then added with a wry smile, "I may take your advice and have a new map produced. Would you send in Major Hay as you leave? And Miss Verin, I'll see to that other matter."

She curtsied and left with Jess, still blushing as Cameron's flattering words repeated in her thoughts.

4

HANSI found her mother cleaning the kitchen house, a small cabin behind their living quarters. Eva Verin smiled faintly and went on scrubbing down the hearth. Breathing hard and repeatedly wiping sweat off her forehead, she continued to work while she questioned Hansi about her morning.

"Did you see anyone interesting?"

"Ever so many interesting people. Captain Taga, for instance."

Eva waved a scrub brush at her. "Stay away from that rogue. I know his sort. Seducing females, like as not. And for what? A life on the frontier. I don't trust him and his Long Knives. They think like Indians. And Taga's got Indian blood. Do you want to end up like me?"

Hansi ignored the slur on her father. "The Indians hate Jess and his Long Knives. But I saw others today. A Puan. And Major Hay, the colonel's new aide. Many people."

Her mother stopped working. "And?"

Hansi smiled, enjoying the suspense. "Yes, mama. And

Colonel Cameron. And I know he likes me. He calls me
Fire-Dawn."

Eva Verin struck the hearth with her brush. "Well, it's
a beginning, though these aristocrats always marry their
own kind. Still, the fact is his precious aristocrat females
can't be with him now, and you can. It must be your task
to make him forget his aristocrats."

"Oh, mama, don't!" It was sickening when her mother
suggested she go to any lengths to trap a kind and decent
man whom she truly cared for.

Hansi left the kitchen cabin abruptly. Her father's
whole life centered on his getting one smile or kind word
from his wife. As she passed her mother's cracked and
unsilvered mirror, she examined her own reflection, wondering what there was about her that could possibly make
Shelby Cameron care deeply about her.

She pulled a comb rapidly through the tangled auburn
lengths of her hair. It should be smooth and neat like the
hair of the young women at the fort, she thought.

She made a face at her reflection. Nothing in that
mirror resembled the features of ladies she knew—the
kind of lady Shelby Cameron's wife should be. She had
always considered herself lucky to possess this face and
features. She had heard a soldier call her mouth "tender"
some months ago and had regarded this as a compliment,
but this day none of her features seemed right.

Through the open flap of deerskin used to cover the
window she heard a voice that startled her. It sounded
like the man in buckskin speaking in French to Nick. She
went to the window and looked out, taking care not to be
seen. Her father and a heavy, bearded man in buckskin
breeches were discussing the bed coverlet of skins that
Nick Verin had painstakingly made for Eva. The man
was admiring the robe.

"You are a fool, my friend," he said in his rapid,
colloquial French. "You should let me sell this robe in
Fort Pitt or, better yet, in Philadelphia. Then you can go

with your woman and daughter to live in one of those pretty French towns on the Mississippi."

"No, Daniel," Nick said firmly, "the robe is for my woman. When it rains, she will be warm."

Thank God! At least her father and the bearded man were not talking treason or the sale of human scalps.

The bearded man slapped the robe, shook his head and stalked away toward the fort. Hansi waited until he had passed the corner of the cabin. Then she went out to her father. He showed her the robe proudly. She tried to admire it, but immediately knew Eva would reject it as she had all Nick's attempts to please her. She could not bear the thought of Nick's happiness once again crushed by Eva's bitter anger. Besides, she was anxious to discover the identity of the bearded man he had called "Daniel."

"Who was your friend, papa?"

He caressed the robe. "Daniel Greathouse. A trapper from the Muskingum country. He is a trader now. They promise to make him sutler here at the fort."

"What blood has he?"

Her curiosity baffled him. "French blood. And some English, maybe. And some tribal blood. What tribe I don't know. Why do you ask questions? Because you don't like the robe?"

"Papa, I love the robe . . . but wouldn't it be better to use it as a cloak for yourself when the snow comes? Or to sell it for a lot of money? Money would give mama a chance to visit New York and see all the places where she grew up. Then she would see it isn't so grand compared to our great street—the river out there."

Nick shook his head emphatically. "No. She would not come back. I would never see her again."

Hansi touched his strong, dark hand. She tried to hide the aching pity she felt for him and show him only her love. She hugged him.

He could not be cross with her for long and gradually raised one arm, patted her shoulder. "Well . . . well . . . you are a good girl."

It was not until they separated and Nick returned to

sizing the robe that Hansi saw a shadow falling across the cabin's ground. She moved in time to catch a glimpse of Daniel Greathouse as he was admitted to the fort. He had waited and heard her entire conversation with her father. Was he suspicious of her? Had he any reason to believe she knew of his meeting with the Puan and his damning conversation about a Hairbuyer?

She shivered as she remembered Shelby Cameron's warning of her danger.

Shortly before sundown while Hansi was basting the venison haunch on its turning spit, she was startled to see a ruffled Dolly Abernathy come fluttering out of the fort, rushing toward the Verin cabin. Eva Verin went out to meet the girl and Hansi was impressed anew at her mother's grace and elegance in the company of her own kind. They spoke for a minute or two.

When they came in Eva was angry and resentful, Dolly twittering as usual.

"Mother bought the silk for me! And father gave me a guinea-piece. Here it is, Hansi. Now you have to make me a gown."

How easy it all was for girls like Dolly Abernathy! The silk from one parent, the money from the other, and easy access to Shelby Cameron. It wasn't fair, Hansi thought. But I know about the Hairbuyer and Daniel Greathouse! I could see Shelby Cameron this very minute if I chose to. . . .

Dolly slipped the guinea-piece into the deep pocket of Hansi's pinafore. Hansi had a strong impulse to tear it out of her pocket and throw it in the girl's smug face. Hansi's fingers curled around the coin.

Eva said abruptly, "My daughter is too busy. She cannot help you, Miss Dolly. Another time."

But Hansi had a better idea. "Mama, I must collect the dress lengths and the pattern doll. May I go to the fort with Miss Dolly?"

Dolly clapped her hands. Eva shrugged, stepped aside, and watched the two girls leave.

"Hansi, I will look divine," Dolly gushed. "I know it. Colonel Cameron adores me in blue."

"Has he told you so?" Hansi asked sourly.

"Certainly not . . . yet. It would be most improper. But he said he liked the color sky blue. And in less than an hour we shall all be dining together in his quarters. That is the first step."

Once they were inside the gate, Hansi said, "I'll come to your quarters later, Miss Dolly. I have business with Colonel Cameron."

Dolly protested. "But you cannot see the officers at this hour, Hansi!"

The girl was right. By the time Hansi reached Colonel Cameron's quarters through the smoke of campfires and the succulent odor of roasting meat and fish, the commander's area was cordoned off by redcoat soldiers. She tried to peer between the warped shutters but a soldier set his rifle against the wall and gently lifted her off the narrow plank walk onto the ground.

"Orders, Miss Hansi. Sorry."

The door of the colonel's quarters opened and Captain Jess Taga came out, talking to Major Hay. She stepped behind the stacked rifles of the Redcoat soldiers now at mess.

"The only fact we have is the buckskins," Jess said. "May I point out, major, that it is going to be difficult to find a man on the Ohio who doesn't wear them."

"I do not wear them, captain."

Jess Taga laughed. "It would take a herd of buckskins to cover that splendid frame of yours."

"At all events, you wear buckskins and I do not."

"Others besides my men wear buckskins upon occasion."

"Frankly, I do not know one of your men from the other, captain."

Jess considered him with interest. "You are trying with such relish to make me your Hairbuyer's friend, I think you must really believe in the story."

"Don't you?" the major asked.

Jess Taga said nothing.

Hansi caught her breath. Jess had obviously guessed a part of her danger from the moment he rescued her that morning. But how had Major Hay discovered it except by his own guilty knowledge? She was only partially relieved by Jess' remark when he caught sight of her. It was as if he tried to warn her.

"My men have been through the thickets a dozen times today. Any of them might have seen the Puan and our friend in buckskins. If the colonel won't say where he got the information, how can I be expected to guess, major?"

"Well, Taga," the major announced, puffing out the pouches of his squirrellike cheeks, "I suggest you discover which of your men is the informer and which the man in buckskins that he saw."

Jess grinned. "Oh, in that matter I am like you. I don't know one from the other. They are all alike to me."

The major snorted his contempt of this evasion. "Between you and me, I think Colonel Cameron's informer was one of the children attached to the fort. Perhaps, as I suggested before"—his pale eyes flicked over Hansi with only the vaguest pause before his gaze encompassed others of the fort's civilian population—"perhaps any of the females one sees everywhere underfoot."

Jess shrugged. "Possibly. By the by, major, your redbelly boys look very like my own Long Knives when I see them outside the fort in buckskins, as I saw them today."

"Nonsense, captain, nonsense. I must be off. We regulars do not have the free time of you lucky Virginians."

Jess asked airily, "Off to find the Puan's buckskin friend—the arch-villain in this little melodrama?"

The big major hesitated. "And who might that be?"

"The employer of our man in buckskin. The one called the Hairbuyer."

The major dismissed this with contempt. "I have strong doubts that any such creature exists. Hairbuyer, indeed! Whose hair would he be purchasing? We are not at war with anyone. Unless it be the Shawnees across the river."

"You forget the colonists, the settlers," Jess reminded him. "My men coming in from Fort Pitt tell me the Massachusetts Colony has been in a state of rebellion since mid-April when they fired on the regulars." His easy chuckle followed the major, who went haughtily on his way.

Treating Hansi with the same familiarity he had used toward the lordly Englishman, Jess said, "Come along, infant. This is no place for you without protection. What ails that fool father of yours that he lets you wander about alone?"

"My father knows perfectly well that I can look out after myself. And I daresay I am a deal more safe among these redcoats than among your Long Knives."

"Certainly . . . certainly. My Virginians can appreciate a beauty through any disguise."

"Disguise!"

"What else would you call that faded horror you are wearing? It may have done very well for a thin-blooded Dutch woman like your mother, but you deserve better."

She colored and tried to think of something equally insulting to say to him, but he had disarmed her with his implied compliment and she ended with a cowardly shrug. Nor did she make the indignant complaint she should have made when he put an arm around her waist and escorted her through a crowd of his own Virginians, who stopped eating long enough to gape at them and call out friendly if lewd suggestions.

Hansi savored his company, feeling the sinews of that lean, tough arm that encircled her waist so warmly. That arm in its worn, fringed buckskin . . .

She assured herself yet again that he could not be connected with Daniel Greathouse. On sudden impulse she asked, "Do you know a trader—French, I think— called Greathouse?"

She was surprised by his easy response. "Fellow has bribed someone in authority at the fort. He is to be appointed sutler by the army. Your father, among others, recommended him. Why?"

That silenced her. She could only be thankful that fate

had kept her from reaching Colonel Cameron this evening.

A minute later they were accosted by Mrs. Abernathy, who popped out of her lodgings demanding to know what had detained Hansi. The woman was still wearing her day dress of flowered challis with a knit shawl over her thick upper arms, but her iron gray hair had already been arranged for the dinner in the commander's quarters, piled high on her large, strong-jawed head.

"Hendrickje, where are your wits? You must come and iron today's wash. It has been sadly treated. And here is the material for Dolly's gown—the ribbons and silks and all you will need."

Then she excused herself to Jess and drew Hansi aside. "My child, you allow that ruffian great familiarities. I am persuaded your dear mother would not approve. Whatever her misfortunes, your mother has always behaved like a lady."

Furious at her words, Hansi looked up sweetly and with a touch of innocence in her voice said, "I understand, ma'am. I will remember in future to be seen only in the company of gentlemen like—Colonel Cameron." She bared her teeth at Mrs. Abernathy's retreating back to Jess, who grinned broadly.

"Give 'em as good as they send, Hansi," he advised her. "Never let the old biddies get the better of you or they'll tread on you every chance they get."

"All the same, I wasn't a lady. It's awful, Captain Jess. Do you know what I wish for more than anything else in all my life? I wish I could sweep into a ballroom where all the crystal lusters are blazing, and everyone is looking at me. I am in a splendid ball gown, and—" She thought but she did not add, *and I am on the arm of Colonel Shelby Cameron.*

As if he read the dreamy look in her eyes, Jess shook her in a friendly way.

"In the end you would come back to your own kind. The world of the Abernathys and the Camerons is not half worthy of you, Hansi. It's a tight, closed-in, stifling world. Remember that when you bloody your fists pounding on their door."

Nick Verin came toward them as they crossed the fort. There was a long-time, easy camaraderie between him and Jess. They never stood on ceremony and, unlike Eva, Nick hoped his daughter would marry Jess Taga. Their friendship baffled Hansi, who knew that most men with Indian blood on the frontier feared the Virginian.

Nick said, "My thanks, captain. My girl should not be out after sunset, and well she knows it."

Jess gave him an informal salute and turned Hansi over to her father. His golden eyes narrowed as he warned Nick, "We may be in for a renewal of scalp buying."

While Hansi watched her father anxiously, he sucked in his breath with genuine dismay. "Buying the hair of the settlers and other whites? But the army—can it not stop this thing?"

"My men have just brought news from the coast. The rebellion is spreading like grassfire. Virginia has been on the verge for months. Why should the army protect those at war with them?"

Nick considered the rapidly darkening forest beyond the river. "It will be bad, Jess. Worse than before."

"Have you any notion who might be back of this hair buying talk?"

Nick took the bundles from his daughter's hand. "Your mother worries. Come." To Jess he said, "I do not know yet, but it may be I can learn something. There are those in Upper Shawnee Town who will talk truth to me."

"Good. I knew I could count on you to take me to Chief Cornstalk. He'd never accept me alone. . . . Good-night, infant."

On Eva Verin's cleaned and polished stone stoop Nick left Hansi for a moment. "I will give the bed robe to her before we eat and she will smile and the meal will be very happy. You will see."

Hansi had learned long ago that her mother was a creature of many moods, dominated by an almost constant gloom. Because she hated the pain her father suffered from Eva Verin's bitter tongue, she tried now to postpone this moment which meant so much to her father.

"Papa, wait until she is in a good mood."

"This is for making a good mood. See? A beautiful thing. You enter first. I come after you with the robe behind me. Look! Have you ever seen a more beautiful thing?"

"It is very beautiful, but this may not be the time."

Hansi hurried into the cabin and tried to placate her mother who was setting out plates of savory meat, with winter turnips and potatoes from the root cellar.

"Let me help you, mama. I never meant to be late, but that wretched Mrs. Abernathy stopped me."

"And you went walking out with the Long Knife." Her mother looked at her sharply. "Did he offer you any familiarity?"

Hansi knew that Jess Taga's arm around her waist might be construed either as a man's way with a child, or a prelude to shocking familiarities, so she lied. "Oh, no, mama. He kept calling me 'infant.' "

"Well, that is something, anyway. Perhaps you are not his sort. I pray God you are not. Did you see anyone else at the fort?"

"Mama, do sit down. You look tired to death."

"I am a little tired. Will you serve us, dear?"

The unexpected endearment touched Hansi. For an instant she felt the disastrous tears of pity and unexpressed love for her mother welling up inside her. She blinked rapidly and laughed. "Supper looks wonderful, mama. You are the best cook in all Virginia."

This made Eva laugh. Then her laughter broke off. She caught her breath, staring at Nick in the doorway with his robe of precious skins. There was a long silence and Hansi could hear the noise from the fort.

Eva Verin cleared her throat. The sound was harsh, rasping. "What is that vile odor?" she said.

With a deep, sick feeling of pity for her father, Hansi knew at once what Eva meant. Nick Verin stood there, looking around in confusion.

"Get that thing out of here!" his wife yelled. "The smell of those awful skins makes me sick."

"Mama!" Hansi began on a desperate hope. "Isn't the robe beautiful? Did you ever see anything so lovely? Touch it."

Eva got up so quickly her chair fell over with a crash. "Get it away from me! It stinks of blood and death. Like you!"

Nick flinched as if she had struck him. He stared down at the robe, his fingers absently caressing the skins. The truth finally cut through to the core of him. His frame shuddered. His hands crushed the borders of the robe, and he roared, "It was for you. I made it for you. Long ago, I should have let the tribe have you. You are no woman for a man. You are nothing!"

He burst out of the cabin, dragging the robe along behind him across the ground.

5

HANSI started after her father, then thought better of it.

"He will come home drunk," Eva said, after a long silence.

"Can you blame him?" Hansi asked, hoping her ruthless, seemingly unfeeling reaction would shake her mother out of her maddening mood.

"No, I cannot." And, deliberately ignoring responsibility for the situation, added, "It is his wretched weakness for rum. What else can we expect?"

Hansi ate little that night and her mother ate even less. During the evening Eva walked about the cabin like a stalking forest cat. Light, lilting sounds of dance music drifted over from the fort. Hansi's feet tapped the rhythm. Dolly Abernathy might be swinging her golden hair as she danced a jig with Colonel Cameron at this very minute. Hansi had risen to her feet, and followed the music, her body moving with a natural grace.

Eva came in and watched from the open door. After a moment's silence, she said, "You should not be dancing here."

Feeling foolish, Hansi stopped. "But I thought you liked to see me dance."

"So I do. In the right places. You should be inside the fort, dancing."

Hansi cut her off. "You know quite well why I can't go to that dancing party."

Eva struck at the door in her frustration. To Hansi's amazement she suddenly rushed into the back room and came out waving her best lilac muslin gown with a white fichu and sash.

"I'll lace you into this. Wear it," she announced.

"No, mama!"

"Wear it!"

Hansi wanted to, desperately.

In short order, she was dressed for the ball. She had no shoes suited to a ballroom, even a ballroom of logs. There was nothing to be done but to borrow Eva's old shoes, which would be painful, for Eva's feet were smaller than Hansi's.

"Now," Eva gave orders like a general, "you are searching for your father. You come by accident into the ballroom. Someone is sure to see you. But make certain Colonel Cameron knows you are there. He is too polite to throw you out. Even if you are not allowed to dance there, he will have seen you looking your best—better than any girl there." She took Hansi's face between her thin hands. "You are never going to be beat down, as I was. You are going to rise above this vicious, unspeakable frontier world."

Hansi felt the tears come and could not blink them away. "Dear mama . . . don't you see? I can't—"

"Yes you can!" Eva slapped her cheek lightly, and on an impulse kissed the same spot. "You are the prettiest girl in Virginia. Never forget that."

The ballroom had been constructed so that it could be used to feed a company of soldiers or for a social occasion. On a little platform at one end of the room a violinist, a tambour player, and a drummer produced the

loud and not always tuneful music that had drawn her
there. By ill luck, the first person to notice her was the
eagle-eyed Mrs. Abernathy. She stopped in the midst of a
lively conversation with two other portly matrons, caught
her breath, and sailed over to block Hansi's further pro-
gress into the room.

"Hendrickje, my dear child, you must not come into
this area while you are working, you know. Have you left
the laundry at our lodgings?"

She managed to withstand Mrs. Abernathy's honeyed
assault with the denial, "I came only to see if my father
was inside the fort, ma'am."

Everyone was looking at her, gossiping behind their
fans.

"But my child, your father—forgive me—none of the
Indians are likely to be found here. Stand still, Hendrickje.
Your sash seems to be wrong side to. But don't you
worry. It looks just as charming on you as it does on your
good mother. Let me turn the sash here and there. Yes,
and that bit of mud on your hem. What a pity! But there,
child. Run along now. It must be far past your bedtime."

At that moment the door opened. She stepped aside
and found herself face to face with Colonel Cameron in
dress uniform. His serious expression softened so quickly
at the sight of her that she felt her calamitous visit might
turn out to be worthwhile. Mrs. Abernathy swept forward
in time to hear Cameron say to Hansi, "You are not
leaving, Miss Fire-Dawn? I hope to stand up with you
in the next set."

"I am afraid I must go. I only came to find papa."

Mrs. Abernathy fluttered into the conversation. "Yes,
yes, my dear sir. We mustn't detain the child. She is
dreadfully concerned to find her father." She reached for
his arm. "Do let me show you off to all these pretty young
ladies, Colonel Cameron. Colonel—"

He had already turned to follow Hansi. He made the
brief, polite explanation, "I may be able to locate Nick
Verin for her. Forgive me, ladies."

Hansi could scarcely believe what was happening when
the colonel suggested, "I had best go and fetch your

father myself. I imagine he must be exchanging tall tales with the militiamen. Can you wait here while I go into the taproom?"

The thought of him finding her father drunk, and then having to carry him back to the cabin was too humiliating to endure. "No, please don't. I want him to enjoy himself with his friends." She looked up, trying to put a light-hearted quality into her smile. "I've nothing to fear, from the gate to the cabin."

"I'm sure you are right, but a lady should always be escorted to her lodgings."

As they crossed the dark clearing, she tried to think of something witty and entertaining to say, but could not. It did not seem to matter because when he said good-night to her she could see that he too had enjoyed the walk. For a long, breathtaking minute she thought he was going to kiss her. He did not, but the warmth in his look as he left her was hardly a disappointment.

Hansi started into the cabin, then discovered that her mother had gone out again. She went to the wardrobe, found her mother's winter cloak, and went out to look for her, with the cape as an excuse. After a few unnerving minutes she came upon Eva at the far end of the clearing.

She threw the cape around her mother's shoulders. "Do come inside now. It is dangerous, mama. You know quite well someone may be waiting out there to send an arrow through us at this very second."

"More likely a knife." But Eva Verin went along with her, slowly.

Hansi looked over at the saplings. Their leaves fluttered in the night breeze. Was there something peculiar in the noise? She pushed her mother inside the cabin.

"What is it?" Eva whispered. "Did you see anything?"

Hansi shook her head. "I don't know. Something is out there. It may only be a painter-cat."

"I wanted to see the stars. Those same stars shining somewhere over the cities on the coast . . . the very same. . . . Who do you think it is outside?" She began to panic as the true threat of danger penetrated her dreamy mood. "The long rifle. On the wall. Can you shoot out there? I'll help you load."

Hansi stopped her. "Have you thought? It might be papa."

They looked at each other. Eva leaned against the table, her head lowered, leaving action to her daughter. Hansi pinched the candle and cautiously looked out the south window. A man was out there, and no mistake. She made out the lean form, still thin after a bitter winter of bad hunting. The scalp lock divided a shaven skull that gleamed in the starlight. He wore a long hunting knife and carried a musket, probably remaining from the old alliance with the French. He staggered across the end of the clearing.

"Drunk," Hansi whispered.

Eva raised her head, her eyes wide with terror. "Not Nick?"

"No. He has a scalp lock. A Shawnee, I think. He may be hoping to get more rum from someone at the fort." She thought he would hardly walk about in that disorderly fashion if he were on the warpath. The Shawnee Nation was far too intelligent and well disciplined for that.

Eva stared in the opposite direction, toward the fort whose high walls were vaguely illuminated by lights from the dancing party inside. The men on guard duty above the walls were in darkness and their silhouettes could only be made out by moonlight or unusual illumination from inside the fort.

Eva pulled aside the skin curtain on the fort side. "Do you think anyone is up there? Can they see us?" she whispered.

"Not if they are watching the dancing," Hansi muttered. She watched the intruder circle the cabin. She signaled to her mother, whispering, "Load papa's musket."

Eva had just gotten the musket loaded when the intruder fell against the door, rattling the entire room. Hansi reached for the musket, then decided it would be better to frighten him off. She took the musket to the window on the fort side and aimed at a tree across the clearing.

The smoke and the noise of the explosion aroused the fort. The music stopped instantly. Lights flashed. Soldiers rushed out into the clearing in various states of undress with fully loaded muskets. Hansi could see Jess Taga as he rushed out of the fort between several confused soldiers, calling out, "Don't shoot the Shawnee. He is drunk."

Meanwhile, the Indian moved away from the door and scrambled to get in by the small window. Eva screamed. He stared in beyond her at Hansi, steel scalp knife in hand. He hefted the knife to throw. Hansi remained absolutely still as she had been taught by her father, waiting until the last second before she moved and thus provided a fresh target.

After that, everything happened at once. Jess called out, "Hold your fire!" and, having reached the Verins' cabin window, started to lift down the scratching, scrambling Indian. At the same time a man shot out of the fort and rushed toward the Indian trying to get in through the window opening. There was a thud, a scream. The women inside heard Jess Taga's voice calling off the soldiers.

"All's well, lads. Just a drunken intruder hanging about the Verins' cabin. Nick's taken him in tow."

"My God," Eva cried, "it was Nick who flew at that fellow. He's out there fighting the creature."

Hansi was already pulling at the bolt on the door. She rushed out into the clearing, now ablaze with lights and shadows. Jess caught her and pulled her back against his body. "Take care, Hansi. Nick is in a temper. He's had a kegful."

"Please stop them. The other one is drunk, too, and he has a knife."

Jess held her back. "Nick knows what he is about," he said.

Soldiers, militia and a few fort wives began to make a semicircle around the two fighters. Hansi struggled impatiently. "No. I want it stopped. When he's drinking he's not himself."

"They are two men and they are fighting like men, infant."

She tried again to tear away from him. Violence and bloodshed. Jess was no better than her father.

Nick and the unknown Indian rolled and twisted in the dirt. Nick was fighting for his family, for her mother, and for Hansi.

Then a calm, quiet voice, well known to her, cut through the turmoil. "Separate those two men. They are still on Fort Blaine ground. . . . Do you hear me? Separate them!"

Two of the Long Knives looked to their captain for orders. Jess' hands squeezed Hansi's shoulders. "Colonel Cameron seems to agree with you." Then he raised his voice. "All right, lads. He outranks me. Stop them."

Hansi swung around excitedly, saw Shelby Cameron in uniform breeches, boots and a shirt, but without his jacket. He had come out in a hurry. So he had not been dancing with Dolly Abernathy. Hansi tried not to let this wholly unimportant information please her too much.

Cameron reached the combatants before Jess' men did, and jerked the top man off. Lantern light gleamed on the blood-stained scalp knife in the hand of the fallen Shawnee. Hansi cried out a warning to her father and Cameron. Elbowing aside his own men, Jess grabbed the man's wrist and got the knife.

Hansi knelt by her father, who had collapsed against the cabin wall. He opened his eyes with an effort. "Will she forgive me, do you think?"

"Of course, papa. Are you hurt?"

She looked up. Jess stood over them.

"Hansi, I think he has been stabbed." He tried to examine the wound but Nick pulled away, suddenly transformed, trying to get to his feet as Eva pushed her way through the gaping crowd and started to kneel before him.

"No. It is not right for my woman to be in the dirt. Help me. I will walk."

Everyone offered a hand but as he staggered to his feet, Eva cried out, "He is bleeding. Look at his side. Nick, you are hurt."

Nick reached for his wife, but his legs went slack. Jess

let him drop easily onto the ground, and examined him, while Nick insisted, "It's a scratch, I tell you, nothing more."

Jess agreed. "He may be right. The knife pierced the flesh but seems to have been deflected by a rib. You'll be right as a trivet in a week or so."

Hansi looked around at the chattering, dispersing crowd. Shelby Cameron had the staggering Shawnee by one arm. She said, "What will you do with him?"

The Shawnee shook his head in confusion and muttered, "Thirsty. Give me drink."

Cameron looked at Hansi. "What does he say?"

"I think he wants more rum."

Cameron said grimly, "Not tonight. He is going to be locked up until he sleeps this off."

Hansi said to the colonel, lowering her voice, "I think he came only for liquor. Do you know a trader named Daniel Greathouse? A bearded man who wears buckskin?"

The colonel studied her face with that special keenness she had noticed on other occasions. "Do you think he is the one?"

"I'm sure of it."

Jess Taga looked up. "Colonel," he said, "who is to shoot that poor devil? Not one of your half-blind Redcoat sharpshooters, I hope."

Colonel Cameron said calmly, "Certainly not. He will be set free when he has sobered up."

"Set free!" Jess started up angrily, but Eva protested, "You will hurt Nick," and he let his Long Knives take up the chorus instead.

As Jess lifted Nick into his arms with admirable ease, the colonel said sternly, "We can hardly go marching into a Shawnee camp talking peace when we have just shot one of their tribe. In any case, if you think we shoot men for getting into drunken brawls, you do not know Redcoats." He turned and strode back to the fort.

Jess called after him, "If you think mercy will appeal to his people, you do not know the Shawnees."

Hansi followed her parents and Jess into the cabin. It was ironic but she realized her father's slight injury had brought him and Eva together again.

Nick was put to bed, the wound washed and dressed. Eva laid a wet cloth across Nick's forehead. He looked up then, and murmured Eva's full name: "Evaline." He always called her "woman" or "wife," and it touched Hansi to hear the longing in his rough, deep voice as he spoke her name. Eva's reaction, the gentleness with which she applied the cloth to his head, made the moment perfect for their daughter.

Satisfied that his scout was mending satisfactorily, Jess Taga started to leave and looked pleased when Hansi walked out with him. On the stoop he said, quietly, "You are very happy for them, aren't you?"

"I used to worry. I don't . . . I didn't know why they ever married. They never understood each other. They had nothing in common."

"Except you."

"Yes, but that wasn't always the case. I mean, why did they marry. Sometimes I wonder . . ."

He looked at her softly. Hansi was uncomfortable, wondering what made him look as if he pitied her. It was not like the tough Long Knife. She was relieved to find a subject that would break the awkward moment.

"The Shawnee lost his rifle. There it is in the shadow against the cabin." She stooped to pick up the gun. "If Colonel Cameron frees the fellow, I suppose he may as well have his property, too," she said.

Jess relieved her of the rifle in a flash. "Our noble-hearted commander may find himself shot by his ex-prisoner."

Hansi watched the flickering light through the open window slant across Jess Taga's features, accentuating the ridges and hollows. She said abruptly, "Did you really want that Shawnee executed tonight?"

"One less Shawnee to shoot at us from ambush next time we venture out."

Hansi found herself unexpectedly angry. "Is it only

Shawnees you hate, captain? Because my father is Indian. And I am Indian, too. Or is it that you hate all Indians?"

She thought for an instant he was going to laugh, but he did not. "There is nothing complicated about my feelings. I am like the Shawnees. I hate what threatens me. If I were a Shawnee, I would hate Virginians. And I would certainly never free a Virginian to use his long knife on me again."

Puzzled, she murmured, "You have the mind of a savage. Much more so than papa."

"Now don't look so disturbed. I am not quite the savage you think me. I can be more gentle than your hero."

"M-my hero?"

"The noble colonel. As a matter of fact, I suspect your dearly beloved is a lot harder than I. He is not as easily swayed by those moist pink lips of yours as I am. And your hair. I doubt that he even sees it."

"He calls me Fire-Dawn, as my father does." She liked the spectacle of a jealous Jess Taga.

"Fire-Dawn. That may be. But he doesn't see you, infant. Not as I do." He took a great handful of her hair and gently tugged her head back into the hollow of his arm. "Someday, when you are grown up, you will come to me. When you are no longer a half-savage child."

"I am not a savage and I am certainly not a child."

He let her go abruptly. "I'll leave a man on watch, though there should be no more trouble tonight." He glanced at the clearing, and startled her with a quick, harsh laugh. "I seem to be too late. The colonel acted first." He left without another word.

She went back to the cabin. Since her father had been placed on her bed in the front room, she lay down to rest on her parents' bed in the back room. Over beyond the walls of the fort she could hear the music of violins and tambour take up again and wondered if Shelby Cameron had gone back to dance with Dolly Abernathy. And she remembered the Indian who had stabbed her father.

Could he have been sent by Greathouse to kill her instead? There was that moment when he threatened to throw the knife at her. Or was the Puan behind the attack, or even the mysterious Hairbuyer?

Eva came in and Hansi noticed that her knees were shaking.

"Mama, if you could only forgive him! He tries so hard to please you."

Eva waved a hand vaguely, but the hand too was shaking. "You know nothing about it. Nothing of my life before."

Hansi sat up, anxious about her mother's nervous reaction. "Of course, I know nothing. Mama, how can you expect me to understand what you feel and why you feel it? Papa said to me once, 'Nobody knows what anybody else thinks.' But I feel torn between you. I love you both."

Eva ran a hand wearily over her face, tried to smile at her daughter. "You are a good girl. And Nick is . . . what he is. I pity him."

"Pity!"

The older woman sat staring at her shaking hands. Without looking up, she said, "There is no hell worse than being bound to a person you pity, a person who clings to you with no pride, no ability to live for himself. Always clinging, always needing you. I cannot understand a person so . . . so unselfish."

Hansi sat up, trying to absorb all this.

"You cannot love papa because he loves you too much?"

"A man like that is half a man." She reached for Hansi's hand and caressed it with her quick, almost frightened touch. "Never use pity, my dear. And never let pity use you. Remember that always."

Hansi's chin went up. "I could never mistake pity and love. Never! And I have too much pride to hold a man by such a means."

"I hope to God you are right. But you are your father's daughter."

Just then, her father stirred. She went to him. "How are you, papa? Do you need anything?"

"Water," he said in the French dialect he had spoken around the forts of his childhood.

She brought a dipper of cold water and held it while he drank thirstily. "I sold the robe," he said.

"Oh, no, papa! It was so beautiful. Who did you sell it to?"

"Friend. From the old days."

She had a depressing idea that the friend was Daniel Greathouse. "I hope he gave you what it was worth. Papa, that robe would be worth a small fortune!"

His eyes avoided hers. She pursued the subject. "What did he give you for the robe?"

"A bottle of rum."

When her father was asleep again, Hansi steeped two cups of tea and carried them into the bedroom.

Eva sipped the strong, dark tea and studied Hansi thoughtfully. "What I told you a few minutes ago has shocked you, hasn't it?"

"No. It is excellent advice. Only I don't think it is fitting for me. I shall take care not to make mistakes in judgment. That is what happened to you, mama. You made a misjudgment long ago."

Eva laughed, harshly. "Do you think I chose to mate with Nick Verin?"

"But you must have felt something for papa! Didn't you like him at all when you met him?"

Eva drank deeply, then burst out, "I was living with my brother and his wife at Fort William Henry on Lake George. That is in upper New York."

"Yes. I know where it is—or rather, where it was." Hansi set her cup down. It rattled in the saucer. Like every other frontier child, she knew too well the massacres during the French and Indian Wars. After a long and terrible silence, she said, "Was papa at Fort William Henry?"

Eva nodded. "I didn't see him until after the horror. My brother Willem and his wife were killed by axes, and so was my two-year-old niece. I was knocked unconscious. The attackers took me with them. They fought over me. Then I saw Nick. He bought me from them. I am worth two beaver skins."

Hansi reached for her hand but she pulled away.

"Even then, he was gentle. He protected me from the others. But he could not protect me from himself. I tried to escape. I actually tried to kill myself. I used his scalp knife. I bled. But, even so, he wrapped my wrists and my throat. He cared for me. And then I found I was with child. His child."

"Oh, God, mama, no!" To be born of such hatred, such loathing, was worse than all else.

"He was so happy. How I hated him! He offered to live in a white community, to be anything that would satisfy me." She drank the dregs of tea. "I should never have agreed, but I could not murder the child. And I could not return to the old life. My people were dead. There was only my cousin Joseph, far away in New York. Nick took me to a French priest in Fort Pitt. We were married, and Nick went to work scouting for the English. You were born. Habit is a strange thing. A human being can grow accustomed to any horror. Just a matter of habit. Now, there is no other life possible for me. It is too late."

"Poor papa!" It was said without thought because, to Hansi, the greater horror was Nick's fate of a life with someone who despised him. Yes, Hansi thought, it was worse for her father.

Eva repeated incredulously, "Poor papa? Not poor Eva?"

"No, mama. You are stronger than he is."

"Hansi, you are too young to understand what I have told you, what it did to me. The fault is mine. I should not have told you."

Perhaps that was true. Hansi knew she should feel the tragedy of these two people she loved. But one thought haunted her: *I was born of this hatred. I should never have been born.*

6

AT sunrise, the world looked clean-washed and far more cheerful than the sad, sinister dark of the previous night. Hansi was outside, as always, awaiting the new day.

Her dreams for herself had grown more confused since her mother's disclosure. She was more than ever determined not to let Jess Taga, the aggressive, teasing Long Knife, pursue his flirtation with her to its obvious conclusion. She was not certain she would ever fall in love or marry, after what had happened to her parents. But that did not mean she would avoid Shelby Cameron. Since he was clearly beyond her hopes, she told herself it was safe to enjoy her dreams.

She located the vagrant Shawnee's powder horn at the far end of the clearing and set off for the fort. She almost walked into Shelby Cameron who had just come up from the riverbank with one of the Redcoat Regulars. Flustered, she pretended she did not recognize him until he seized her by her forearms, amused at her preoccupation, and lifted her out of the path.

"Good-morning, Mistress Fire-Dawn. You put us to shame. You are always out so early."

"And with treasure," she announced brightly, offering him the powder horn. "Is the Shawnee prisoner still here?"

"No. We let him go as soon as he had slept off that monumental thirst of his."

But she was not thinking about the Shawnee prisoner. She had been unnerved as she always was by the proximity of this gentleman so unlike the men she had seen all her life. She was not fooled by his friendliness, his gently humorous manner with her. She knew she was just one more of the females he treated with the same seeming romantically interested manner. It was sickening, but Hansi told herself she believed in facing facts.

"May I see your father today? We are anxious not to postpone the talks with Chief Cornstalk. We can't afford to let them think we are hesitating, or that there is any trouble between our regulars and the militia."

She was thinking about the way his dark hair curled on his neck at the edge of his stiffened uniform. Even Jess Taga wore his bronze-colored mane bound with a doeskin thong at the nape of his neck. In so many ways Shelby Cameron was different from the others. After a pause, she thought to ask, "*Is* there any trouble between the English and the militia?"

He smiled. "Certainly not! You are an army child. You know quite well I would never say yes to such a question. Have you any notion of where your father's sympathies might lie, if the rebellion should spread to the frontier?"

She flashed her best answering smile. "But you just said there was no trouble of that kind at the fort."

He received this with a good humor that she suspected was forced. The Redcoat behind him snorted as if he too had been upset by her evasion. Cameron was growing impatient. The matter must be more immediate than she had suspected.

"I would appreciate it if you could find out in some way, Hansi. I don't suggest you ask him directly, but you may get an indication. Not that it is necessary to gather in our friends and reserves, but one likes to be prepared."

"Ay, sir. Papa isn't awake yet. I'll try and see what I can learn."

He took her hand, took the powder horn, and looked at her with a mysterious gaze. "You are very good," he said. "I will count upon you."

He completed her happiness by bringing her hand to his lips and then he strode on toward the fort's river gate.

She returned to the main cabin, dreading the encounter with her parents after her mother's terrible story. She was amazed to find her mother sitting on the side of the cot, holding water to her father's lips. The sight relieved Hansi and at the same time puzzled her.

Eva looked about calmly, as though nothing unusual had happened. She seemed surprised that her daughter should be staring at her.

"You've brought my tea. Thank you, dear. And your father's breakfast. Nick, are you feeling well enough to eat?"

While they ate, Hansi took the opportunity to approach the matter that interested Colonel Cameron.

"Papa, they say that beyond the mountains, all along the coast, more people are rising against the government. It is disloyal. It is actually treason, papa. The British have always defended us out here on the frontier. These colonials want only more land. They don't care about us. Papa! What will become of us if the Redcoats and the militia turn against each other?"

She watched Nick for a sign that he would remain loyal if rebellion came to Fort Blaine. In her own mind she had exaggerated the danger. Surely Jess Taga and his men would not desert the settlements of Virginians in Kentucky County!

Her father reached for his steaming mug of rum and herbs and let out a bellow of pain as his movement pulled on the tight bandage around his middle. He seemed to Hansi far less recovered than he was pretending to be.

Eva had already made up the big bed in the back room

and was now beginning to complain that she had not cleaned the two rooms yet. Nick reached for her hand and, with an effort, squeezed it.

"I will sleep a little. I do not need it, but it is good to be prepared. They will need me tomorrow."

7

DANGER was in the air. The fort buzzed with activity.
Knowing that whatever happened, water would be all-
important, Hansi filled two pails and started up the path
past the fort, toward the cabin. She tried to keep out of the
way of running men, some dragging an old cannon on
wheels. The high walls and towers of the fort were already
manned at double strength. Three of the Virginia Long
Knives trotted out of the fort with their commander, who
asked Hansi as he ran past her, "Can your father talk to
me?"

"I think so. He has difficulty moving, but—"

Jess was already nearing the cabin. He burst in as Eva
came out with a load of bedclothes and one of her favorite
Sabbath dresses, which she guarded as another would
have guarded gold.

"We are to go into the fort, Hansi."

Hansi's muscles tightened. She was aware of a stiff,
tense readiness for action that at the same time did not
preclude terror. "Does papa think they will attack today
in force?"

"He thinks someone has been advising Cornstalk—
someone from outside the tribe."

Could the outsider be Daniel Greathouse? Or the one called the Hairbuyer? This was a special dread for Hansi. With an effort she pushed her fears to the back of her mind and followed her mother into the fort.

By the time the Verin family was settled in a one-room shack, the fort was prepared for an assault from the river. It would be much easier to take the fort by land, and Jess spent an hour trying to discover all that Nick Verin knew, all that might be useful for defense of the land approaches on the Kentucky side. As the fort's interior buzzed with activity of civilians and soldiers, Hansi was called to head-quarters.

She followed the soldier sent to fetch her, not knowing whether to worry about the unexpected summons or to be cheered by the fact that Colonel Cameron might be present. By the time she stepped into the office, she felt fairly confident. At least in his presence she would be at her best.

The room was dark after the piercing sunlight of the open quadrangle. She blinked and saw several vague faces. Men were standing like sentinels and all of them staring at her. But she saw neither Shelby Cameron nor Jess Taga. Presiding at this interview was the huge figure of Major Geoffrey Hay. She felt his cold eyes observing her every move. She bobbed a slight curtsy and asked, "Excellency, you called on me to see you?"

"You are a loyal child? One may count on you?" Major Hay stretched a huge hand across Colonel Cameron's desk. She did not touch it, but looked around, innocently. She was very much on her guard. She saw no face that she trusted.

"Ay, sir."

"You reported seeing a hostile redskin on our shores yesterday?"

Continuing in her sweetest, most childlike voice, she said, "The man was drunk, sir. He came looking for rum from the fort."

The major's heavy lips fell open. He glanced at one of the two soldiers standing behind Hansi. The soldier cleared his throat.

"The wench refers to the fight last night between the half-blood scout, her father, and an unknown redskin. Colonel Cameron freed him this morning."

Major Hay considered Hansi. "We are not discussing that regrettable episode, young lady, but rather a redskin you allegedly saw yesterday morning on the shore. Precisely what did you see?"

Obviously, in spite of Colonel Cameron's efforts, Major Hay knew the whole truth. Hansi held her hands close to her sides so Major Hay would not guess at her fright.

"No, sir. There is a mistake. I saw no one except the Indian. A Puan. He spoke in French." That was half true, but the only one who knew better was Daniel Greathouse and he could hardly give himself away. "Puans attacked Colonel Cameron on the trail several months ago, and I thought this man might be a spy for the Shawnee Confederacy."

Major Hay examined his large flat fingernails. His voice was low and gentle, but she remained tightly on guard. "He spoke in French, you say? Yes. Very possibly working for the Shawnees."

Someone breathed a sigh as if relieved that the major seemed less explosive. He looked up at her with a suddenness that sent panic racing through her body. "And to whom was this French addressed? You say you merely overheard it. You saw nothing. Do you suggest he held this curious conversation with himself, girl?"

"N-no, sir. Another man. But I have no notion who he was," she lied quickly. "There were the rushes and dogwood, and . . . and trees between us."

"Sounds reasonable, major," an all-too-familiar voice broke in. She swung around wildly. Even before the big, bearded man's face took form in the half-darkness of the major's quarters, she recognized Daniel Greathouse. "Anybody here know any damned Frenchie hanging about the fort? Frenchies ain't as common in these parts as they was some years gone by, major. You redbelly boys seen to that."

"That will do," the major cut him off impatiently. "I'll make my recommendations to the colonel. Girl, you heard an Indian speaking French, that is all. Frankly, I suspect this story of yours is an effort to cover up some negligence in your work. You are a laundress, are you not?"

"Yes, sir." Curious that, faced with attack at any moment, he had not asked the substance of the conversation. Or had he forgotten that Nick Verin's daughter understood French?

The major dismissed his men. The soldiers left for their posts. Hansi was following them when Greathouse blocked her way, his teeth glittering within the dirty, food-stained beard.

"Clever little wench, ain't you? Make a nice morsel for one of them savages out there. Best take care how you go prowling about, eh?"

"As you say, sir." But she knew quite well how dangerous her position was until she or Shelby Cameron could find proof against the Hairbuyer.

When she came out onto the grounds again the general panic of activity had subsided. Jess was up in the west river-lookout with Shelby Cameron. They appeared dangerously open to attack.

Dolly Abernathy came running out to Hansi. "Oh, heavens! What will become of us? Hansi, can't they make peace long enough to get us safely out? If only I could be somewhere else! What will they do to us?"

Poor Dolly, Hansi thought . . . I've found someone more frightened than I am . . . She tried to reassure the terrified girl, as well as her mother, who rustled out to ask indignantly, "What have those fools done to cause this outrage? Undoubtedly the fault of the wretched militia—always running about shooting redskins!"

Hansi was about to explain to Dolly that there had been no attack yet, and very possibly would be none at all, when the girl clutched her hands. "Hansi, you did save my gown, didn't you?"

With her mind full of images of scalpings, burnings and torture, Hansi could not imagine what gown this might be.

Bewildered, she began, "I think I brought everything I had washed yesterday."

Dolly shook her head in a frenzy. "My blue gown! The new one, you foolish thing! All those lengths of blue silk. You did rescue it?"

Hansi pried herself away from the girl. "I haven't the least notion whether it was rescued or not. You are the silliest girl alive. It would serve you good and proper if some Shawnee snatches your head off."

"Oh," Dolly gasped. Mrs. Abernathy exclaimed, "Hendrickje!" and then added, surprisingly, "Not but what she is right, Dolly. You really are too tiresome. Go along, Hansi. We all have to do our share, though the Good Lord knows I detest using ramrods and paper wads and loading those enormous rifles and muskets they insist on using. How much nicer if everyone still fought with bow and arrow!"

Hansi found her mother working to make the single room habitable. It was not an easy task. She said, "How is papa? Has he talked with Captain Taga?"

"I talked," her father put in from his bed in the far corner of the room. "When I am on my feet tomorrow, I will go to Chief Cornstalk. He trusts only me. You see, woman? I have important things to do. I am somebody at Fort Blaine because the Shawnees put much faith only in my word."

"Yes, yes. We know," Eva mumbled, absorbed with the order of the tiny room.

Hansi had been thinking about the situation and asked him urgently, "Papa, how much danger are we really in now?"

Proud to be called upon as an authority, Nick tried to sit up, groaned, and sank back. "I know Cornstalk would listen to me, but he is getting advice from others. I do not like that. My friend Daniel believes we should give up the fort and go up to Fort Pitt. But he is wrong. I do not know why he says this."

Hansi did not reply to this and spent the next hour helping her mother and the other women who were busy organizing for a siege. Tense, nervous hours passed. Hansi was aware of being watched and several times saw Daniel Greathouse's hulking figure threateningly nearby.

Late in the afternoon Colonel Cameron called Hansi away for a minute or two. "I have not thanked you for your help," he said to her. "You were quite wonderful."

She reddened with pleasure. Any praise from him was welcome, hoarded in memory and thought over later. In replying, she lowered her voice. "May I ask you something?"

He put his arm around her, drew her out of sight of the courtyard.

She wanted to ask him what could be done since her father's injury, but even in these moments of potential danger she let herself enjoy the warmth and protection of his arm and the special tenderness she found in his smile.

"Hansi," he went on, "Hansi, what a pleasure it is to look at you—the only beautiful thing that has happened to me since I arrived at Fort Blaine. Now, what is your secret?" Before she could answer, he said suddenly, in the chilling, aristocratic voice he had never before used with her, "What are you doing here? Do you want to speak to me?"

"No, sir. I'm here to walk Nick Verin's pretty wench back to her father."

Hansi tensed, feeling once more the terror inspired by the voice of Daniel Greathouse.

"Miss Verin is my responsibility. I suggest you see to your own part in the defense of the walls."

"Ay, but first . . . old Nick asked me to look out for his child. Come, girl." Daniel Greathouse reached for her, flashing his repulsive grin.

The colonel said casually, "Be about your business." He added, "That is, if you do have business in this fort."

Greathouse's grin faded. "No, sir. I'd as lief stay in the fort, thankee, sir." He retreated, not even glancing back.

Colonel Cameron drew Hansi farther out of reach of the activities in the compound. "I have discussed Great-

house with Captain Taga. We have very little doubt he is
the man you heard talking to the Puan." She started to
mention her recent interview with Major Hay, but he put
one finger over lips, silencing her. "We know what he is
about in frightening you. I have had him followed since
you spoke to me last night. The difficulty is, we have no
firm proof of guilt. He spoke of a Hairbuyer, you said.
There are a good many interpretations for that, and in the
end it is your word against his."

She laughed uneasily, "I trust even my death won't provide the needed proof, sir."

He turned her toward the main gates, which were now
closed and bolted. She felt his cheek brush briefly against
hers as he asked her to look where he indicated, at Jess
Taga's friend, the powerful, amiable Kentucky Helm. The
Long Knife was standing in front of the gates, legs apart.
Seeing their attention upon him he nodded.

"What does it mean? Does he know what we are talking
about?" Hansi asked.

"Certainly. I talked it over with Taga and we decided
to set a watch on you as well as on Greathouse. The soldier you saw following Greathouse a few minutes ago was
present when Major Hay interviewed you. He tells me you
conducted yourself like a skilled campaigner."

She did not like to disturb his delicious nearness. By
rising on her toes she might very easily touch his cheek
with her lip, but she did not feel brave enough to try.

He said a bit huskily, "You cannot imagine I would let
anything happen to you, do you, Mistress Fire-Dawn?"

She smiled up at him, trying to make her smile as winning, as inviting as possible, but as she might have pre-
dicted, any further action between them was cut off by
Captain Jess Taga.

"Here I am bumbling into your little romance, Cameron, but there is a fort to defend, and we may as well get
about it."

To Hansi's surprise the colonel took his sarcasm well.
He let Hansi go without haste, saluted Jess and agreed
jokingly, "Ay, captain. At once, captain. Your orders for
me, captain?"

Jess grinned with some reluctance, then looked from one to the other of them. "Have you told her she is under protection?"

Hansi put in, "And he tells me nothing can be done about Daniel Greathouse yet. Oh, Jess, I'm certain he isn't here for trading rights! Isn't it possible he may have something to do with our Shawnee trouble?"

"Possibly. But I can't see how he gains by it. He is being watched, too," Jess added. "As well as any contacts he makes inside the fort."

Hansi said, "Including Major Geoffrey Hay?"

She felt the sharp recoil in both men. Jess Taga's tawny eyebrows raised as he watched the colonel's face. Cameron stared at her with an intensity she found unnerving.

"What made you say that? Is there something you have heard?"

"Nothing, sir. It is only that he seems to make such a vigorous defense of Greathouse."

The colonel asked sharply, "Have you any idea what such an accusation could mean, made against one of the highest ranking officers on the frontier? And at a time when there is such mistrust between the colonials and the army?"

Jess put in, "I'm sure Hansi meant nothing of the kind, Cameron. She was subjected to an unpleasant experience at the hands of this major of yours, so naturally she has little use for him. Can't say I blame her."

It was infuriating that both men should dismiss her suspicions. "No! It isn't that way at all! I think Major Hay found out what I told Colonel Cameron, and warned Greathouse. Why would he do that?"

Jess said, "Come, Hansi. The colonel has to put his lads to bed. If there's no attack within the hour we may win a night's sleep."

"Yes, but . . ." She looked at Shelby Cameron. His very manner frightened her.

"Say nothing, Hansi. Promise me you will say nothing until we can prove it."

"You had better promise," Jess advised her.

"Of course, I will. It was only a thought. I am glad you consider it important."

"Thank you."

When they were beyond his hearing, Jess said, "I wonder what he will do if the rebellion spreads to the frontier and the Redcoats make a separate peace with the Shawnees. Can you imagine what that would do to the settlers and fort civilians here?"

"They would be massacred. But Colonel Cameron would never permit such a dishonorable thing."

"Maybe it won't be for him to say. If he died—in line of duty—naturally, we'd have the good major in control. I wouldn't give a brass farthing for that boy's honor. He'd take his regulars, march out of here and leave the gates wide open for Cornstalk."

They passed a crowd of women looking anxious and strained, twisting their pinafores in nervous fingers.

Hansi muttered to him, "Be quiet. They've enough to worry about."

"Hendrickje," one of the women called, "are we in danger? Will they attack?"

"I don't know. I can't say."

"You ought to know, Hendrickje. Your own Pa being one of them redskins."

Hansi slowed her steps, lest they dare to imagine she ran from them, and then went toward the Verin shack. Jess turned and left her, moving through the crowd of women as they besieged him for comfort.

Late in the afternoon, comforting rumors swept through the civilians of the fort. "Shawnees crossed the river to deliver our men safely," they said. "A pair of Shawnees is with Major Hay now, getting our thanks. Looks like to be no war today."

Hearing the news, Nick Verin muttered, "This is not like Cornstalk. What do the Shawnees gain from such a show of weakness?"

Although the fort remained on the alert, there was a decreasing tension, especially among the regulars. In the evening Eva prepared supper over the fire outside the shack.

The explosion of a rifle in the woods beyond the clearing startled them all. Across the table Eva and Hansi groped for each other's hands. They waited. Running steps echoed across the ground outside. Eva ran to look out.

"That soldier who has been outside our door all afternoon is gone. Must be running to see what the shot was about. But why has he been here so long?"

Hansi knocked over her chair, rushing after her mother. "He was guarding us. They were afraid Daniel Greathouse might kill me."

"But why?" Nick began to struggle, trying to sit up. "Old Daniel kill my Hansi? Woman, bring me my gun. The musket."

There were shouts of "All's well" across the parade ground, but Nick, struggling against Hansi who tried to make him lie down, demanded, "What is happening?"

"Papa, has your friend Greathouse said anything about the Shawnees siding with the regulars against us, if the rebellion reaches here?"

"What are you talking about? The Redcoat regulars protect us. The Shawnees have no use for them. Girl, are you mad!"

Behind them, Eva screamed. Hansi whirled around.

Daniel Greathouse's bulk filled the doorway.

"My good friend Nick, I am glad to see you are so sensible. I will take your little girl to the Redcoat major and she will tell him what you say. It is dark now, girl. I will take you safely where you are to go. Isn't that so, friend Nick?"

8

NICK shot up to a sitting position with a fierce effort. "Daniel, what are you doing here?" he demanded in French. "What was the shooting out there?"

"My friend, you must not let a bit of noise make you afraid. Probably just one of those redbellies falling on his gun." His ugly grin turned upon them. "You see, Miss Fire-Dawn? I speak of the redbellies with contempt. So how can you say I take their side against the colonials?"

Hansi felt her panic rising.

He went on, "And your little girl says I am friend to the Shawnees as well as the redbellies. But Nick, it is you who have the half-blood. Not me. I am friend to all men. But Major Hay told his men tonight, 'It is Nick Verin who is Indian, Nick Verin who is French.' You see how it is . . ."

"You accuse me?" Nick cried.

"No, no, friend. I say only to send your daughter with me to explain your loyalty. Let her speak for you. I will guard her."

"Fire-Dawn, it is good sense. Daniel will see you across

the grounds. It is growing dark, not safe for you to be alone."

"I won't go with him!" Hansi shouted.

"Daughter!"

"I will go screaming through the grounds that he wants to kill me. They will believe me because I am young, and have friends among the regulars and the Long Knives."

"Friends, ay!" Greathouse sneered, losing his temper for the first time. "Nick, what kind of a father will let his child choose lovers like the Long Knife butcher, Jess Taga? Or the commander who will take her and abuse her honor?"

Hansi grabbed up her wooden trencher from the table and would have thrown it in his face but he avoided it and lunged for her. While Nick tried vainly to get off his couch, Eva ran to her daughter's rescue, surprising Greathouse as Hansi slipped out.

Jess Taga elbowed his way through the crowd to reach Hansi. "Are you all right?"

"I am now. Greathouse intended to kill me. I know it!"

"Where the devil is the soldier guarding you?"

"The shooting sent him off to the walls."

"Is Nick able to move yet?"

"He can't get up, but he is better."

"Then I'll have to parley with Cornstalk alone. We have to talk immediately. I want the Shawnees neutral if this rebellion against the Redcoats reaches us on the frontier."

"But they hate you. No Long Knife would be safe without a guide the Shawnees trust, like papa. Or . . ." She took a firm breath. "Or me. They trusted me two years ago, when papa was sick."

"No! We were not at war then."

"We were hardly at peace. And we are not technically at war now. They will accept Nick Verin's *son*, as before. I must only wear male clothes and be addressed as Nick's son. They know I am a female. They simply cannot admit it. Cornstalk won't speak on terms of equality to a female. But after that time two years ago they assured papa repeatedly that his 'son' had served well and my word was good."

"Are you sure Nick won't be able to act as our agent? My scouts brought in two Piankashaws. They will talk to us only through Nick."

"Then I will go, as Nick's son."

He hesitated. "It may work. I hope to God it does." Quickly he maneuvered her through the crowd outside the protective walls of the fort. Whatever Jess Taga was about, he clearly wanted it kept secret from the Regular Army.

"Where are we going?" she whispered, but understood a minute later as they moved silently along the path beneath the walls heading toward the Verin's abandoned cabin.

It was difficult to see inside. One dim candle flickered and gradually revealed the room's occupants. Facing Hansi across the room were two dignified Indians still holding their long rifles. The Indians, with their long, greased braids, status feathers and leggings were obviously from country far above the Ohio. Did this mean that even faraway tribes had now joined against the small defending force at Fort Blaine?

She was reassured by the sight of Kentuck Helm, easy and solid, standing behind the two Piankashaws. The Indians appeared to look through her. She knew the contempt with which they regarded a female acting in any official capacity.

Jess looked at Kentuck Helm. "Have they said anything more?"

"Won't say anything without Nick Verin translating. I've explained to them that Nick has been wounded. It is impossible unless we bring them inside the walls to meet with Nick."

One of the Piankashaws made rapid chopping gestures of dissent, which told Hansi they understood English and would listen carefully to her translations. Then the Piankashaw spokesman said, "We have found the word of Nick

Verin true to the words we speak. We accept the son who is of his blood."

"I will speak in my father's name and with his words."

Both Piankashaws nodded. The spokesman said, "We bring facts to the Long Knives. Though the Long Knives boast, they do not see what is close. They are blind to their friends, the Redcoat soldiers."

Hansi began to translate but saw that Jess was not surprised. To her, he said, "There is certainly something going on between the regulars and the Shawnee Confederation, something the regulars have not seen fit to discuss with the militia."

Kentuck silently raised a corner of the skin curtain at the window and peered out at the fort's great, shadowed wall.

Jess asked, "Anyone out there?"

"Hard to tell. Pretty dark already. Nothing seems to be moving around the fort, though."

The Piankashaws looked at each other. The spokesman smiled faintly, almost triumphantly, Hansi thought. She asked him, "Is there more to your message?"

"There is more. The Piankashaws are sometimes neighbor to a wandering tribe called Puans. Once they were a great people, but now they are like scattered seeds. The Puans go with any tribe that will have them. Many are boasting they may soon be brothers to the Redcoat soldiers. These Puans share their camps with the Shawnees."

"Did they say they would be brothers only to the Redcoats?" Jess asked in the Piankashaws' tongue.

The Indian answered, "We have not come here over this long trail to be brothers to Long Knives. They kill our game and send their people to make longhouses on our ground. If the Shawnees and the Redcoats join, they will sweep across the frontier. Together they will be strong enough to march over our land and join their fortress of Detroit."

The room was silent. The horrifying implications of such a treaty had caught them all.

Kentuck raised one hand and indicated the covered window with his shaggy russet head.

Hansi stood motionless. Jess Taga's moccasins moved soundlessly toward the door. He motioned to Kentuck, but before the Virginian could snuff out the candle, the door was thrown open and a tall man stepped inside.

Jess recovered rapidly, but, as with Hansi and the others, the sight of Shelby Cameron had been a shock to him. He said, "A good evening to you, colonel. Were you curious about our little meeting?"

Cameron glanced past the Piankashaws and Kentuck Helm, and spoke directly to Hansi. "I saw Greathouse enter your cabin. When one of my men saw the light flickering, I thought you had come here to hide."

Jess cut in. "Something important came to my attention, colonel. We needed an emergency interpreter."

"Well, in God's name, close the door now. You are a fine clutch of conspirators, meeting so close to the fort and raising curtains so that anyone of us may see you. And of course it was necessary to take a female interpreter. None of my own well-equipped men would do." Cameron's contempt cut at them all. Even the Indians looked disturbed. One of them raised his rifle, hefted it slowly, but Cameron ignored them. Hansi was terrified for fear one of them would attack him.

To cover the truth, Hansi quickly burst out, "The Piankashaws were telling us they have found Puans sneaking about the fort recently. They thought the militia—that is, the army—should know."

Cameron stared at her. His jaw muscles tightened. She had never seen him really angry before and she suspected he could be as ruthless as Jess Taga, if provoked. "May one ask why these men, with their message, were intercepted in secret?"

He stepped to the center of the room. The two Piankashaws, startled by his abrasive voice and movement, raised their weapons, but Jess got between them, speaking to the Indians in their dialect. This time, they made no pretense of needing Hansi's translation. "The colonel is our chief. The chief of all the Redcoats and the Long

Knives on this part of the frontier. He has great power. He loses face when you come to us instead of to him. But now that you have completed your report, I reckon there's no more to be said."

When Hansi translated to Cameron a minute later, he smiled at her. She felt slightly optimistic for the first time that night.

Kentuck moved over to join Hansi and Cameron. "I allow I thought you were like other lobsterbacks, colonel, but if you mean you'll take the word of these Piankashaws because they're our friends, then you won't have any separate dealings with the Shawnees."

"It may be very much to the interest of these Indians to cause a rupture between the army and the militia," Cameron returned grimly.

Jess said something to the Piankashaws and turned back to Cameron. "Then you don't believe there are secret dealings between some of your officers and the Shawnees?"

"If you have proof of your accusations, show it to me and I will act. Otherwise, send these Indians about their business and end this ridiculous charade."

Jess took out his long hunting knife and examined its blade. "Our Piankashaw allies don't want us to let you return to the fort."

Hansi gasped. Cameron looked amused. "Are you going to assassinate me now? You would only prove me right and you wrong."

"Cornstalk's scouts shot your men today, colonel."

Cameron turned as if to leave. None of them knew what he would do, whether he would betray their meeting, or if he believed any part of what they had told him.

The two Piankashaws slipped around either side of Cameron, cutting him off from the door. One of them raised his rifle, but the other motioned it away, took out his scalp knife and put its edge to Cameron's throat. The Englishman looked around at the others with such contempt even Hansi was silenced. Kentuck had applied painful force to her shoulders so she did not move.

"Easy, girl," he whispered. "Jess'll see to it."

Jess Taga strolled over to the group at the door.

"The colonel's right. We'll take his word that there's no secret treaty, and that his officers are innocent, until we can prove otherwise to his satisfaction. How's that, colonel? The rest of you, put away your blades."

Without waiting for a translation, the Piankashaw removed his knife from Cameron's neck.

The colonel said, "I give you my word. I will take no action about this meeting, but end it. There will be no next time." He looked at Hansi and abruptly went out into the clearing.

Hansi walked with Jess Taga back through the river gate toward the fort. After the nerve-racking hours she had spent since Daniel Greathouse burst into the cabin, Hansi had not had a moment to think her own thoughts. Walking in silence with Jess' strong, comforting arm wrapped around her, she could no longer avoid the strong image of Shelby Cameron.

Hansi glanced at Jess, whose contagious grin told her he had not taken offense at her daydreaming. She thanked him for accompanying her home and slipped inside. Minutes after Jess Taga had left, one of his Long Knives came to lounge outside their door with his huge rifle, bayoneted, pointing up at the starry sky.

Hansi slept on a pile of skins and dreamed strange dreams. Whispering voices seemed to intrude over her dream. She awoke with a start.

Shelby Cameron. She would know that quiet, special voice out of a thousand. She stood up, stepped into her moccasins, pulled the blanket around her and listened, trying to discover whether she had dreamed or heard the English colonel's voice.

She pushed the curtain aside and suddenly saw him wrapped in his dark blue cape leaning against the wall. She stepped outside, not sure of what to expect. He was a reserved man who undoubtedly set much store in propriety, but when she appeared before him in the silent, moonlit night, she could not mistake the glow in his usually somber dark eyes. His look totally encompassed her, from her tousled hair down to her well-shaped bare ankles and moccasined feet. Excitement raced through her body.

With uncharacteristic hesitancy, he spoke her name. "Hansi . . ."

Fearful of breaking the mood, she began, "I . . . I was afraid. I heard the soldier leave. I thought perhaps Greathouse had come."

"No. I am relieving the soldier. I began to think about your danger." He smiled. "I had a dream about you. I was afraid you might be in danger." He moved slightly closer to her. "A dream," Cameron repeated softly, raising her chin so that she could not avoid him. She trembled at his touch. She scarcely dared take a breath for fear she would shatter this exquisite moment.

As his face approached hers, she closed her eyes. When his lips touched hers, she expected the cool, restrained absence of passion that marked his military activity. But as he kissed her, drawing her body to him, his hard, unexpected strength caught her unawares. The blanket slipped from her shoulders, tumbled in a heap around her feet. She scarcely noticed.

She had never been kissed with such bruising force. His lips lingered over her mouth, then were upon the hollow of her throat and down to the soft warmth between her breasts.

Through a blur of happiness, she told herself she had reached the crowning point of her life. What other love could infuse her entire body with this glorious heat of desire?

All too soon he let her go. Now, reluctantly, she felt her body slowing separating from his. She longed to remain a part of him, to have him take her as she was now, and damn the consequences!

Instead, he loosed his grip on her shoulders and, looking down at her, and murmured, "How lovely you are—and how pitifully young!"

She was crushed. And angry, too. Before she could get out more than a furious stammer, he had clasped his hand over her mouth and whispered, "Hush," and softly kissed her hot cheek. Then he picked up her blanket and wrapped her in it. "Do you know what would happen to your good name if you were seen with me here at this hour?"

"I don't care!"

"I do. Hansi, you are not going the way of other girls with mixed blood. Do you understand me? *You are not.*"

Did this mean that he cared what happened to her? She was too dazed to argue. She retreated inside the cabin without looking at him again. Would she ever understand him, she wondered, drifting off into delicious sleep.

9

HANSI was awakened by piercing sounds in the darkness of the forest. Eva, fully dressed, urgently shook her.

"It's an attack! Someone firing at the lookouts." She stepped outside, onto the grounds.

"Shawnees," Nick called, climbing out of bed with difficulty.

Hansi stood in the doorway with her father, watching the night sky light up with puffs of smoke and gunfire.

"Daughter, bring me my musket! They will need me. The fire is coming from both the clearing and the river. I must get to the walls."

"Papa, in your condition you couldn't hold a musket, let alone fire it. Go back to bed."

"They need me. I must—"

Eva came back then, forcing her way through the panic-stricken civilians. Her order, which echoed Hansi's, was listened to, although it was impossible to expect that he would go back inside the room while his army fought for its life.

Mrs. Abernathy rushed past with her hair bouncing wildly, her ample figure swathed in a dressing sacque. "I was given to understand that redskins did not attack at night," she babbled. "Indeed, one can no longer trust the word of these savages."

Eva held Nick back when he tried to rush out and join the soldiers. Meanwhile, Hansi dressed quickly in her hunting shirt and pantaloons of doeskin. As quietly as possible, she slipped by her parents and joined the rapid movement of soldiers and waterboys.

The British regulars fired systematically, changing rifles or muskets for reloading by the women and boys at their feet. The militia, both Long Knife Virginians and Pennsylvanians, fired in their own manner, sharp-shooting.

Kentuck gave Hansi a little friendly nudge. "Good lass! We can use you. But stay down."

Hansi knelt between him and Shelby Cameron, who had mounted the tower to discover why his own men were having less luck than the militia at picking off the enemy. She wondered if he remembered their embrace a few hours before. As she got busy with the ramrod, the powder and wad for the rifles, Cameron smiled down at her, which made the night seem slightly less nightmarish.

A well-aimed musket ball passed between the stakes of the high wall, carving a fiery red streak across Cameron's boot and lower right thigh. As Hansi cried out, he went down on his left knee. She was about to drop the rifle she had been loading but he stopped her brusquely. "Go about your work."

Meanwhile, he discovered that the ball had cut through the flesh of his leg but not the bone. He wiped blood onto a handkerchief, then casually removed the piece of leather that had adhered to the bloody wound. With some difficulty he finally climbed down the ladder, and limped across the quadrangle to the dressing station. As Hansi handed another rifle to Kentuck, a Redcoat regular fell, pierced through the throat by an arrow.

After an hour's time all activity from the Shawnees ceased.

Cameron had returned to the wall, limping. He gave orders for the removal of two bodies from the tower.

In the yard below there was a sudden commotion at the river gate. For one terrible second it looked as if a Redcoat might fire at the man sneaking in through that gate, but a Long Knife near him held the soldier's arm as Jess Taga came dripping into the quadrangle. Everyone crowded around him in the lantern light, joking with a touch of hysteria and inquiring how he liked swimming at midnight.

Hansi looked down from the high walk and called to Cameron. "What has Jess been about?"

"Spying on the Shawnee camp. Captain Taga is an extraordinary man."

"I've known that since I was born." Hansi shrugged. "He must be the most remarkable man on the frontier."

Cameron was watching her with interest. "You dismiss such a paragon as if he were no more than the rest of us."

"But Captain Taga is . . ." How could she make him understand? Jess was simply Jess, the dashing bronze hero of all the girls on the frontier. What the colonel seemed to be asking was why she had not fallen in love with him.

"You see," she tried again, "Jess is just somebody in my life. Someone I would go to at once if I were in trouble. Like my father. He is always here. It would be dreadful if anything ever happened to him. But . . ."

"But you are not in love with him? I understand most of the fort's young ladies are."

"No, no." She turned away, embarrassed. "Captain Taga belongs to everyone." And besides, she thought to herself, loving a man like Jess meant fear and hardship. Se could not bear to become a bitter, unhappy drudge like Eva.

He laughed. "I suspect you are right. Now, Fire-Dawn, you look dead to the world. Go and rest."

She protested, importantly. "They need me. I must be ready."

"Nonsense. Go along."

She blushed and went happily to the Verin lean-to.

In spite of all dangers outside, she dreamed blissfully of Shelby Cameron and herself. She wore the blue silk gown she had promised to make for Dolly Abernathy.

The Englishman called her exquisite. He had reached her bosom with his lips when the shrill call of fifes and drums awakened her.

"How bad is it?" she asked Eva as she splashed cold water on her face and blinked to arouse herself.

"Four dead and a dozen wounded. Hansi, we can't hold out at these odds."

Her father put in, "A thousand Shawnees and their allies are out there."

Hansi turned to look at her parents. "But that's impossible. Nobody's ever seen a thousand in one place."

"We see it now," Nick remarked. "And Colonel Cameron needs me at the wall."

"Papa, no!"

"I am needed. Would you make me a coward?"

With his dark head held up in pride he marched out carrying his musket as he had in the French War, back when he won Eva as his prize. The once unwilling captive hurried after her husband.

"Take care, Nick. Take care."

Hansi shivered and scooped up a handful of cold venison. Half of this she dropped in the cartridge bag slung over her shoulder. The rest she chewed as she joined the defenders at the blockhouse where she was detailed to help care for the wounded. She felt great sympathy for the suffering men with torn flesh and broken bones, but she had become spoiled by the militia and soldiers who motioned her up to the fighting line as one of them.

Mrs. Abernathy was busy organizing all the women and children. Eva Verin was binding the shattered remnants of an English soldier's leg while the boy polished off a bottle of Spanish run to kill the pain. With a distinctly officious manner, Mrs. Abernathy ordered Hansi to assist Dolly make and stack bandages.

"There is a terribly charming young Redcoat over in the corner," Dolly chattered. "Not badly wounded, either. But you know mama. I can't get near him because his shirt was torn off. His shirt, mind! Lud, Hansi, after all I have seen—" Catching the gorgon's eye of her mother across the hospital room of the blockhouse, she lowered her voice. "I've seen a man—you know—nude. What a silly business the human body is!"

A young Pennsylvanian was standing beside Dolly, bleeding all over the board floor from a hand wound. Delighted to have her very own patient, and one fully dressed so her mother would not interfere, Dolly forgot all her objections to male bodies and began her ministrations.

While Dolly and the young soldier worked on his medical problem and built up an acquaintance, Hansi moved to others awaiting treatment. There were no beds within the dim, airless room. Bodies were thrown in like slaughtered meat. Eva and other wives had brought in their own bedding. The moment one man died or was sent back to the line, the bedding would be used for the next case. It was practical but unpleasant, Hansi thought, for the normal dirt and lice on one body seemed to be communicated to the next man who occupied the bedding.

Moving to her next patient, Hansi recognized her young admirer, Albion McAndrews. Someone had thrown a blanket over the lower half of his body, already drenched with blood. Probably a stomach wound. The pain would be excruciating. Hansi knelt beside him and ignored Mrs. Abernathy's severe throat-clearing.

"Miss . . . Hansi?" She held one of his hands, with her free hand stroked his face. "Promise . . . you won't let them take me alive. If they come—if I can't be moved . . . promise?"

"I promise. Now, don't think of such things. They won't take the fort. Your beloved Captain Taga won't let them!"

" . . . Water—Miss Hansi . . ."

She knew he could not even keep water down, but she reached for a dipper. He muttered hoarsely, "Don't go. I'm—feared when I'm alone. Talk . . . to me."

"I'll be here." She wiped her fingers on her hunting shirt, then dipped them in the water and moistened Albion's lips. The pain twisted his frail body. Hansi called to the surgeon, "Master Brenner! Please come. He needs you."

The surgeon complained querulously, "What would you have me do? I am attending Captain Tarleton."

Hansi got up despite the weak pull of Albion's fingers. "Stay, miss. Do."

"I'll return. Don't fret, Master Albion."

Hansi confronted the harassed Master Brenner. "May I have a few drops of laudanum?"

"There is only enough for those certain to live. That Long Knife boy will not live. I cannot waste my laudanum."

Hansi thought of the gentle, loyal boy doomed to suffer a terrible death. She moved to the surgeon's other side, found the small bottle behind his blood-stained saw, and took it. She brought it quickly to Albion who was writhing in quiet torment.

He opened his eyes. "You came back."

She touched his lips with a drop of the drug, and dispensed drops to others before returning it to the indignant doctor.

Suddenly Eva screamed. Hansi looked up. Three Shawnees were scrambling over the west wall. A soldier immediately shot one, but two were running through the panic-stricken crowd in the quadrangle. They obviously intended to open the main gate. Kentuck Helm fired from the wall and brought down another. The other turned, let fly his ax and caught a Redcoat deep between the shoulder blades. The grizzled Englishman's back arched, and he plunged off the catwalk as the Shawnee screamed in agony and dropped with a musket shell in his skull.

But there were hundreds more outside the walls. Canoes filled the river.

Eva Verin joined Hansi. "Have you seen your father? I warned him he was no match for those young men."

Hansi looked up at the walls, her heart stopped until she saw Nick. He must be humiliated, she thought, seeing he had been relegated to her old job of loading rifles and muskets.

A sharpshooting Shawnee had climbed up on the roof of the Verin cabin in the clearing, where he lay flat, firing with amazing accuracy. Already, two of the defenders had been hit. Nick, sitting beside Shelby Cameron, took one of the Englishman's rifles and leveled the barrel with the sharpshooter in his sights.

Down below Eva cried, "No, Nick! Stay down! I warned you! Oh, that man!" She started across the quadrangle toward him, holding up her hand to shade her eyes from the sun.

Hansi sighed. "Mama, you can't argue with papa when he wants to be a hero."

Two sharp cracks cut through the sultry air. Nick hit the sharpshooter on the cabin rooftop, and a Shawnee, climbing over the west wall, fired his musket at a Redcoat in the quadrangle. At the last second the Shawnee lost his balance and the musket ball went wild, tearing through Eva Verin's body.

10

FEW people noticed. The men on the walls were screaming congratulations at Nick, who slapped the gun barrel happily, accepting their praise. Soldiers in the courtyard ran to examine the dead Shawnee. Hansi had watched Eva race across the quadrangle. She knew now that Eva cared deeply for Nick Verin.

Hansi saw her mother hesitate as if she had tripped over a stone. Her reed-thin body swayed. Still not understanding, Hansi rushed out to help her. People milled around, paying no attention to a tiny, fainting woman. At any minute Chief Cornstalk's army could pour over the walls. Eva's body sank into Hansi's arms. The girl knelt in the dust, cradling her mother's tidy golden head.

"Mama?" Hansi did not recognize her own high-pitched, desperate wail. "Where are you hurt? Mama, please—"

Eva was having trouble opening her eyes. "My . . . my back. Don't fret, honey, it isn't bad. Hardly hurts." Her lashes flickered. The disillusioned blue eyes suddenly flashed, disturbed. They had never been brighter. "Hansi?"

"Yes, mama?"

"Don't . . . stay here. Horrid place." Her fingers moved against Hansi's body. "Cameron . . . love you. Make . . . yourself worthy of him. Promise . . . promise . . ."

"I promise," she said softly. She called out for somebody to get the surgeon. "Mama, mama, does it hurt?"

"Tell Nick . . ."

"Yes, yes. Don't you move now. The surgeon is coming."

A shadow passed over them as they huddled on the ground. Hansi insisted, "He's here now. He will make it better. You'll see, mama dear." Without looking up, she knew it was Jess Taga's hand on her mother's wrist, his voice gentle, "Be a brave soldier, sweetheart."

Slowly Hansi raised her head. His face was a blur but she knew she could count upon his word. "Jess, don't let her stay out here in the sun. She sunburns so easy."

"Sweetheart, it's too late."

She felt the white-hot light overhead, burning into her own scalp. She bent over her mother. "Please, please, God, don't let her die."

"Hansi, let me take her."

A terrible cry, a howl torn from the lungs of a creature in agony pierced the air.

"No! My woman! Let me by. My woman!"

Hansi saw Jess Taga's hawk face looking down at her tenderly. She wondered if this sweet side of him had always existed. "That was papa. He knows."

Jess nodded. "Let me take her."

Hansi watched him lift Eva's slight form into his arms. The hair came free of its confining pins and fell across his arm. Hansi blinked and looked at the ground. There was surprisingly little blood where Eva had fallen. Hansi gently piled some loose earth over the stain, burying it without quite knowing why. She heard scuffling around her. The firing went on at the walls. Colonel Cameron was trying to restrain Nick Verin as he limped toward his wife and daughter.

"Wait until she is laid down indoors," Cameron said quietly. "Only a few seconds."

Hansi got to her feet, tried to head off her father. "Papa, wait. Stay with me."

She had never seen him like this, even raving drunk. His black eyes were glazed, his leathery face streaked with his grief.

"He took her right away from me. I couldn't touch her. Daughter, I couldn't even touch her."

Hansi tried to speak but her throat seemed to lock. She took Nick's arm and guided him toward the blockhouse. When her knees gave way suddenly for no reason, Cameron reached out to support her.

"Hansi . . ."

"I know. Please don't talk about it. Papa, we'll go and sit by mama until they . . ." The thought was agony.

But there was no time to mourn. By nightfall, the defenders were reduced by half, and Nick Verin, without having said a single word in five hours, was led back up to the wall with instructions to look out for more sharpshooters. Hansi followed and loaded his weapons for him. He fired blindly, but the whole fort heard the shriek of the enemy hard upon his shots. Now and again, between shots, he reached his hand down, seeking the comfort of his daughter's presence. Her fingers closed on his, and then he took up his rifle again.

Gradually the firing ceased. Hansi turned to look down at the quadrangle with her usual and largely unconscious thought, "I wonder if mama . . ."

Realization intruded and the black pall of grief fell over her spirit. She tried to concentrate upon the immediate activity below. Colonel Cameron and Jess Taga were deep in conversation, with Jess gesturing toward the river wall. Some of the numbness she felt over her mother's death vanished now in the chilling knowledge that they could never hold out another day.

She stared between the weather-warped slivers of the palisade but could make out no movement among the Shawnees in all that vast darkness beyond the walls of the fort. Yet she knew Cornstalk's army was out there. In the far distance through the trees she finally made out the gleam of a campfire, small and easily contained like all

Indian fires. The Shawnees had not abandoned their prey. Would tomorrow bring a repetition of the horrors her mother had experienced during the massacre at Fort William Henry on Lake George? Hansi felt a chill run down her body. *No,* she vowed, *I won't let it happen to me. I'll kill anyone who tries to take me as mama was taken. . . .*

Through the flickering lantern and torch lights, she could make out the frightened white faces of the women on the parade ground. The word had already begun to spread. Mothers were gathering their children urgently. A terrible scramble ensued as civilians ran in every direction, colliding with soldiers.

Cameron relieved Kentuck Helm who had subsisted twenty-four hours on dried venison, corn and the Holland gin called Blue Ruin. The colonel said nothing to the numb and silent Nick Verin, but touched Hansi's hand sympathetically. She wished he had not done so, for the tears blinded her at once and she had to look away.

"It's bad, isn't it?" she said hoarsely, frantic to avoid the subject of her mother.

"Very bad, I'm afraid. My officers want to ask Cornstalk the terms of surrender, but I agree with Taga. There is no hope in that. Cornstalk made a treaty with Major Hay, which he considers we broke. It's possible he will spare the women, but—"

"You don't believe that anymore than I do."

He drew her aside. "Taga has a plan. Quite mad, of course, but that shouldn't surprise me. He wants to evacuate the entire fort."

She swung around, stared at him. "We are surrounded and Jess wants to evacuate? How? Through the air?"

"The river. Since the northeast corner is nearly impregnable, with the high wall and the river depth, it's impossible for them to scale. Jess thinks a handful of Long Knives could surprise their sentries at that point while we get all the civilians out by the river. If we can, the military will follow. Once we get beyond the Shawnee lines, we take to the forest and march overland to Fort Pitt."

"Is it possible?" she asked, her mind racing on to picture the evacuation. "But no. The children will babble. The mothers will talk. The Shawnees would be onto us in a minute."

"All the same, I think it could be done," Cameron insisted quietly. "So does Helm."

"And your officers?"

He shrugged. "They say Captain Taga is mad. They don't believe we can count on silence and discipline from the civilians. Carleton agrees with Major Hay that it would be better if we parley with Cornstalk."

"But, colonel, surely your officers won't take the word of a traitor like Major Hay."

"I'm afraid they're not as strongly against the major as you. They claimed Hay made a *misguided* peace effort with the Shawnee Confederation. Hay's offense, according to the army, is a crime of military protocol. He went over his colonel's head."

"Dear God!"

"Yes, you might say that. My own vote, for whatever it is worth, is unquestionably for Captain Taga's plan. It is daring, but that may be its best feature. The Shawnees will never expect it."

Hansi thought of her mother's body. What will be her grave? How can we bear to leave her here, in this ground she hated?

Cameron explained the situation to each man at the wall. By the time a half hour had passed without a shot fired Hansi guessed that all the English regulars and the militia had been informed of Jess Taga's plan and knew his own part in that perilous effort.

Late in the evening Hansi was ordered to join the other civilians in the long, barnlike room where the fort routs and dances had been held. She expected to find women and children huddled together crying. She was ashamed and relieved to find the children, wide-eyed with fear, on their best behavior, with no squirming or whispers. The adults, especially the women, stood stiffly at attention, like new recruits on parade.

Mrs. Abernathy, who had been organizing the civilian company, bustled over to Hansi. "Dear Hendrickje, allow me to express our sorrow for your tragic loss. What a perfectly dreadful thing to happen! You must let me look after you now, my child, as I am sure your dear mother would have wished."

Each mention of her mother was a twisting, tearing pain. "Yes, ma'am. Are we to meet someone here?"

"The dear colonel, but as I was saying, when I saw dear Eva run across the parade ground and then sway—just that graceful way she seemed to lean forward and then back—I said to myself, 'even when she is bleeding and torn, she manages to—' "

"Excuse me. I'm needed." Hansi walked rapidly away, with her hand clasped around her throat. This pressure eased the intolerable ache. She had never hated anyone, not even the man who killed her mother, as much as she hated the well-meaning Mrs. Abernathy.

Dolly and the young man she had found in the blockhouse-hospital were whispering in a corner. The young soldier called to Hansi. "Miss, could you tell me, how is that young militiaman, Albion? He took a nasty musketball in the gut. Nasty!" He glanced at his companion. "Begging your pardon, miss, I'm sure."

Guiltily, Hansi realized she had not thought once of the suffering young Long Knife in all the hours since morning. "I am afraid I haven't seen him since early today. I will go as soon as we leave here."

Dolly put in nervously, "From here we may have to leave the fort at once. It will be very difficult not to make a sound. Some are sure to cry out, if they miss their footing, or are frightened, or any of a thousand things."

But her young Redcoat would have none of that. "I'll be there to see to you, Miss Dolly. Don't you worry."

It was strange that life could go on quite as though nothing untoward had happened, as though tomorrow morning Eva Verin would be outside her cabin scrubbing the stoop as usual. As though she would once more kiss

Hansi good-night brusquely, without warmth, then perhaps touch her hand in that odd little secretive gesture, as if she were ashamed of her own sentimentality.

And the scoldings . . . if she would scold me now! Hard. Order me about. Frown. If she would only walk in that door this minute! If only . . .

Captain Carleton strode in, pulling down the tail of his jacket, stiffening his shoulders, looking as if the last thing in the world he wanted was responsibility for the safety of these scores of civilians. Everyone quickly gathered around him. He began to explain the situation in harsh, cold tones. He was obviously not used to dealing with terrified women and children. By the time Hansi reached the crowd he had made his definitive statement: "Therefore, the evacuation of all army personnel will be under my command. Captain Jess Taga and his lieutenant will be responsible for the women and children."

"And the wounded, sir?" Hansi put in nervously, remembering Albion McAndrews.

Captain Carleton looked at her, clearly puzzled by the sight of her in the clothing of a Long Knife. From the look in his eyes, Hansi knew he disapproved.

"Naturally, all wounded capable of being moved will be taken out by the army under the supervision of Master Brenner, our surgeon."

Mrs. Abernathy was not intimidated by the captain's severity. She pushed her way to the front.

"I am certain there must be instructions for the ladies and their little ones, sir. Are we to hear these instructions from you or Colonel Cameron?"

"From the commander of militia, Captain Taga. I ask you all to hear him out as though his instructions came from me. Your lives—all our lives—will depend upon your following his instructions to the last detail." He inclined his head stiffly, and repeated, ". . . the last detail, mesdames. Impress this upon your children."

As the captain descended from the musicians' platform, Jess passed him but stood among the attentive women to speak with them.

"If one of you sneezes, we all die. If this pretty little

lass, or that fine upstanding lad over in the corner there should cry, or even moan, she—and he—will die. All of us. And horribly." He tilted up the little girl's chin, which quavered, although the child was now all eyes, mesmerized by his every move, every word. "Do you understand me, child?"

"Ay, sir."

"Two nights ago I saw a child your age with her skull crushed by a Shawnee hunting party. Do you know what that means?"

"Should you remind them?" Hansi asked. "She is so young, it will give her nightmares."

"That is better than she will receive at the hands of the enemy."

Hansi said no more. He was right. Everyone's life depended on silence during the evacuation. Then Captain Jess spoke individually to each child and adult, impressing upon them the hideous fate of the entire company if even the tiniest sound was made.

In every case, as Hansi noted carefully, the child was treated like a grown-up, told the truth and the danger. As a result, each child became an adult, serious without panic, giving his word, and aware of the immense importance of what lay ahead.

Hansi breathed with relief. They knew that, incredible as it seemed, they could trust their children who had been bred to frontier warfare.

11

THE young soldier with Dolly Abernathy asked, "Pardon, captain, are we to leave no one in the fort? Won't they be suspicious if there are no sounds from here?"

Jess grinned. It may have been a grim smile but it cheered them, giving the company a sense that he would always stand between them and the enemy. Hansi shared their feeling. Seeing Jess before them looking cheerful and supremely self-confident, she thought for the first time since her mother had died in her arms that there might be sunlight in the future, that it would not always be a starless night.

Jess raised his hands in a jovial, carefree gesture. "I'm asking for a dozen volunteers to stay behind to provide a certain amount of—shall we say jollification, until shortly before dawn. Those who remain will find it a near thing when they leave." He looked over the crowd. "Believe me, we will perform so well Governor Dunmore will ask for an encore in Williamsburg, and even King George may want us for his summer follies."

This produced a laugh from everyone, even the English.

Hansi's heart jumped unpleasantly as a languid, bored voice from the back of the room called out: "Who is to choose the manner in which the fort will be evacuated? By Gad, that should have some slight importance."

Jess glanced at Hansi briefly. She did not know why until she looked around to see big, stout Major Hay, whom she regarded as a murderous traitor to the people of Fort Blaine.

"Sorry, major. That choice has been pretty well made. Colonel Cameron will lead the first contingent of regulars, in case they're needed to clear the way. They will be followed by the civilians. Lieutenant Helm will aid you, major. He'll glue himself to your side during the whole evacuation." He looked at the others, who listened anxiously. "We hope the soldiers won't be needed to silence you folks. A bayonet in the belly isn't a nice business."

They looked at each other uneasily. Was he joking? There was no doubt. Without a word, everyone knew: *He means it. He will do it!*

Jess spoke a few words to the women he had not individually warned earlier. Hansi watched Major Hay turn and leave the room. She waited, hoping to catch Jess alone, but he was surrounded by questioners. Outside, she found the fort grounds in chaos, men running everywhere in eerie silence, tightly clutching sword scabbards with one hand and uniform hats with the other.

Hansi was more troubled by the decisions she felt she must make than by the problems facing Jess and the British regulars. She knew she must go and see to the poor Long Knife, Albion McAndrews, but she was still haunted by the anguish of leaving her mother in this place that she had so bitterly hated. If she could have chosen her mother's resting place, it would be somewhere beyond the Blue Mountains, the magic coastal land she had longed to return to for most of her life.

"And I promised her I would make myself worthy of Shelby Cameron. But what if he doesn't want me that way?" It was too much to hope for, that the gentlemanly and tender Shelby Cameron should actually make an urchin in deerskin like herself his wife.

She went into the Verin shack, where her mother had been laid out on the bed. Her body was covered by her best embroidered coverlet. Hansi reached under the coverlet, took her mother's hand and held it for endless minutes. Her thoughts were too chaotic for prayer. Despite all the scurrying figures out in the quadrangle, she still could not spur herself to action.

Gradually she became aware that she was not alone with her mother's spirit and her own painful memories. She looked over her shoulder. "I will go in a minute. I only came here because I didn't know what to do."

"I know," Shelby Cameron said. "When I lost my father—I was perhaps your age—I was very bitter. I had been in Canada and my father in India. I admired him very much, you see, and he was betrayed by the villagers. But no matter. I meant only to say I understand." He put his hand on her shoulder and she wanted to jerk away, to say, *Don't be tender and kind. Don't make me cry. Make me hard for what must be done.*

Instead, she asked him, "Did you ever reconcile yourself?"

After a moment's pause he said unexpectedly, "I don't believe so. I never forgave them. But why should I think of it now? It is all long gone by. Hansi, something must be done. I've tried to reason with your father and I believe he understands. But I need your permission too. Do you know what I am trying to say?"

She had not wanted to face the inevitable. "I know. She mustn't be left there. They might—"

"She must be buried. And immediately. The fort will be deserted in two hours."

She looked down at her mother's hand, caressing it between her fingers. "What shall we do?"

"Come with me."

She crossed Eva's hands on her bosom. Cameron drew the coverlet over the quiet, colorless face, then led Hansi across the quadrangle.

"Where are we going?"

He brought her to the small plot of spaded ground beside the blockhouse. The children of the forest planted whatever they chose here. Cornstalks were beginning to shoot up—and two rose brushes, and bluebells. Hansi understood.

"It is almost like a garden beyond the mountains, where she was born."

"Do you have a Bible?"

"Of course. Mama has."

Two of the regulars on the run knocked against Hansi as they passed on their way to the river gate. Cameron reminded her, "They are beginning. We must hurry."

He commandeered one of the soldiers to help him dig the grave and brought out Eva Verin's body, using the coverlet for a shroud. Hansi led her father over to the narrow grave and held his hand tightly while Cameron quoted from memory, "I will look to the hills, from whence cometh my salvation . . ."

Hansi shared her father's numb disbelief in what was happening. She had been terrified that she would weep and perhaps plunge her father into an awareness of his loss, but the bizarre circumstances of the burial made it impossible for her to feel anything. With disaster hanging heavily in the air, she was grateful for her numbness.

Nick Verin spoke suddenly. "She is not there, daughter."

"No, papa, she is in heaven."

He said nothing to that. She wondered if he actually understood what was happening. Obedient to Cameron's suggestion, she dropped a clump of earth symbolically upon the body. That could not be Eva. This morning she had been alive and sharply reminding Hansi that she must get more rest. It was not mama lying there. Hansi looked away.

"You must both go and join the others," Cameron said firmly. "The evacuation is under way."

She avoided the open grave, cleared her throat, and asked, "Will you . . ."

"The sergeant and I will attend to everything. You go and see Captain Taga. I know you can help him. He has the wounded to worry about as well as the women and children."

She tried to lead her father away but was shaken when he said suddenly, "No one but me must see my woman to Manitou's place."

He had understood then. She glanced at Cameron, who nodded. She left the small plot and after a few steps began to run from the anguish of the open grave. For the rest of her life she would regret that she did not have the courage to look back one last time.

She passed silent women and children hurrying along like phantoms in the black night. They were being led out of the fort by the seldom-used northeast gate, directly into the water. Some of them were swimming. Others were taken off in boats. She heard an oarlock squeak once and then the strange, unnatural silence again took over the fort.

Inside, the walking wounded were being helped out by soldiers and militiamen detailed to the task. Many of the injured winced as their broken shoulders or stumps of severed limbs were pushed and shoved, but no one protested. The horror of what would happen to them if they remained was vivid in every mind. None of them had forgotten the nightmare of Fort William Henry on Lake George. The hospital looked empty, but Hansi saw Jess at the side of Albion McAndrews, lying among soiled rags on the dirt floor.

Hansi looked at Jess, who hid one hand behind him as she approached.

"Hansi, he will be dead by this time tomorrow. He is beyond hope."

Frantic, she cried, "You can't leave him here. You know what they will do to him." It was as if, in saving this young militiaman, she might turn back time and save her mother.

"I've given him as much laudanum as we can spare.

But it isn't going to be enough to keep him unconscious for very long."

She moistened her dry lips. "What will you do?"

"You know what I must do, what he begged me to do."

"No!"

He looked more grim than she had ever seen him. "Hansi, your place is with the living. They need you." He brought his hand into sight. He was carrying a heavy pistol.

She drew back, feeling a revulsion toward Jess that she had never thought possible. "You can't!"

"I promised him. Go out and join the others."

She moved away slowly trying to think of some way to prevent his ruthless act of murder, still unable to believe he would go through with it. Unable to restrain herself, she glanced back. Jess had placed the muzzle of the pistol against the unconscious boy's temple. She rushed out onto the grounds, swept along by the running civilians. The pistol shot reverberated through the blockhouse. She shut her eyes tightly, letting herself be pushed down to the river gate.

Her mother had always been right. She hated the frontier for its brutality, its raw cruelty. She had always disliked Jess Taga, saying that he was a symbol of this life that would end by making a savage of Hansi herself.

At the river's edge Major Hay startled her by appearing suddenly in all his stout importance and offering to put her into a flatboat already overloaded with silent women and children who scarcely breathed. As the boat swayed with the current, she thought of her father and drew back.

"Not yet. There is someone else." She climbed the slope back into the quadrangle. It looked calm and deserted under the rising moon. The golden moonlight cheered her for a moment, until she remembered the target the boats would provide. There were occasional stirrings and sounds inside the fort which she supposed were the activities of the remaining men trying to fool the enemy into thinking that all was normal inside the fort.

She headed for the children's vegetable plot. Nothing seemed to move in those deep shadows. A mound of earth remained against the blockhouse wall.

"From mama's grave," she thought, and almost turned back. But some instinct made her approach the ground.

She realized then that the mound of earth was a man kneeling. Her heart twisted painfully and she went to him and put her arms around him, stepping on the edge of the grave to reach him. He needed her now. Her mother was beyond help.

"Papa, come with me. Everyone is gone."

"I do not leave her here alone."

"She isn't here. She is in heaven. Come, father."

He raised his head but did not look at her. "I know where she is." One of his hands caressed the loose earth beside him. "In the night she was always frightened until I came. Did you know that, daughter?"

"Yes, papa, but . . ." The night hung ominously still about them. She looked around, wanting so much to scream out her despair, her terror of the future for herself as well as for Nick. How would he survive without the one person for whom he had existed? She tried the only persuasion left to her.

"Papa, dear, I need you. Please, come with me. Cornstalk's men are liable to break into the fort at any time."

"They will not touch her." For the first time he looked at her, raising one hand to touch her face. "Daughter, I cannot leave her here alone. They may find her . . . her body."

She caught her breath. She had not thought of that. "They are human. Chief Cornstalk would not let them do such a thing. He is a civilized man. Papa, I need you too. Don't you understand?" She tried to shake his shoulder but it was like shaking the great, rough trunk of a valley oak. "Do you want to make mother terribly unhappy? Why must you die and make her so sad?"

Did she sound as though she were reasoning with a child? She prayed that he would not notice. She need not have concerned herself. He paid little attention. She forgot the moment, the danger, everything, and cried, "There isn't a minute to lose. You must come, father. Now!"

She could have moved a rooted oak more easily than Nick Verin. She backed away from him, avoided her mother's grave and went into the blockhouse-hospital. Albion's body had been removed. The deserted room stank of blood, urine and abandoned bandages, but she saw no one. As she came out again, not knowing what to do, she saw Jess Taga. He had been heading for the river gate but turned abruptly at the sight of Nick Verin.

She tried to say something, to plead with him for help. He waved her to silence and came on to the kneeling scout. Hansi was shocked when he cuffed Nick across the back in a comradely way.

"You will need a good swig of rum to keep you through the night. It looks to be cold."

"No. She would not like it. She does not like me to drink rum." He raised his head, added plaintively, "Or Blue Ruin."

"Quite right. But surely you will join me in a last toast to Mrs. Verin's memory. Your daughter will join us. It is the custom, you know."

Nick hesitated. At another time Hansi would have been proud of his resistance. Now, as the moments edged closer to dawn, she became frantic. Clutching his own shoulders and hugging them, Nick repeated, "No. She would not wish it."

Jess Taga's voice came, cold, sharp and contemptuous. "Do you think she will be proud of you if you keep trembling like that? She will not believe it is the cold. She will think you are a shivering coward."

"It is a lie! I am no coward."

"Prove it. Take a drink and you will stop shaking."

To Hansi's intense relief, Nick Verin got up from his knees.

"I will take one glass, because they must not see me shiver when they come."

Hansi followed them into the militia headquarters next

door to Colonel Cameron's cabin. One of Jess' Long Knife lieutenants was gathering up extra ammunition stored in front of several jugs of Spanish rum. Jess reached for one of the rum jugs, slung it over his shoulder and asked his man for a mug.

Nick Verin straightened his shoulders. With that rare and occasional dignity that his daughter always loved and admired, he scoffed, "You think I need a mug? A cup? Like a female? Here." Jess passed the big jug to him. He slung it over his shoulder, brought the lip of the jug to his mouth, and took a long swallow. Hansi shuddered.

Jess walked toward the door, motioned for Hansi to join him. Nick looked up, called out militantly, "Wait. Where do you go with my daughter?"

"What's it to you, Nick?" Jess smiled wickedly. "Your child is nearly a woman. She needs a—shall we say—a friend?"

"Now, see here, you'll take your hand from my child!" Nick dropped the jug and started after them. Hansi gasped. There was a hideous crash as the jug broke and rum splattered all around. Nick ignored the crash, charging after the others indignantly. Jess took Hansi's arm and hurried her along, across the quadrangle, down the slope to the river gate. Captain Carleton signaled to them from a little skiff pushing against the stockade walls.

"Be quick, captain. We've had to get rid of the fifth Redskin. He was on guard at the east wall. Two or three might go unnoticed, but five!"

Nick lurched down the slope after them. "You! Jess! Take your hand off my child!"

By the time he reached the skiff Hansi was in the boat. Under Captain Carleton's astonished eyes, Nick lunged for his daughter and was struck a fast, hard blow by Jess' strong fist. His head snapped back, and he collapsed into the skiff where Hansi caressed his tousled head and shed a few relieved tears.

The little boat passed by under the great stockade walls. The only sound echoing over the water was the creak of oarlocks. A minute or two later Hansi's sharp eyes made out the bodies of several Shawnees scattered beneath the east wall. They had been strangled. She saw the contorted faces and the protruding tongues like ghastly masks under the moon. Jess Taga's doing, she decided. Jess and Kentuck. She was grateful to them for saving her father, but all that her mother had believed about their brutality and ruthlessness was true. They had to live like this because they lived on the frontier. But she would not become an animal too. It was what her mother had struggled against all her adult life, and with that dying promise to her, Hansi had set the future pattern of her own life.

They were all safe now. She knew it even before the skiff pulled into a little cove. Now, only the march to the Fort Pitt Trace lay between them and safety. And civilization . . .

"I will do what mama told me in the last minutes of her life," she vowed silently, "I must go over the mountains and learn to be what she wanted me to be. A lady, God help me."

And what of Nick Verin's life? How could he possibly be contented beyond the mountains, among townspeople? The great black forests of the Ohio were his whole life. He had spent his life out here in the vastness of nature. Could he ever fit into the life of a townsman?

What could she do about him? Surely, somewhere there might be a life for Nick and herself if, as was highly probable, Cameron decided that amid the polite and proper surroundings of a civilized town there was no place in his life for a frontier wife. Would she be his mistress?

"No!" she thought. "If I am not good enough to be his wife, I am still too good to be his mistress."

Soon it would be dawn, and Hansi's courage was restored. It was the wonderful thing about the sunrise—a new, unused, unscarred day lay ahead.

12

IN a lifetime of seventeen years on the frontier Hansi had never dreamed of anything like Fort Pitt, with its population of over two hundred souls on a normal trading day. With a village and numerous trading posts hovering around its small fortress, Fort Pitt faced at once east and west. It was the doorway to both the highly civilized coastal colonies, and the trackless wilderness that stretched the length of the Ohio to the mysterious waters of the Mississippi that the Spanish had discovered and the French settled.

The injured were removed from the flatboats first, then the women and children. At its busiest the old fort town had never heard such a hullabaloo as came from the throats of a few children when, for the first time in more than a fortnight, they could speak above a whisper. Now they might cry if they wished, or shout and scream. Surprisingly, few did cry. There was a new, tense and adult look about the children now that had not been there before and which in some cases would remain with them throughout their lives.

The hospital areas were soon overcrowded. Hansi was

sent first to attend the dying with Père Gilbert, the French priest. It was a gloomy, hopeless effort, with its constant reminders of Eva Verin's death. Hansi was much relieved to be put to work caring for those wounded who were not beyond help.

The Abernathys, to Hansi's surprise, had come through the ordeal of the flight from Fort Blaine with colors flying, but once they reached Fort Pitt Mrs. Abernathy resumed her hateful position as social dowager of the dressing station. Captain Abernathy had caught an arrow in his shoulder in the battle, but his proper wife was careful not to show partiality. She bustled busily around every other patient in the room, until many patients complained they envied Captain Abernathy because he received so little attention.

The room had been a prison barracks. It had an earth floor. Tiny, barred windows, high overhead, prevented the room from getting much direct sun. It was unbearably hot by day and dank and cold by night.

The barracks room was already overcrowded with survivors of a company of colonial troops who had lost a skirmish with the blood-hungry Shawnees. Lying on beds of straw and rags, men were briskly shoved together to make room for the newcomers.

Recognizing a natural, if officious, leader in Mrs. Abernathy, Hansi tried to obey her, meanwhile wondering what had happened to Nick and Colonel Cameron and Jess Taga. Hours later, toward darkness that closed in around the long spring evening, she met Jess Taga as she came off duty. They stood in the dusty wagon ruts formed months before by the winter mud, while he patiently answered her worried questions.

"Nick has been burying the dead out along the Monongahela. Looks as if two of the Redcoats were gone before Cameron got this far. And old Mrs. Jermyn died just when she reached the fort."

Hansi wiped her sweating face on her pinafore, and pulled the clean night air into her lungs. It felt pure and comforting, peppered with the smell of meat roasting over low-burning fires. Overhead the night-blue sky was ablaze with stars.

"I don't like papa burying people. He might begin to remember—"

Jess shook his head. "He wanted to. For some reason it comforts him. He's going to be right as a trivet, you'll see. He just needs something to occupy him, something to make him feel useful. Have you seen the colonel since we arrived?"

She did not want to let him see that she was hurt because Shelby Cameron had said almost nothing to her since escaping Fort Blaine. She knew he was much too busy getting everyone through that dangerous trek to safety. She was comfortable in her relationships with Jess and the other Long Knives, who were frontier folk and treated her as one of them. But Shelby Cameron was different. Remembering his recent attempts to treat her like an uninformed, inexperienced lady, Hansi felt anger rise up in her. It was all right to be treated daintily once in a while, but it didn't stop her from understanding other things. Gentlemen, she realized, could be infuriating.

"I haven't seen the colonel," she said coolly. "But I daresay he has been busy. As I have."

Jess grinned down at her. "Been too much the gentleman for your taste, has he? Hansi-girl, you'd do well to keep to your own kind." He laughed softly and patted her hair. It felt good.

Removing his hand, and forcing herself to sound calm, Hansi asked, "And what precisely is my kind? Am I so much inferior?"

"Your own kind—you vixen—is a man who sees you as a female, not as one of those—what do they call them?— pattern dolls."

"Never mind." She looked up. Never had she seen a night sky more beautiful, more filled with shooting stars leaving white milky tails streaking out behind them. "Shooting stars are a bad sign, papa says. Do you believe that?"

He cocked an eyebrow in the general direction of

heaven. His mind was clearly on something else but he answered, "I've heard Indians say it happens when there's a major tribal war about to explode. Some whites agree. It's a sign of war."

She looked around anxiously. She never doubted Jess Taga's word. "A war with the British, or the Indians?"

"Both. The Redcoats are marching back out of Pitt as soon as they can get fresh supplies. They'll take up stations at Fort Detroit. And there's little doubt they'll carry out that Hairbuyer Hay's treaty with the Shawnees. We colonials may have our war, but the minute we do, we've lost the frontier to the British and their Indian allies."

This was all too complicated for Hansi. For once, she could not decide who was right and who was wrong. Either way, there were more important matters at hand. "Captain, you wanted to tell me something?"

Reminded of the urgent matters at hand, he laughed shortly. "Considering that your beloved colonel will soon become my enemy, I ought to find it good news. But—"

"But what? What is it? Jess! Is it about Shelby Cameron?"

"Your precious Redcoat? Have you noticed how badly he limped along the entire Trace, until they reached the flatboats? A dozen people have told me so."

Alarmed, she remembered how Cameron had tried not to favor his leg. Was it really that bad? He needed her, and all the time she had not noticed. She had been everywhere except where she could help the most.

"I'll go at once. How bad is it?"

"He says there's nothing wrong, and I don't advise you to approach it straight off. But Brenner, the surgeon, says that it's badly infected. All the dirt and water the fellow went through. It's swelled up and green and . . . no sight for a lady."

"I thought we had agreed I was no lady. Where is he?"

"Best to wait, infant. He's with Nick and the priest, burying one of his men—a sergeant, I think. And don't mention me in the affair."

She picked up her skirts and started along the riverbank

between rows of apple trees that formed a skimpy-looking orchard. The burial ground was deserted by the time she arrived. She hesitated, turned and walked back between the rows of the dead.

The still beauty of the night, the protective rise of forested hills to the north, behind the fort, and most of all the fact that those she loved had reached safety gave her a sudden sense of security and optimism. Shelby Cameron would be well. Her father would recover from Eva's death. Jess was his unruly but familiar self. She gazed at the serene sky and felt the comfort of her mother looking down upon her, content at last, in heaven.

Out of the shadow of a wooden grave marker half sunk in moist riverside earth, a man seemed to rise up out of nowhere, standing before her. Badly shaken, she would have cried out, but as he took several hasty steps toward her she saw that he limped.

"Please, don't be alarmed. I am Shelby Cameron. What in God's name are you doing out here alone at this hour?"

She caught herself before admitting the truth. "I was looking for my father."

"Nick has gone to take a well-earned bottle of Blue Ruin. Don't worry. He'll give himself a good sleep, which he certainly deserves." She didn't like the idea, but dismissed Nick from her thoughts as he slipped his hand under her elbow, escorting her grandly over the ground as he would any lady. Ironically, she remembered she had searched him out to do quite the reverse. After all, it was he who needed her help. He walked with deliberate steps, straining to hide his injury.

"This is good luck, meeting you alone out here," he said as they neared the little village of hovels crowded around the fort on three sides.

"Then I am glad I came."

He looked up at the storm lantern that illuminated a wooden sign: TRIANGLE AND CROWN. This was the local inn, an imposing wooden building of two stories, which was the center of the town's activities. The word "crown" was nearly blotted out by clods of mud that seemed to have become a part of the wood.

"These are the only decent lodgings in town, from what I have been able to discover." His hand closed painfully on her arm. "Wait. I've made plans of my own for you, but where have they housed you and Nick?"

"I've no idea. The Abernathys and the other officers' wives are assigned to quarters vacated by the British officers. The militia women—" She hesitated, not knowing his feelings about the female hangers-on at the fort, women of loose morals and vagabond ways who served only one purpose for the men in the militia. "With the British leaving," she continued and found it an even less happy subject, "that is, there should be considerable space."

He ignored the political implications of what she said. "See here. I must talk to you. My orders will send me to Fort Detroit. With this fort in the hands of the rebels, God knows when I may see you again. I want you and Nick to join the Loyalist settlers making their way to the French settlements on the Mississippi. That is, if you still feel loyal to the Crown."

"Papa does. And I do. Remember, papa is half French. But—" She felt shy of explaining further. "Will we ever see you again, sir?"

"Can you possibly call me something besides 'sir'? It makes me feel—"

"Like a commander?" She smiled.

"Just so. And I prefer to be your friend."

"Thank you. You have always been that."

"And in future, something much more. If I knew you were safe at Kaskaskia, or in one of the other French towns, I could accept that desolate command post out in Fort Detroit without any qualms. As to seeing you again, you must believe me. I promise you we will soon meet in Arbreville or Kaskaskia."

Did the Redcoats intend to take over all those peaceful French towns along the Mississippi? It was grossly unfair. The French settlers had made no trouble for anyone. They provided the one civilizing influence between the Great Waters and Fort Sacklin in the Ohio Forest.

"Even if papa and I lived in one of those towns, we could never be like your people. Your world isn't mine. My manners, for one thing."

"Do not contradict me." She raised her chin, but he cut off her protest with a strong finger pressed over her lips. "I find you the most enchanting creature on the frontier."

His words, intended to please her, gave her a quick stab of pain. Unfortunately, he had proved her worst fears—that she did not fit into Colonel Shelby Cameron's world, and never could.

"Come," he said suddenly, moving her toward the door, "we will find your father. I sent him here to the tavern."

At the same time the inn door opened and a pair of militiamen stumbled out. They crashed into Cameron and Hansi saw him wince and stagger as one of them accidentally hit against his injured leg. Hansi's entire body shivered. She felt the pain he must be enduring. If she did have some influence upon him—and he had certainly suggested that she did—she was determined that he not go marching out of her life with an injury that threatened to cripple him.

The two militiamen recovered their balance as best they could and turned to survey the obstacle in their path.

"Well now, colonel laddie, I reckon we don't salute you anymore, do we? What d'you say, lobsterback? I give you a fortnight before we're at war with you in real and earnest."

Cameron's face looked drawn. His strong jaw set as he fought to hide the stinging pain in his leg. Finally he managed a cool, scornful reply. "In that case, farewell, gentlemen. We have nothing more to say to each other."

Weaving tipsily, the second colonial piped up, "We're the ones ordered *you* out of Fort Pitt and don't you be so proud as to be forgetting it. We don't need your kind to fight heathen redskins. We'll have you, and that king of yours—plus the damned Shawnees—on the run inside a month."

"Not if you drink as much as you have had tonight," Cameron coldly shot back, turning on his bad leg to walk into the taproom with Hansi. Although he dragged his leg he stood with his usual straight military stance as several men and two women, gathered around the roasts on a turning spit, eyed him curiously.

In the far corner of the hearth Nick Verin sat cross-legged, his head bowed against his knees. Neither the buoyant chatter around him, nor even the aroma of wild turkey glistening brown on the spit, aroused him.

"It must be the gin," Hansi explained when she crossed the room with Cameron following close behind.

"Perhaps he should eat something."

She shook her head. "I'll get him to bed. He did well today. He must be so tired . . ."

"You think I am not grateful?" He looked at her. "Nick is my friend too, you know. The two of you will have a room above stairs. I've seen to it."

It was more than she had a right to hope for. Never in her life had she been permitted to sleep in a private bed-chamber of an inn.

"Sir, you are very good."

He seemed to need her praise and to thrive upon it.

"Go along. I'll get Nick on his feet and bring him up."

"No, I had better do it. I am used to—that is, papa drank even before mama died." She took her father's arm and shoulder, aware that others were watching her activities with interest. She wouldn't have minded, had Cameron not been there. It was just another instance in which she and Nick must appear common and vulgar, far from the heights of dignity Shelby Cameron demanded.

Nick's dark head slowly began to rise. He easily maneuvered himself out of her grasp. "No. Not to bed. She will be angry."

"Papa, she isn't here. You must get some sleep."

Cameron bent over him. *"These are orders, Verin!"*

Hansi resented his sudden, officious tone with its crisp accent. She was astonished when, under the lash of

Cameron's voice, Nick struggled to his feet, stumbled against Cameron and mumbled, "Sorry, sir."

Again Hansi put out her hands to help, but Nick waved her aside, accepting Cameron's arm instead. Turning to the officer, Nick whispered confidentially, "It is not good for women to be allowed where men are drinking. Better for us men too, no?"

"Quite right," Cameron agreed, with a brief grin. Hansi shrugged and let them make their uncertain way upstairs.

As she followed them, a soldier at the bar stared at her and said, loudly, "Damn! That colonel's still collecting strays. Fellow's got a great heart, Jamie, you'll admit."

"Or he's the greatest fool on this cursed frontier."

Hansi stiffened. The two Redcoats merely winked and laughed. She knew from long experience that there would be nothing gained by exchanging insults with two drunken Redcoats in uniform.

By the time she reached the upper floor, Cameron was edging Nick in through an open door opposite the stairs. Both men disappeared into the bedchamber, whose roof was so low Cameron had to duck to avoid hitting his head. A tallow candle on the roughly carved bed table cast a pleasant flickering light.

Hansi came in to find Nick stubbornly wrestling with Cameron. "What the devil ails him?" he asked her, with irritation in his voice. He looked haggard and worn, his patience nearly spent.

"He wants to sleep on the floor. He's like a child. Papa, for heaven's sake, behave!"

Between them, Hansi and Cameron managed to get Nick onto the bed. He was lying crosswise on the scrambled coverlet and he kicked out at the nearest obstacle—which proved to be Cameron's bad leg.

The colonel fell against the lower bedpost, in such excruciating pain his body seemed to be struck numb for a moment. Hansi rushed to help him, thoroughly angry and disgusted with her father. She was shocked to find Cameron unable to speak. She persuaded him to sit on the edge of the bed. He tried to say something but caught his breath and closed his eyes.

Hansi hurried out to the staircase, calling over the rickety balustrade to the British soldiers in the taproom below.

"Fetch Master Brenner, the surgeon!"

"What? For a drunken redskin? Forget him, girl. Come down. We'll show you a better time."

"It is for the colonel, you fool! For your own Colonel Cameron."

The two soldiers exchanged glances, then, with one accord, they dashed out toward the fort.

Hansi ran down the stairs, hoping to find more help from other of Cameron's men, but the only persons left in the taproom were Americans, militia or local traders, and she did not trust them to help a man who might turn into the enemy at any minute. Inside, she found Cameron trying to put some weight on his injured leg. Seeing her, he reassured her about Nick, to divert her anxiety.

"He is asleep. He shouldn't give you any more trouble for some hours."

He took her hand in his, smiling but silent. She lowered her head and touched the back of his hand with her lips. "Sir, you are very good to me and mine. I won't forget that."

"Will you love me?"

It was abrupt, not even romantic, but it touched her heart. She looked up. "I have always loved you, sir. The very first time I saw you."

At that precise second they were interrupted by Dr. Brenner, the surgeon, running up the old creaking stairs and dashing in through the open door. It was awkward to be caught kneeling on the bed almost in a position of obeisance to Colonel Cameron. At the same time she was delighted by his quick appearance, in deference to Cameron's authority. She would never forget or forgive the surgeon's indifference to poor Albion McAndrews.

Brenner ordered him sharply, "You had your orders, colonel. No walking. I'm told you've marched halfway to Philadelphia."

Cameron smiled with an effort. "Not quite, Brenner, but there were things to be done."

The surgeon tried to take his arm. Cameron drew away, stood up on his good leg and would have fallen if Brenner and Hansi had not quickly stepped to catch him. Together, they thrust him back onto the bed, just missing Nick's body. With an enormous effort Brenner pulled off Cameron's boot.

Cameron groaned, trying to camouflage the undeniable pain with a cough.

"Brenner, I must be ready to march the day after tomorrow. Do not make complications for me."

Hansi pressed her fist against her mouth at the sight of his green, mottled flesh. She was not surprised when Brenner said in his emotionless voice, "Not only will you not be marching, sir, but you are very likely to be invalided out of the army—the shorter by half a leg!"

13

TWO days later Shelby Cameron was still securely bed-ded down in the private parlor of the PATRIOT TRIANGLE, while his men prepared to march out of the fortress and halfway across the continent. Hansi hoped to be permitted to care for him, but she had Mrs. Abernathy to contend with and that formidable lady firmly established golden Dolly in the colonel's quarters. The first night it became clear to Mrs. Abernathy that Hansi and her father, who had the room next door to Colonel Cameron, would be more "useful" in other quarters, out of the inn and well inside the fortress.

She failed to have the Verins removed from the inn, due to Shelby Cameron's insistence in the matter, but she was determined that Dolly nurse the colonel. She tried repeatedly to have Hansi and Dolly exchange rooms, in her typically heavy-handed way, as she fussed over Cameron.

"Perhaps my Dolly would find it easier to attend you, colonel, if she is moved into the room the Indian and our dear Hansi share." She added with her fat chuckle, "Naturally, it would be most improper if a young lady of

Dolly's age were placed in such close proximity to an eligible gentleman like yourself. But I would be willing to play the chaperone. We wouldn't want Fort Pitt to acquire the notion that my Dolly and our commanding officer were . . . ah . . . had come to an understanding beforehand, as it were, would we?"

"Indeed not," Cameron agreed quickly.

"Though of course the two of you are eminently suited to each other."

Cameron glanced at Hansi. She read the amusement in his eyes, though he replied to Mrs. Abernathy with his usual good manners. "You flatter me. I am far too old for a pretty little child like Miss Dolly."

"Dear me!" Mrs. Abernathy was taken aback. "We've overstayed our visit, I can see. You do look tired, colonel. We'll just leave you alone until Dolly can come and see to your comfort." She reached out for Hansi, got a grasp on her shoulder with a thick thumb and forefinger. "Hansi, child, come along. Other of our brave lads have been pining after you all day. We mustn't disappoint them."

Hansi wondered what would happen if she honestly answered the woman, but the kind of resistance that might defeat Mrs. Abernathy would unmask her most unladylike qualities. After all Shelby Cameron's compliments and gentleness, she could not bear to have him witness the angry, fiery part of her that Mrs. Abernathy brought out.

Keenly aware that Cameron had propped himself up on his elbows in bed to watch her leave, Hansi curtsied low to him and followed Mrs. Abernathy. In the fortress, she was assigned to the prison barracks where most of Fort Blaine's refugees were rapidly recovering. She had learned long ago that there were no lengthy convalescences on the frontier. Those who were ill or injured either died immediately or recovered in spite of their medical treatment. These patients were recovering. The critically ill and wounded had already died.

On the day of the Redcoat army's departure, Hansi was headed for the inn to eat her midday meal just as they marched out of the fortress. The sounds of fife and drums seemed to create disparate moods—one happy, one ominous. Until this moment she had not realized the full signifiance of their departure. Now, as the bright, newly brushed uniforms passed, she knew that all that remained of civilized discipline and law was leaving the frontier she had known and cherished all her life. But for the others—the colonials, the militia, the traders, the wives and other women—one would have thought they were celebrating a great victory. The bright summer air was full of laughter, ironic cheers and jeers, and shouts of triumph as they sent the lobsterbacks out of their lives. Hansi felt more inclined to weep than to laugh.

A disturbance at the window of Colonel Cameron's room drew her attention. She saw Cameron's face at the open window, pale and drawn. His hands grasped the wooden frame tightly. Someone behind him was trying to get him away from this painful sight of his departing comrades. Hansi wanted desperately to comfort him, but he did not look as though he would welcome any consolation. Suddenly, he swung his arm back rudely, smashing against someone—a man who appeared to be the surgeon, Brenner.

Hansi heard her name called out by Jess Taga, who had come up behind her. Startled, she found that along with his rifle, canteen and skinning knife, he carried double shotbags, one slung over each shoulder, the bands crossed on his breast. The extra shotbag doubtless contained food for a journey. He was wearing his big-brimmed black hat with his hair neatly queued out of his way.

As always when she thought of Jess going away, she felt helpless, alarmed.

"A journey?" she asked unnecessarily, raising her voice to compete with the fifes, drums and marching boots.

"Up to Philadelphia. There is a Colonial Congress going on. They'll vote war powers and an army, sure as shooting. They want to conquer our Redcoat friends as bad as I want to conquer that frontier out there."

"Jess! They say it's half a continent. You'd have to

fight almost every Indian tribe between here and the Mississippi, as well as the British Army."

He poked his hat brim up with his thumb and squinted at the sun overhead. "I can do it. Or—we can do it. We need money. Not a great deal, but enough to get good equipment. If the Congress doesn't know the value of all that land out there, I'll get help from the Virginians alone. Virginia Colony knows how important it is. I only need about two hundred Long Knives as good as—"

"You?"

He grinned. "Better, I hope. That's all it would take. Every settlement on the Mississippi would go over to us if they were given a choice. All those villages above St. Louis are French. They're certain to come over to our side. Even St. Louis. None of them like the Redcoats any better than we do."

She was startled and uneasy. Did he suspect the plan of the British Army to seize the French towns?

"You don't speak for me. Or for my father."

He put his hand under her chin. "Nick belongs to us. Not to your friend Cameron. You had better be sure which side you belong to, but don't force Nick into something he would hate, something that would kill him."

She glanced up at the window across the road. Cameron had turned away. He was talking to someone behind him. One fist still clutched the rough, warped wood at the bottom of the window embrasure. She knew instinctively how much he suffered at the loss of his command, and with no certainty that he would not lose his leg as well.

"I think it is a tragedy, this rebellion everyone is so keen to fight," she surprised herself by saying. "I think when it is over and you men must come dragging back to the Crown, you are going to wonder why you ever fought."

He pretended alarm. "Not so loud, you Tory vixen, or they'll be heating the tar and collecting the feathers to decorate that pretty flesh of yours." As she looked around anxiously, well aware that he was right, he demanded, "Am I to get nothing but politics before I depart for the wilds of Philadelphia?"

She softened at once.

"Everything is sure to be in a dreadful state while you are gone," she grumbled. It would be hard to feel safe when there was no Jess Taga to go to with her troubles and fears, no Jess to quarrel or laugh with.

"Ah! That's better." Jess lowered his head to kiss her, the big brim of his hat concealing their faces from view. Hansi had intended to kiss him in a spirit of comradeship, but she liked him too much for that. As she realized he was actually going to leave her, she put her arms around him.

"Please do take care of yourself," she whispered, a trifle hoarsely.

How warm and comforting—how right!—his lips felt, but without the romantic, magical quality she sensed in Shelby Cameron. With his lips against her cheek, he murmured, "Am I to understand you will miss me?"

"What a silly thing to say! Of course I'll miss you. Everyone will."

He raised his head, indicating the upper floor of the inn. "There is someone who won't miss me."

She swung around in time to see Cameron back away from the window, but his hands remained on the sill, grasping it so hard she saw his knuckles gleam white against the weathered tan of his flesh. Panic stricken, Hansi tried to pull away from Jess.

"I'm sorry. I forgot he might see. He looked so shocked!"

Jess laughed shortly, without humor. "Shocked! He looked angry to me. And jealous."

"But he is so ill. Last night he was quite feverish. I had best go and explain."

Jess let her go with a push that almost sent her to her knees. "So I am someone you must explain to your lover, is that it?"

By the time she reached the inn door and looked back, thinking to soothe him with a wave or a smile, he had stalked off toward the Philadelphia Trace and the blue hills beyond Fort Pitt. It was disappointing but not surprising that they should part on an angry note. She shrugged and ran up the stairs to Shelby Cameron's room.

She found the place in confusion. Brenner had apparently not yet won over his patient, who was hunched up on the bed, hugging his injured leg as though he expected it to be taken away from him.

"Very well, sir," the surgeon said. "If you persist in committing suicide by putting weight on that leg, there is nothing I can do to stop you. But that leg has got to come off."

Hansi cried out. Dolly Abernathy was sniffing and gulping in a corner beside the wooden pegs where Cameron's cloak and tricorn hat hung. She scrambled across the creaking floorboards and flung herself on Hansi.

"Hansi, you must do it. I can't! Master Brenner says there is no more laudanum. He says I must assist, but if he saws it off—oh, I can't! I shall faint if I get all that blood on me. I know it."

Hansi shivered. She looked over the girl's head at Brenner. "Is it true? Must you?"

Before he could speak, Cameron broke in, demanding in an icy voice, "Was that tender kiss some sort of betrothal? Or do you embrace all your admirers in public?"

"Sir!" Brenner began, "Miss Verin's affairs have nothing to do with the matter. Now, about the—"

Hansi crossed the room and went to Cameron on the bed. "Sir, I was saying good-bye to my dearest friend in the world. Captain Taga has left for Philadelphia."

Cameron looked relieved, despite his pain, as he reached for her hand. "Is it true? That he is only a friend?"

"Yes, sir." His fingers were dry and hot on hers. He must have fever again.

She looked down at his injured leg. A stocking had been slipped on over his foot and lower leg to cover the bandage. It was clearly totally inadequate. The wound had swollen grotesquely. One of his knee-breeches was stained with blood and infected ooze. A sweet stench from the wound had apparently kept Dolly away from her patient.

"I'll do anything I can to help Colonel Cameron, if Miss Dolly can take my place at the barracks dressing station."

"Oh yes, please. May I go now?"

Brenner suggested to Hansi, "We may need a strong man. Can we count on your father?"

"He is cleaning the officers' quarters in the fortress."

"Very well." Brenner waved away the trembling Dolly. "Miss Abernathy, go and send Nick Verin to us."

The girl rushed out and clattered down the stairs, the palm of one shaking hand over her mouth. Meanwhile Cameron recovered the superficial calm that served him in so many bad situations. "I have lost my entire command. I fought to gain that command for years. Since I was fifteen. To be what my father was before those vile people—villagers—betrayed him to his death. I wanted to carry on for him. I cannot lose this leg, Hansi! Don't you see?" He sounded so reasonable as he pleaded with her. If he allowed himself to explode over painful or unpleasant matters as Jess did, Hansi thought, he might avoid the terrible anguish and tension that always seemed to grip him.

"My darling," he assured her, though his hand shook as it gripped hers, "I am not going to let them take my leg. I would rather be dead."

Brenner ignored them. He began to unwrap the wound. It was hideous, even to Hansi, who had seen such injuries all her life. She swallowed rapidly and brought her other hand around to imprison Cameron's fingers between her own. All the same, she shared Cameron's desperate hope that something could be done. The sunlight glittered on the small saw that lay on the table beside a pewter bowl of water with summer flies lazily wandering about its rim.

The flies were attracted to the blood and putrefaction in Cameron's exposed wound, and Brenner angrily brushed them away. After a thorough examination he turned away. "If it is to be done here, we must have a fire. I won't answer for his life if I must operate without cauterizing the instruments and the stump afterward. I've had too many men bleed to death otherwise."

Hansi tried to free herself from Cameron's tight grip to fetch the fire maker, but he would not let her go. He said nothing, simply held on. His face, usually so pale in contrast to his hair and eyes, was now bright with fever. She drew his head to the cool bosom of her faded gown. She wanted to draw out the pain and relieve him with the comfort of her love. Her eyes pleaded with the surgeon, who stared back at her coldly and then began to unfold a large, threadbare coverlet and a heavy weather-cape. It was obvious to Hansi that these items were meant to absorb the blood and gangrenous draining from the wound. The hideous business began to seem far too real, too certain.

Nick Verin arrived in the room in his silent way, typical of him when he was sober. He saw and understood everything at a glance and set about making a fire in the grate. By the time the wooden chips and heavier branches were glowing, Brenner had several other instruments spread out on the table, including a thin-bladed knife which he carefully rubbed across his dusty breeches.

Cameron began to struggle again. Nick came to the bedside to lend his firm support to his daughter's. The sick man was helpless between them. As Brenner approached with the coverlet and sheet, he found Nick studying the wound. Green and bright yellow-orange poison seeped out around the stretched and horribly distended skin. The odor of putrefying flesh rose to Hansi's nostrils and she turned her head.

"You do not cut," Nick said suddenly.

Hansi swung around. "Papa, is there hope? Any hope at all?"

Even Brenner waited in suspense, with his hands full.

Nick said, "I think, maybe. Master Brenner, you heat the blade and open the swelled flesh. Here. And here. You wash the wound and we keep the flies off. Flies on the wound are bad luck. No flies."

To Hansi's amazement, Brenner hesitated. "You have

seen wounds like this heal without killing the patient?"
he asked Nick.

"Many times it kills. Many times it saves the leg. And
the life, too. Many times."

Cameron raised his head, struggled to speak. "You say
there is a chance?"

Nick shrugged. He pressed the back of his hand
against Cameron's forehead. The sick man twisted to
avoid him, insisting, "It is better to die. I order you.
Don't—"

Nick said to Brenner, calmly, "Do it as I say. It can't
be worse."

The surgeon had made his decision. "Where do you
keep your rum, colonel?"

Cameron pointed to the cupboard against the far wall.
The possibility of saving his leg seemed to rouse him for
a minute. He tried to smile. "I'll walk out of here on two
legs . . . as I walked in."

Hansi held him tightly as he began to lose consciousness. She thought she could never love anyone as she
loved this suffering man, who had been so exalted, so
superior to her in many ways, yet was now so helpless
in her strong arms.

Brenner laid the blade of the double-edge knife on a
glowing sycamore branch in the fire. Nick knelt with one
knee across Cameron's good leg, ready for a violent reaction when the knife entered the wound.

"He will live, won't he, papa?"

"Hush. You talk too much."

She prayed then, to her mother's god and in a kind of
jumble, to her father's god as well . . .

Master Brenner, having wrapped himself in an old
homespun sheet, returned with the knife and a long,
strong needle like those used by ship's carpenters on
canvas. Hansi tightened her grip on the unconscious man.
She sensed, rather than saw, the heated knife approach
the swelling. As the stench of burning flesh arose, Cameron cried out and struggled so frantically that Nick had
to apply all his weight to hold him down. Brenner

squeezed the flesh between needle and knife, and applied a wad of homespun to the wound. The cloth was saturated in minutes.

The room smelled vilely of burned flesh and decay. Hansi glanced at the open window, wishing for a breeze, but only summer heat poured in. No one said anything for several minutes. The surgeon removed the second saturated cloth, and washed the ragged wound. Then he spread basilicum powder over the wound, in the hope of coagulating the blood, and wrapped the leg loosely. He looked up.

"I can do no more for the time being. If the swelling recurs, the leg must go. Tonight." He sighed. "I should have done the thing now, while he was unconscious. You realize that if the poison rises, it will kill him."

Nick replied somberly, "It is in the hands of Manitou. You have done the best thing. My daughter and I, we will watch over him."

Brenner shook his head gloomily. "This time tomorrow we will be burying him, I make no doubt."

Hansi felt the hot tears blinding her. She was shaken out of this mood of despair by Nick Verin's voice, harsh and deep, as she had never heard him. "You weep and I am ashamed for you. Come. Have faith."

She nodded and gently touched Cameron's burning forehead.

14

CAMERON was roused to consciousness by a grinding pain that seemed to eat into the bone. Incredibly enough, it made him happy. It proved that his leg had not been amputated. Hansi sat on the side of the bed fanning him, now and then wiping a hand across her own sweating face.

"What if he dies?" She had asked herself this all the afternoon. "I will have murdered him. This kind, gentle, fine man who never treats me rudely as his officers or the Abernathys treat me. And he never despised papa. He helped papa the other night when he was drunk."

She knew it was these qualities as much as his exceptional good looks that made Shelby Cameron her idol.

He awoke when she was not even looking at him, and he lay there watching her. He studied her, seeing her as she really was, her faded dress stained with his blood, her hair wild and unconfined, her forehead gleaming with sweat. Yet his hand sought hers and she could have sworn that when he looked up into her eyes he truly loved her as she was, a dirty, unkempt daughter of a drunken half-blood.

Still stiff with pain, he managed to whisper, "I adore you."

She turned to him, gazed down at their interlaced hands and whispered, "No. It is the other way round."

He seemed to understand and she was certain that he loved her better for her confession, even though everyone knew that females did not say such things to men.

Wincing, he considered his loosely covered leg, lying there in plain view on top of the weather-cape. "I still have my leg. I remember, I owe that to Nick."

She watched him, wrenched with pity for his suffering in spite of his elaborate pretenses. "I'll get you some water. You must be thirsty."

He clutched her fingers even more tightly than before. "Don't go," he said.

She assured him gently, "I promise. Two seconds."

She returned from the table with fresh water Nick had fetched in the afternoon. She started to raise it to Cameron's lips. He took it from her with a hand that shook, but managed to caress her fingers as he did so. Afterwards, he said, "I take it there is still no laudanum."

She knew this meant that the pain must be excessive. It was sickening but she admitted, "The last was used yesterday morning on amputations after the skirmish up the Monongahela. But there should be some coming in any day, down the Allegheny from the Coast."

He grimaced. "A little late, I'm afraid. I expect to be on my feet by then."

She felt tenderness for him swell within her. "Yes. You will. I know you will."

"Meanwhile, perhaps we could make do with some of that ginever my men call Blue Ruin."

"Of course. That should do it." She knew it would give him the kind of headache her father suffered through in numerous aftermaths, but perhaps, in some small way, the headache might take his mind off his leg. She went back to the room she shared with her father and found his bottle of gin behind his low trundle bed. She brought it back and poured the watery liquid into a pewter cup and offered it to Cameron.

This time he slept through the surgeon's evening visit. Nick came in during Brenner's examination.

"Daughter, there is a hot supper for you in the room he gave us. Thieves have been there. This place is full of thieves. They took my bottle."

Hansi waved the gin bottle, in which only the dregs remained. "If it was this, papa, it's been put to good use."

He looked at the patient, shrugged and agreed, "Good. It does the job better than rum."

Hansi watched the surgeon nervously. "The swelling? Has it come back?" She did not like the dour look on Brenner's face as he fingered various spots on the bandages, but she noted that his touch was feather-light, involving just the balls of his fingers.

"What do you think, sir?"

Brenner looked over at Nick. "You seem to know your surgery, man. To this moment, at least, he does well. The swelling is congealed blood, for the most part. Naturally, I can't guarantee anything tomorrow. We'll see."

"Oh, sir! You work miracles!" Hansi hugged him, to his astonishment.

He released himself with dignity. "In the hands of the Almighty, girl. Nothing more." He cleared his throat. "Run along and eat your supper. Verin will watch over the colonel. I'm off to get my own mug of Somewhat."

Hansi went to enjoy her late supper. When she returned, after a delicious ragout and cold ale, she was surprised—and not at all happy—to see Mrs. Abernathy's lumpy form hovering over the patient.

"Hush!" the lady warned Hansi as she came in. "You will disturb the dear man."

Hansi refused to let herself be intimidated. "Is he awake yet? We gave him some Holland ginever for the pain. He went to sleep again."

"Heavens! What a disgusting thing for a gentleman like Colonel Cameron. I daresay it is the first time he knew the revolting fluid existed."

"There was no laudanum, ma'am."

"Yes, yes. What a pity dear Dolly cannot abide the sight of blood. She would have been so entirely suited to care for him. And I assure you, Holland gin would never have occurred to her. Ah! He's coming around."

Still with his eyes closed, Cameron felt for the woman's hand, clasped the thick, strong fingers, which included a wedding ring.

Startled, he opened his eyes, saw Mrs. Abernathy and immediately closed them again.

Hansi made an effort not to smile. That lady was completely oblivious.

"I think you are disturbing him, Hansi. You had better run along to bed now. I'll just sit here and keep him company. I want to be certain he needs no further help." She permitted herself a small titter. "I shouldn't like to see the dear colonel reduced to drinking some more of that dreadful Blue . . . Blue Ruin, or whatever it may be called."

"Yes, ma'am. Good-night." But Hansi could not resist tiptoeing over to see if Cameron was aware of her presence. While Mrs. Abernathy's bosom swelled with impatience, Hansi looked down.

"Good-night, sir."

Cameron's eyes opened. His forehead was drawn in pain, but he managed to wink at her as his hands sought hers. "Don't leave."

"My dear colonel," Mrs. Abernathy assured him, "you would wish the girl to have some rest, would you not?"

"Yes, of course. Forgive me, Fire-Dawn."

Hansi squeezed his hand. "I will see you soon," she almost whispered, and left the room, not quickly enough to escape Mrs. Abernathy's basilisk eye.

Two mornings later Cameron was back in firm control of himself and his leg, and again became the calmly imperious colonel. He awoke and, finding himself alone, called out several times. Failing in this, he banged on the floor with the empty gin bottle. When that produced only a cracked bottle, he drank the last of the warm, stale water in the pewter carafe and attacked the floor again, having better luck with the pewter.

The tapster arrived demanding, not too enthusiastically, if the gentleman was in pain.

"Yes, but you can do nothing about that. I am starving, and am persuaded you can help me."

"Ay, sir. Battered eggs and ham, a slab of pork, and a pannikin of stewed corn, maybe?"

"Anything. Is Miss Verin up and about?"

"I believe so, sir. Off to the fort she is. They fetched her over there. Something about making up a blue gown for that little pretty Abernathy lass."

"I should have thought the Abernathys would be moving east, after the captain marched out with my troops yesterday."

" 'Fraid not, sir. Cap'n Abernathy's stayed behind to join what they're calling a Continental Army. Them that's getting set to fight you. Already fighting you up in the northern colonies, from what I hear."

"Unfortunately, I am in no position to fight them back today. But in a month, I devoutly hope . . . well, no matter. I can see I'll get no good wishes from you. Staunch colonial, are you?"

"Staunch patriot, sir. That's what we call ourselves."

"I'm certain you do. Just send us whatever food there is, no matter what you call yourself."

Over the tray of his arriving breakfast half an hour later he saw the sweet face and bouncing blonde curls of Dolly Abernathy. She had the grace to be ashamed of her quick departure three days before, and apologized with many charming little pouts and airs of regret.

Cameron asked with ironic politeness, "And are you ready to care for this unpleasant wound of mine? I shouldn't think it would be your sort of charity, Miss Dolly."

She had remained all eagerness, well schooled by her redoubtable mother.

"But I assure you, I shan't fail you again. When Master

Brenner comes to change the bandage, I'll remain in this very room. And afterward, I'll read to you if you like."

"From that lively tale by Mr. Richardson that the Coast is reading so avidly?"

Dolly looked at the door with an anxious shudder. "Not if mama could hear me!" She added on a flirtatious note, "So you would like me to read *Pamela* to you. What a naughty suggestion!"

He had sighed at that. "Then what would you suggest reading to me?"

"Well . . ." She brightened. "A trader from Philadelphia brought in several pamphlets yesterday. 'The Power of Virtue' was one. And then there was 'The Frugal Housewife and Complete Woman Cook.' It has been popular in London since 1772, they say." She looked down at him soulfully. "Every prospective bride is given a copy, so I should think it might be most edifying."

"But I am not about to become a housewife. Nor yet a woman cook, whether complete or not. Now, may I have the tray?"

She giggled. "I'm so sorry. I forgot." She started to set the tray on his legs. He shouted at her an instant before she set it down. With shaking hands she dropped it on the bed beside him. But still she remained, fussing over him, apologizing again and again, insisting that she was there to make him more comfortable.

Realizing that more drastic means must be employed, he took up the two-pronged fork and began to eat. After a minute he groaned, and murmured, "It's of no use. I can't ask you. Such a dainty creature as you!"

"Ask . . . ask me what?" She was trembling in advance.

"The surgeon insists the wound be reopened. With a needle, I believe." She gasped. He went on reproachfully, "He seems to think you would prefer to assist him. You will wear your oldest gown, of course. And you must—" He considered. "Now what was it you were to do? You would not object to an indelicacy if it were to aid me?"

"I . . . I don't think . . . mama might not . . ." Curiosity got the better of her. "What indelicacy?"

"You must sit upon my good leg and hold the other down. I may become violent," he added on an inspiration.

She backed away, eyes widening.

"Perhaps you had better speak to mama first. Perhaps you would find me terribly inadequate. I never . . . I couldn't . . ." She groped for the door.

"Send me Miss Verin," he called after her. "She is the sort who deals with these things."

"Yes." Her face cleared, relief washing over her. "Immediately."

"Good girl."

The door slammed behind her as he began to laugh. He could not stop laughing until the physical strain reached his leg and he groaned, but went on smiling.

"I thought myself very clever," he told Hansi when she arrived. "Perhaps I have missed my true vocation. I belong at Covent Garden. Or New York's John Street Theatre; don't you think so, Fire-Dawn?"

She brushed aside his attempt at humor.

"Shelby Cameron! Do you know I ran all the way to this room? And I find you making jokes."

He pulled her down upon the bed, overturning the platter of ham. "Say it again, and this time, please, my adorable tigress, do not scowl."

It was hard to scowl when she was so happy, but she tried to occupy herself with rescuing the ham and other overturned food on the bed. "I find you making jokes, sir?"

"Before that, you called me by my name. Say it once more."

She knew suddenly that what he asked was impossible. "I beg your pardon, sir. I cannot. You must understand why."

He seemed to understand. His smile appeared, the gentle smile that was so unlike the insolent or sensual grin of most men she knew. "My sweet rescuer, call me whatever you wish. As my wife, your name will be mine."

"Sir! You are delirious!"

"All the more reason why you must marry me. I need you."

She studied his face, feeling herself in the throes of a dream, unable to believe, yet unwilling to wake up. She tried to say something but nothing would come out.

"Won't you at least say that you need me?" he asked wryly.

"Oh, I do! Only you could never marry me. You know why."

He leaned over the tumbled dishes on the tray and kissed her. Once before in the night shadows of Fort Blaine she had felt that unexpected passion, like burning ice, as his lips smothered her protests. She poured all her confused feelings into returning his kiss. She knew she belonged to him.

"I will marry you." He was her romantic ideal, the perfect knight. And he had been her mother's ideal. How happy Eva would have been to know that such a man loved Fire-Dawn.

His lips lingered upon hers and then, more briefly and in fun, he kissed her on the cheek and the nose and held her away from him without releasing her.

"Have you said yes?"

She managed to nod, and he drew her to him. Conflicting emotions swirled inside her. This was the height of all her dreams, her distant hopes! Yet Hansi Verin could not possibly become Colonel Shelby Cameron's lady-wife, and he must know that. Then, with her lips pressing against his warm throat, she wondered, "Will I ever be this happy again?"

15

HANSI said nothing to anyone, not even Nick, about Cameron's proposal. She felt that Shelby was far too much the gentleman to jilt her, but the least she could do was to give him the opportunity of pretending the scene in this room had never happened.

She did not know what his thoughts or plans were. He had been visited that afternoon by Captain Abernathy and a group of well-meaning colonial patriots hoping to win him over to the side of the rebellious colonies. They spent nearly two hours with him. Hansi heard the result of the meeting later in the inn's kitchen.

"They'll never win the colonel. Not that'n," said the cook. "I know the stripe of them Redcoats. Good fighters but not too much above decks, if you know what I mean." He tapped his forehead.

Hansi was indignant. "Colonel Cameron is a brave, loyal officer of the Crown. He took an oath to defend it. If he came over to the rebels he would be a traitor. Can't you see that?"

"Whew! There's a temper under that pretty silken red head of yours, lass. All the same, they'd best be looking into his mail. He's already sent off a runner to the Tide-water. Ten shillings says he's sending off secrets to some Tories in Williamsburg."

She remembered Jess Taga's half-joking remark about tar-and-feathering Tories and realized that even if Cameron's leg mended, he would remain in great danger at Fort Pitt. He was worse than a Tory-sympathizing Ameri-can. He was the *enemy*.

She started up to her room and saw Nick at the tapster's bar below the stairs. He was listening to two trappers boast of their beaver catch the previous winter. She watched to see if he was drunk and finding that he was quite sober, felt a surge of affection for him that was partly rooted in guilt. He had a rum mug in his hand but was paying little attention to it.

Dear papa! She knew then that she would never let any-one separate her from him—not even Shelby Cameron!

One of the trappers, a Frenchman, turned to Nick. "What you say, Verin? Next season the country beyond the Muskingum? A world of beaver there, eh?"

"No. Not the drowned lands," Nick replied quickly. "Between Fort Sacklin and the Mississippi, it is all drowned lands at the end of winter."

"You see?" said the Frenchman to his friend. "No one knows that country like this fellow Nick."

Hansi was impressed by Nick's reputation among all those who knew the frontier, but she also remembered Jess Taga's words: *Nick belongs to us. Don't force Nick into something he would hate, something that would kill him.*

"Damn Jess!" she said to herself. Why did he haunt her life, her opinions and thoughts? Would she never be free of him?

If she married Cameron, she need never listen to Jess again. After the time Cameron had seen her and Jess from the window, she was more keenly aware than ever that in spite of Cameron's habitual dignity and restraint, he could become furious in his jealousy. She vowed never to arouse that jealous, cold rage of his again.

But any doubts she might have were banished when, in

the middle of her supper, she was summoned to the invalid's room by Master Brenner.

She asked anxiously, "Is he ill again?"

"No, miss. But he will not be able to put weight on that leg for some time and he refuses to accept it. He believes it will heal in a matter of hours, I think. Talks of going off to Fort Detroit—and not alone."

"If he doesn't take care, he will never walk properly again."

"Precisely. He has already opened the wound with his foolishness and there has been a new bleeding I don't like. All because of some damned female."

"A female?"

"Babbles about marriage." He eyed her in his slightly fishy way. "Anyone you might know? Does he tell you of this newfound ladylove?"

"Somewhat, sir."

He seemed to be taken aback by her frankness. "You?"

"I don't know, sir. He . . . we . . . he has been most kind, but I feel there would be many objections."

"I am not at all surprised. But he wishes to see you now. I suggest that for your own protection, you behave with decorum."

She resented his advice but could not deny that he was right. She started up and was halfway across the room when the surgeon said, "Will you not eat your supper?"

"I am not hungry, thank you." She hurried out to the hall wondering at her own happiness, so soon after her mother's death. Had she lost Eva only to gain the love of Shelby Cameron? It was wrong, perhaps, but she was powerless to do anything about it.

It was all true. The instant she entered Cameron's room he looked around, tried to get up and, failing that, held his arms out to her. She approached him hesitantly. Perhaps he would vanish in a puff of smoke. But his arms were real and his flesh warm, and his welcoming kiss deep and overpowering.

He seated her beside him on the bed, her head against

his shoulder. He lowered his head and kissed her gently, a soft caress, but lingering as he felt her deep bodily response.

"My sweet . . . sweet Fire-Dawn. You must say you love me. . . . Say you adore me. *You must adore me."* As he issued each command his lips touched her cheek, her neck, and then her bosom, the golden swell of her breast, sending tremors of excitement through her.

He had pressed her body against his and now raised his head, his hands forcing her shoulders back. "My little love, you must always remember that you promised. You adore me."

"I adore you." Her voice sounded harsh and unromantic as she said it, but the passion and pounding in her body was present.

He let her go reluctantly, and then brought her hand to his lips in a gentlemanly manner that returned the dreamlike scene to reality. He said, with a whimsical smile, "God knows I am asking a selfish thing of one so young. While this rebellion goes on, while I lie here like a wretched cripple, I have no right to take you off to some Godforsaken frontier post. But I need you so. I've known a great many women"—she raised her head and he caressed her fingers, laughing at her expression—"but never one like you."

A faint uneasiness crept into her happy mood. In a low voice she asked, "Is it me you love, really? Or is it like that night you said you wanted to make love to me?"

He colored faintly, but assured her, "My sweet child, every man who loves a woman wants to make love to her."

Feeling his body hard and firm against hers, she realized that the future Mistress Cameron should not be conducting herself so scandalously on the commander's bed, and she broke away.

"I am going to learn to be a lady for you. You will see."

He frowned. "Never. I have known ladies all my life." As she stared at him, he warned her, "I did not fall in love with a lady." He murmured tenderly as he nuzzled against her cheek. "You must not mind that. Remember, wherever you go, you will want to enter a room, even a throne room, with that pretty fire-red head neatly combed and your figure proudly displaying the finest garments to be obtained. You will be Mrs. Colonel Cameron, my mother's successor."

She wanted to ask him why—what he had possibly found about her to love, but some intuition stopped her.

He did not want her to leave him that night. If she had agreed to stay, she worried that his love might have to change drastically to a mere regard for an animal who furnished him pleasure. Though all her body and her aroused passions urged her to stay, she would not. And later she was relieved at her ability to refuse him.

Shelby Cameron's temper was sorely tried during the following days. With an almost religious zeal he attempted every day to use his injured leg and managed to reopen the wound almost as many times. Nor could he leave Fort Pitt until he received his military orders, and in the meanwhile there were those citizens and a few soldiers of the new Continental Army who regarded him as a fierce and deadly enemy.

Even Mrs. Abernathy became a trifle wary. She continued to visit now and again, bringing a pudding, or a copy of a Philadelphia newspaper in the hope of converting him to the rebel cause. But she no longer urged her daughter upon him, and her husband no longer mentioned his name without prefixing the word which branded Cameron as "that Redcoat."

It was with enormous relief that Cameron limped out of his room, down the rickety stairs and into the public room where he found Nick and Hansi listening to several militiamen reading aloud with hilarious results.

"A pity to interrupt," Cameron whispered in Hansi's ear.

She giggled, moved away from the enthralled audience and then hugged him in her excitement. "You've walked all this way without any help at all. I'm so proud of you!"

She had seldom seen him so happy. "The first steps to

Detroit and my command. And I certainly intend to walk to my wedding."

The militiamen stopped their wild reading of Shakespeare long enough to stare at Cameron and exchange significant looks. Cameron led Hansi and Nick away from the public room. He limped noticeably but tried to hide it. Hansi took care not to notice, but when Cameron slipped as he reached the landing and took tight hold of the stair rail, Nick observed closely.

"It is better to have a cane for walking, sir. You do not like to fall down before these people you visit."

Hansi flinched at Nick's words and was not surprised when Cameron's dark eyes flitted angrily over her father.

"I have no need for a cane, thank you," he assured Nick. "I'm afraid I drank a little too much this afternoon."

This was not the truth, Hansi knew. But his mood rapidly changed back, and when he kissed her good-night he was again his gentle and fond self. Nick had already fallen asleep. Cameron looked after him, then murmured, "This room of mine is enormous, now that I am well. It needs warmth. It needs you, Fire-Dawn."

She found herself unnerved by this new assault upon her own desires. His touch inflamed her, his lips so close to her cheek burned with that remembered and curiously unsettling combination of ice and fire. She managed to say with an effort, "Shelby Cameron's wife should be like our friend Caesar's wife—above suspicion."

Again, she felt that he had been pleased. She was certain that however much he wanted her, he preferred to think of her as Caesar's wife.

Every time she awoke in the night and thought of him, she thought of their marriage and planned all the ways she would make herself worthy of that distinguished title: Mrs. Colonel Shelby Cameron.

"I mustn't walk too fast, or take unbecomingly long steps. I must learn to wear respectable clothes and keep my hair smooth. Thanks to mama, I know how to speak properly. And later I will be expected to act as hostess for Colonel Cameron's—no, Shelby's—fine guests. Mama would be so proud of me!"

She went to sleep counting the things she must do and learn.

She was awakened in the morning by Nick shaking her bed. She opened her eyes, startled, and sat straight up, demanding to know what had happened.

"The war. That is what happens."

She groaned, "Oh, that!" and yawned, but it was clear that Nick had not roused her just to remind her of what she knew all too well. "What is it, papa?"

He went to the window, pushed one of the shutters and looked out. "I hear things. Captain Jess is on the Philadelphia Trace. He arrives tonight or tomorrow. The whisper is that the Congress has called for an army to rise against the Redcoats."

She began to throw on her clothes.

"What will happen to Colonel Cameron? He is surrounded by enemies."

"He will be taken prisoner—maybe even shot."

"No!"

"It is always the same. Long ago in the French War some of the captive officers were shot. At Fort William Henry—"

She shivered, moving rapidly to dress. "Don't speak of Fort William Henry, papa." She remembered all too well her mother's fate when that fortress surrendered to the French and their Indian allies.

"Your mother was with the British and colonials in the fort. I was with the French and the Mohawks. It was very bad."

"How many people know what you heard about this war today?"

"Only the Piankashaw who told me. He will say nothing. These colonials trust no Indian. They would not believe him."

Hansi said sharply, "So much the worse for them. They can never win the frontier without the help of the tribes. I can tell them that."

Nick considered her thoughtfully. "Do you hate Captain Jess very much?"

"Hate Jess?" What an absurd thing to say! She felt so many different things for Jess. He might be fickle, infuriating, dangerous . . . but . . . to hate him? She was impatient with her father's apparent stupidity.

"Certainly not. But I can't let him destroy a brave man like Colonel Cameron. Even if Shelby were only imprisoned, he would be ruined, his career gone. Papa, his career is his life."

Nick nodded but Hansi was disturbed by the odd way he looked at her. She was afraid to ask why. He might provoke a question about herself that she could not answer. She rushed to Colonel Cameron's door. There was no answer and for a few desperate minutes she wondered if some of the rebels at Fort Pitt had already taken him prisoner.

The creaking of the stairs, followed by quick if uneven footfalls upon the floor behind her reassured Hansi. Before she could turn, Cameron's powerful arms drew her to him. He was in deadly earnest despite an attempt at a light, teasing tone.

"My love, you read my mind. I was coming to get you."

"Sir, I've been told that Jess Taga—"

He silenced her with a kiss and then the gentle reminder, "Not *sir*. By tonight, you will be Mrs. Cameron."

"What! But, sir!"

"In secret. By nightfall. The French priest will perform the ceremony."

"No posting of the banns? No—"

He kissed her protests away. She surrendered to his impulsiveness and his mastery as she longed to surrender to his passion. She could not believe that she would actually become his wife instead of a temporary mistress, but if he did do her that honor, she was determined to make him the best of wives.

Hansi felt swept up in her future husband's impetuous plan for their future and found herself almost resentful of her father's doubts when she told him of it as she packed her few belongings.

He had been very silent and thoughtful when she first mentioned the plan. But then he said, in careful words, "You think you will be happy with this man? It is not good to marry when two people are not at all alike. One may grow to hate the other. It is often so."

Her fingers, busy folding a worn fichu, were suddenly stilled. She knew the source of that quiet reminder. He must feel very strongly to have admitted the ghastly failure of his own marriage.

"Papa, don't you like Colonel Cameron? You get on very well together."

"He is my friend. . . . Captain Jess is my friend, too."

She resumed her packing, avoiding his heavy-lidded gaze. She did not want to discuss Jess Taga.

Her father pursued the matter. "You will marry before you see Captain Jess?"

Hansi took a long, sharp breath. "Papa, I am not one of Jess Taga's women. Colonel Cameron has asked me to be his lady, not his harlot. No man has ever raised me so high. Jess would tear me down, drag me after him in the mud. Do you understand that, papa?"

As he made no answer, she turned on him in a sudden, desperate attack. "Tell me, are you loyal to the Crown, or to the rebels?"

He stiffened. "I made oath to obey the king over the seas. Colonel Cameron is his man. He asked me to follow him as his scout. I keep my word."

"Then we are agreed." She hugged his tense shoulders, and continued packing. But her euphoria over Shelby Cameron's masterful plans for their marriage had begun to evaporate. The old doubts, the deep feelings of unworthiness returned.

She wondered whether he might suddenly feel ashamed at the prospect of making an ill-educated, half-blood girl his wife and possessor of his name. But when he spoke to her in public, particularly in Mrs. Abernathy's presence, Hansi realized that his continued pretense that there was nothing between them amused him. He even flirted with the matron, but over her head he winked at Hansi who was too nervous to share his humor. She understood how dangerous his position at Fort Pitt would be if Jess arrived before they left the town.

Cameron went so far as to accept a supper invitation from Dolly Abernathy. Hansi did not know what to think. She was on her way to her room at the inn an hour later when Père Gilbert startled her by materializing out of the darkness of the upstairs hall. Before she could speak, he motioned her to follow him into the colonel's room where she found Nick and Shelby Cameron awaiting her.

Nick, who seemed to have conquered his fears about the marriage, grinned at her surprise as Cameron limped across the room to take her hand. An impressive silver crucifix, two hands high, had been set upon the gaming table and Hansi was placed before the crucifix between Nick and her future husband.

She found herself suddenly panic-stricken. Did she want to bind her life to this mysterious stranger? What did she know of the real man behind the handsome, elegant exterior? She whirled around, desiring nothing so much as a quick escape. But she noted her father's stillness, the priest's gentle, knowing smile, and finally the sharp apprehension in Cameron's dark eyes. It was this latter, and the awareness that her panic must seem like a denial of her love for him, which restored her calm. She reminded herself that he needed her. She remembered Jess Taga. There was no time for doubts. She looked at him, trying to put all her love and gratitude, all her profound admiration for him into her gaze. After all, he was the most perfect male she had ever known. In all things he was the superior of others she might have loved. And at this moment his very uncertainty about her gave Hansi new confidence. Through her fingers she felt him relax.

When Père Gilbert put aside the paper with what she supposed must be the marriage lines that she and Cameron would sign, he began to speak in French. She stood close beside Shelby Cameron, certain now that the ceremony being performed was proper. She would make her husband proud, he would give her dignity and pride. He would make her what Eva Verin had wanted her to be: a lady.

"The two of you are one, my child," said Père Gilbert, closing his Bible. He waited, smiling, as Cameron took both Hansi's hands in his and kissed her tenderly on the lips. She had long since recovered from her early fears and that horrible moment when she had thought she did not wish to marry him. Now she returned his kiss, her warm, full lips clinging to his briefly, aware all the while that she was thawing that careful reserve of his.

She felt another and more curious reaction. Although she knew from past experience that he was a man of passion, his reserve seemed to be so strongly a part of him that he welcomed her initiative in love. He welcomed the passion in her kiss, but it was she who had first given of that passion.

"And now, my children," Père Gilbert reminded them, "there is a carriage I sometimes use to visit the mountain families on the Philadelphia Trace. You must take it as far as the Triangle Trace. A very pleasant tavern for your marriage night. I will fetch back the mare and the carriage tomorrow. I owe that and more to your wife, Colonel Cameron, for what she has done to help us here at the fort." He added quickly, "But for the safety of Colonel Cameron, it is good that you leave Fort Pitt at once, while the town is indoors at supper."

"Yes. At once," Hansi agreed, anxious to leave before there was any chance of meeting Jess Taga. Even so, they would be only a few hours in advance of the colonials if Jess and the others chose to pursue them.

How different her life and her future might have been if Jess had needed her in the ways that this fine, gentle man needed her! But Captain Jess Taga was the one person ruthless enough to be dreaded now. How chilling to fear dear Jess as *the enemy!*

"What are you thinking, my darling?" Shelby Cameron asked her suddenly.

"I was thinking—how very much we owe to Père Gilbert," she lied, and curtsying to the benign priest, kissed his hand, then hurried out between her father and her husband. The fates had decided. She was Mrs. Shelby Cameron. Out of all the females he knew in the world, this great man had chosen Hansi Verin for his mate. But why?

16

Hansi looked out at the moonlight dotting the rows of maple trees below in the inn's courtyard. The filtered rays cast a distinctly romantic aura over the old wooden building. A faint glow seen through the open window of the public room only hinted the place was inhabited.

Hansi was deeply conscious of Shelby Cameron's body beside hers, his heartbeat, the warmth of his arm encircling her as they strolled outside in the courtyard.

He murmured with amusement, "After this ghastly shed, we are certain to find any army quarters vastly superior."

"It doesn't matter, so long as we are together."

It had been the right thing to say. His grip tightened around her waist. "Thank you for that, my darling."

A small stream meandered in front of the tavern. Cameron lifted her over the rivulet directly into the dark entryway. Nick Verin remained behind them, moving silently to help the landlord's boy care for the priest's mare and carriage.

The burly landlord greeted Cameron with controlled

politeness. "None about to do you harm at this hour, sir. Come you in, you and your lady."

"Mrs. Cameron," said Hansi's husband.

"Ay."

Hansi glanced at Cameron gratefully, noting that he was ever careful not to let anyone think the worse of her or—by extension, she admitted to herself—of his choice of companionship. She quickly banished the unworthy suspicion. How splendid he looked in the night, his silvered features etched in moonlight! She still could barely believe the wonder of it all—that Shelby Cameron was her lawful husband.

They went up the stairs to the single, low-ceilinged private parlor and bedchamber that the tavern afforded. She was totally unprepared when Cameron gathered her up suddenly, skirts, petticoats, mantle and bonnet, and lifted her over the threshhold into their bridal chamber.

"For luck," he told her, as he set her back on her feet somewhat mussed, her clothing all awry. "You see, it would be bad fortune if the bride stumbled."

She turned in his arms, kissed him, her eyes excited and lively. "You are superstitious too. Oh, sir, how glad I am that I married you!"

"And that I married you?"

"Yes. Yes! I can't believe it. It's like . . . like a fairy tale."

"King Cophetua and the Beggar Girl?"

She studied his face, not knowing how to take this, then saw the teasing laughter in his eyes. "Very like, sir. Your obedient slave."

He touched her face gently, slowly outlining her features with sensitive fingers. "My slave . . . adorable slave."

Nick came then, carrying her mother's bandbox with its worn ribbons, and Cameron's portmanteau. He kissed Hansi briefly on the forehead and after an awkward moment shook Cameron's outstretched hand.

"Where will you sleep, papa?" Hansi asked anxiously.

"By the fire. It is the best place."

This was true enough, for the private parlor given over to Cameron and his wife was beginning to feel the faint chill of an early fall night. All the same, Hansi told herself, *my husband and I will be warm in each other's arms*.

"Be happy," Nick told her gruffly, and went out into the passageway.

"What else can we be?" She laughed, taking her husband's hand.

"My loving little slave," he whispered. "Let me make you ready. Do not be shy. Never be shy of me." He snuffed all but one of the candles. Only one thin glow illuminated the room, fitfully elongating shadow and light. He was gently removing her mantle, untying her bonnet. "I want you always to show me the passions you feel, the desires you want to express. This world of the body is our secret world, yours and mine. Do you understand what I am trying to say?"

She began to do so. She had several times suspected it of him. He wanted her to know that despite all his careful, surface reserve, he welcomed the heat of passion he found in her. His reassurance added to her joy. Her body trembled under his touch, she made no effort to interfere with the way he removed each of her garments, always managing to brush her flesh sensitively with the ball of a finger or the knuckle of a hand.

Of all emotions, she had not thought she would feel shame at such a moment. She sensed his growing excitement as she stood naked before him, like a slave about to be sold on the block. From the burning brightness in his eyes, she knew he was aroused by her slim, golden flesh, her high breasts, stiff with anticipation, the flat stomach and narrow flanks throbbing with desire, the darkness where the soft body hair, unlike the flaming auburn hair on her head, was shining and black.

She shivered and felt her way to the bed, watching him as he removed his own clothing, never taking his eyes off her. How well he knew women, she thought, intensely aware of his body, while pretending to examine the carpeted floorboards. Tall and trim and imposing, he was everything she could have wished. His flesh was lighter than hers. Would he be aware of the difference, this clear sign that he was her superior in the eyes of society? She lowered her eyelids in panic, aware of a heretofore unsuspected modesty in herself.

All the same she sensed he knew she was admiring him. He must be well used to the admiration and the excitement he aroused in other females. She waited nervously until, with a start, she felt his approach, his hot body against hers, and the throb of his groin as he threw her down beneath him.

She closed her eyes, marveling that this union was so perfect, so different from her mother's tortured first union with Nick. Instinctively she locked her dark, golden legs about his body as he thrust himself deep inside her.

Afterward, they lay together exhausted. Throughout their lovemaking he had never stopped insisting that she play the role of his slave. She wondered if her joy could have been greater with another man, with Jess Taga, who might have regarded her own pleasure with more concern. Shocked at the thought, she opened her eyes and studied her husband's chill features, gleaming with a faint glow of sweat in the cold room.

He put out his hand, wound a strand of her thick red hair across her forehead, and smiled at her. "My adorable slave," he murmured sleepily. "Promise me you will always receive your master as you did tonight. Never be shy with me."

"I promise."

"Think now of a far-off Arabia." He turned and rested on his elbow. "A harem. You must serve and excite your master. Think of ways in which you will win over your rivals . . . new ways, a thousand ways of rousing your master."

"My rivals?"

"Only in your thoughts, my darling." He moved his body upon hers again and kissed the bridge of her nose. "These are games that are played by men and women all the time. I simply want you to learn and perfect them.

Think of all the ways you may please your master in bed. I will help you."

They made love again. Though Hansi's body pleased Cameron, and she dutifully followed all his sharp instructions, a part of her mind remained aloof. Did all men insist that their wives perform so aggressively and even shockingly? He was an active lover. There would be bruises on her body tomorrow. But his fantasies troubled her even more. What made him force her to perform acts he himself seemed to find shameful? Was this to shame her? To make himself even more superior to his low-bred wife?

She banished the loathsome thought.

They went to sleep in each other's arms. When she awoke a little after dawn she found herself wondering again if her husband wanted her to initiate the act. Carefully, she released herself from his hands clasped across her breasts. She assured herself that she had merely behaved as a loving, sensuous and obedient wife. She must not let herself feel shame for acts of love to please him. Still, she was troubled as she recalled his hoarse urgings that she call out *"master,"* and *"sultan"* as he tossed her from one position to another.

Watching him now she found a satisfactory answer for her husband's strange behavior. This man of superior power and authority needed her more than any of those other women he might have chosen, who would be too proud or too inhibited to satisfy him. She, Fire-Dawn, passionate and strong, half-blood Nick Verin's daughter, was different. She must always remember that she vowed to cling to that whenever she felt inferior or degraded. *He needed her.* None of his other possible wives would have answered in public as wife and in private as his harem-slave.

And when they had children one day . . . but she suspected he was a man who would never surrender any of her love or attention to children. He was not a family man.

Shivering in the cool dawn she dressed quickly, glancing back to make certain to watch her husband, beautiful in the defenselessness of sleep. He looked younger than his age, innocent and vulnerable. No one, seeing that face so quiet in sleep, would guess the secret, insatiably dark side of his passionate nature.

I won't betray you, she promised him in her thoughts.

She hurried down the stairs, looking for her father in the public room. She looked around the lower floor, then heard a boy's voice out in the courtyard.

"Pa says we're full up. Take no one, he says. Not 'til after sunup."

Whatever the traveler said, the boy insisted stoutly. "That's as may be, but we're to take in no rebels what's up against the king."

Hansi waited no longer but rushed back up the stairs. She burst in upon Shelby Cameron, who stood barefoot but had already gotten into his breeches and shirt. He dropped the stocking in his hand, seeing her excitement. Before she could speak he drew her to him, stopping her anxious warning with a kiss. "Are you still happy, my darling?"

She loved this side of him, but was too alarmed to waste time in a game. "More than ever. Sir, you must hurry."

"Sir?"

"Shelby. There is a rebel soldier outside. He may be dangerous. Please, hurry!"

She was relieved to see him cross the room quickly to the shuttered window. As with most frontier buildings thrown together in haste, there was no window glass.

He pushed open the shutters. "No escape this way," he said quickly. "Through the kitchen, perhaps."

"I'll go."

"No. I don't want you to risk—"

"They will do nothing to me. Darling, please wait here."

"Since you ask me in that special way," he agreed,

flashing one of his warm smiles that seemed so far from the cruel harem master of a few hours ago.

She found a little winding flight of stairs that led, as she had hoped, into the stillroom and kitchen of the tavern. A pot of porridge bubbled on a crane over the hearth, but the room was deserted. The back door was open. She saw Nick Verin and the landlord out in an overgrown field behind the tavern. They were harnessing the priest's mare to the carriage that had brought the three of them to his inn last night. Thank God for Père Gilbert's loyalty!

Hansi spun around to face Jess Taga standing in the doorway. How long had he been watching her? She was terrified of his powerful presence.

"Well, infant, are you still angry with me? Come. Slap me as you are longing to do, and then let's be friends again."

She felt a sudden, anguished pang at his simple assumption that all was as it had been the day he left for Philadelphia. That day, in his worn golden buckskins, with the black hat tilted jauntily back on his head, he had looked tough and masterful, a vital part of the primitive frontier they both loved. But today he wore white bandoliers and soldier's black boots. Gone were his familiar moccasins and long knife. He swung a Pennsylvania Infantry rifle across his broad shoulders. He had been her best and dearest friend, but he was now her husband's enemy and hers as well.

She started toward him. She tried to return his easy, affectionate, teasing manner, but it was no use. She kept remembering Shelby Cameron upstairs, waiting for her.

"I was looking for papa."

She had nearly gotten past him when he put out his free hand, took her arm. His grin had faded.

"Are you still angry, infant? You mustn't be. We've quarreled before. It never meant anything."

"I know, Jess. I'm not angry. I never was. Please excuse me. I'm in a great hurry. You see, it's . . . it's papa."

He turned her chin up, studied her face. "Sweetheart? Tell me what it is. Are you frightened of me?"

She tried to pass him. "I told you."

"And you lied. Nick is out in the pasture. I can see him from here. The ostler mentioned Tories. King's men. Have you made poor Nick into a king's man?"

"He was always loyal to his oath," she reminded him, some of her normal pride returning. She tried once more to free herself.

Behind them on the staircase that separated the kitchen from the public room, the cool voice of a regimental commander cut into their childish tussle.

"Be so good as to free my wife, captain."

Jess Taga's hard grip on her wrist slackened. It was as if he had been stunned by a blow. After an endless few seconds, without taking his eyes away from Fire-Dawn's stunned gaze, he found his voice.

"Is it true?"

She nodded, trying to get out a simple "yes," but finding herself silenced by the look in his eyes.

"Quite true, captain," Shelby Cameron assured him.

Jess laughed shortly. "I should never have waited. I played the gentleman for once, and you grew up behind my back. Sweetheart, you have made the mistake of your life!"

Cameron caught his breath in a way that was audible to Hansi. He descended another stair. Hansi heard the uneven, limping sound he made as the ancient wood creaked. When he came into the light his sword was in his hand, its tip within an inch of Jess Taga's spine. Hansi cried out.

"No, Shelby! He won't stop us. . . . Will you, Jess?"

She would never know what he might have said or done because Nick came through the open innyard doorway at that moment, with the landlord close behind him wielding a heavy meat chopper.

While Hansi and the others remained frozen, Nick said calmly, "We are friends, captain. Your word is good. You will let them go."

Jess shrugged, then turned abruptly. His eyes blazed with a rage Hansi had never thought possible for him. He struck aside Cameron's sword blade with the back of his hand. A fine line of blood welled up across his knuckles.

"I assure you, Colonel, I would not have fought a duel to hold a child who no longer asks my protection." He paused a second, then added. "Or my love. If it came to that."

"Get out!" Cameron ordered him, pale with anger. "Be on your way."

Jess laughed. "Why not? I have nothing to hold me here." He moved deliberately away from Cameron and strode between Hansi and her father. His eyes reminded Hansi of the Shawnee chief, Cornstalk—opaque, unreadable, deadly.

Ignoring the others, Jess addressed Nick. "When you are done with serving the noble colonel and his savage major, come back to us. We will welcome you." Then he turned and walked quickly away.

It was Hansi who stopped her husband as he leaped off the last two stairs and started after Jess with his naked sword.

"No! We must get away. We have no time to lose."

Cameron thrust her aside. "He will not call me a savage, that damnable traitor!"

Nick Verin's quiet voice stopped him. "He called your major a savage, not you, sir."

Hansi pursued this hope eagerly. "Yes. He said that only to goad you. He is angry because his cause is hopeless, darling."

The endearment and his own good sense calmed Shelby Cameron. He stared at his drawn sword and laughed at his own theatrical display. "Forgive me. But I could not bear his treatment of my wife. As if she were some property to be bartered between us."

And yet, thought Hansi as he drew her into the circle of his arm, *they were both thinking of me as a prize to be defended, as a dog defends his bone.* Nevertheless, she was so relieved that the dangerous moment had passd she could even forgive Jess Taga's insult.

They got their things and started out to the carriage.

Nick dropped behind to finish the dregs of rum in a discarded bottle. Hansi went back to get him.

"Are you all right, papa?"

"All right." But as they followed her husband, Nick murmured, "It is strange."

"What is?"

"I think Colonel Cameron was most angry when he thought Captain Jess called him a savage. Why is that?"

"You have had too much to drink, papa. Come along."

"I know these feelings. I know what Jess Taga feels."

"What feelings?" She had a sudden premonition and prayed he would not go on. A part of her wanted so badly to know as another part told her it would be disastrous to know what Jess Taga really felt for her—for it was too late, and all the rest of her life it would be too late to know.

"Captain Jess loves you. For many months this has been so. I have seen it."

"Don't say such things, papa. They can't be true. Mama used to see him kissing all those wretched women at the fort. She said—"

"My Eva did not know love. She never knew love."

That shook her. She had never heard her father betray such a profound truth about the woman he adored.

"What you say may be true, but it is too late. He never told me so. He never treated me like a woman he would marry. Respect is as important to me as it was to mama. All these things my . . . my husband has given me."

"He gives you these things and he wishes something of you. Something he needs."

"My love. And I have sworn to give that to him."

Nick said nothing more.

Book
Two

1

IN the two years since her marriage, Hansi Verin Cameron had come to learn a great many things. The two years had taught her beyond doubt that her original theory about her husband was correct. The gallant aristocratic man who had done her the honor of marriage desired that she should always suffer an enormous gulf between them. She was still the well-loved slave, he the sultan. It had become an accepted way of life in private, from small requirements like fetching his nightly glass of Madeira, or submitting to his orders within the confines of their bedroom. She told herself she did not care; that he needed and loved her. Daily, she renewed her first vow to Père Gilbert to obey Shelby Cameron as long as life endured. Rarely did she recall the old, grim life from which he had rescued her.

Hansi occasionally dreamed of Jess Taga but never mentioned his name aloud. Jess was becoming one of the most talked about men on the frontier. A brave and valiant raider, with strong allegiance to the colonial army, he and his band were the terror of the British and their Indian allies.

Once, after dreaming that Jess had been calling out for her, lying injured after a raid, she cried out in her sleep. She awoke to find Cameron leaning on one elbow, watching her—a sensation that made her shudder, for all the sweetness and warmth of his behavior afterward.

Colonel Cameron and a motley assortment of British, French and Indian troops maintained a polite control over the occupied French villages along the Mississippi, "to protect them from capture by the rebel terror, Captain Jess Taga." The French ladies of Arbreville delayed paying their social visit to their detested English conquerors as long as seemed politically wise, but a fortnight after the arrival of Colonel Cameron's beautiful, red-haired wife, their curiosity got the better part of them.

It was whispered among their servants that Mrs. Cameron had the best cook and served the best meals in the entire Mississippi area, including elegant St. Louis. The ladies of Arbreville felt, therefore, that they owed it to their own proud tradition to meet this newcomer and judge for themselves.

One sunny afternoon, with their flowered paduasoy hooped gowns floating over the muddy street, and their flat-crowned hats gently flapping in the breeze, the ladies arrived at the neat gray stone house that the colonel had commandeered for his wife and his staff, since the old French fort on the south border of the town was hopelessly antiquated and uninhabitable.

Upon meeting their hostess, the French ladies were at a loss how to proceed, for red-haired Mrs. Cameron behaved with alarming freedom, as though she did not regard their visit as a great social triumph.

Hansi had discovered that social distinctions were never more harshly enforced than in these tiny outposts of civilization. None of these plump little ladies appeared as formidable as the still vivid Mrs. Abernathy. They seemed unusually keen, asking about her housekeeping and servants this afternoon, and Hansi sat back to wait for the usual questions about her family background and life before her marriage.

Even her own secret knowledge of Shelby Cameron's peculiarities had not prepared her for his delight in publicly revealing every facet of her past life. Only her hard work in the sick wards of Montreal and later at Fort Detroit helped her overcome that first shocking impression she had made when her husband presented her to society. He so relished the retelling of his young wife's wretched past! Whatever his feminine listeners thought of red-haired Mrs. Cameron after the story unfolded, their admiration for her husband was boundless.

The chatter continued for nearly an hour. Hansi struggled to pay attention, lest she make an embarrassing mistake. It was the fat, haughty Madame de Rochblave who finally asked the invasive question. Hansi smiled to herself. These women were so predictable.

"We met at Fort Blaine on the Ohio River," she explained, pouring coffee into dainty porcelain cups.

"Oh! The Ohio River," the woman exclaimed as if it were practiced. *"La Belle Riviere,* as we call it, madam. Isn't that the lair of this terrible fiend called Taga? One should know what to expect of a man with such a heathen name. Indian, I have no doubt." The other ladies mumbled in agreement.

Hansi set the china coffee container upon the little taboret. Her hand trembled uncontrollably. The night before she had had another nightmare that Jess was lying alone, injured and calling for her. As she thought of it, she lurched over the tray. The ladies squealed in unison, "You spilled it."

Hansi was surprised by her own clumsy reaction. Recovering gracefully she slipped into private thoughts as the women fussed over the coffee-stained rug.

Why did Jess loom larger and larger in her life after two years of separation? She could not keep him out of her dreams and now he was popping up in ladies' tea conversation. But the reason for the public preoccupation with Captain Jess Taga was not a mystery. Long ago, he and his men won control over Fort Sacklin in the name of the Continental Army. Regaining that fort was Shelby Cameron's sole military objective and Hansi knew plans were already under way. Nick was on a scouting expedition at this moment, hoping to report on the size of the force left under Lieutenant Kentuck Helm's command at Fort Sacklin. Cameron was determined to win the frontier for the Loyal forces. Fort Sacklin was the key to the entire frontier and all his best plans and determination would go into this campaign.

Hansi shuddered involuntarily. She prayed that Jess Taga would not be destroyed by a British victory. There were times when she scarcely recognized in the savage forest fighter, Jess Taga, the man who had been kind to her, occasionally brusque, but always direct. Never double-tongued. He had once said he loved her. That she tried to forget. The memory remained, however, and all her efforts at confession in the privacy of her thoughts had never obliterated it. Even the memory shamed her; for she knew Shelby Cameron loved her and was loyal. He never lived a lie with her. Could she say as much for herself? She had loved Jess—in quite a different way—yet she married Shelby out of some terrible, driving need to be recognized for what they called her now, a lady. For the deception she had unconsciously practiced on Shelby, she now owed him all her loyalty and devotion. It was a bargain she made with herself sometime during the last two years.

Madame de Rochblave tittered behind her lace glove. "But it is not surprising that Madame Cameron's hand shook. This Captain Taga has that effect. No British soldier will admit it, but we are told that the terrible Captain Taga is excessively handsome."

A pleasant male voice in the open doorway behind them startled the ladies. "You must ask my lady-wife about that, madam. Mistress Cameron was once a friend to the terrible captain. What do you say, my love?"

All aflutter, the ladies turned. Long-cherished and yellowed fans were set in motion as Colonel Cameron in uniform, moved across the rush-covered floor to drop a kiss upon his wife's lips and to place his hand around the nape of her neck in a tenderly proprietary gesture. His smile as he greeted his guests confirmed their portrait of him as the ideal husband.

Hansi was puzzled at his intrusion, especially on the subject of Jess Taga. The name had seldom been mentioned between them in two years.

"Good-day, Madame de Rochblave. Ladies. I see I was not misinformed. They told me that the fairest flowers of France were to be found in Arbreville."

The women giggled in pleasure and Hansi devoutly hoped the subject which had brought her husband into the room would be forgotten. Feeling his fingers tighten playfully about her neck, she was not surprised when he repeated, "My love, what do you say to the ladies? They are eager to know what Captain Taga is really like."

She remarked coolly, "I am sure I could not say. I believe you were the last to see him, sir, and that was some years past." She reached for the tray of small iced cakes and offered it to him. "Rebel soldiers can hardly concern us here, so far from the battlefields." It was not true. Fort Sacklin was some ten days' march from their quarters on the Mississippi, and Hansi knew Cameron planned to march his men south, taking the villages along the way, as soon as conditions were right.

With his free hand he took up one of the cakes and considered it. "On the contrary. They will concern us all very shortly. It seems that the so-called Governor of Virginia Colony, Patrick Henry, is sending Taga and his lieutenants to discuss terms for an amnesty with me. They want to propose an armistice throughout the Ohio River Forest."

Hansi set the tray down with special care, keenly aware that she was under close observation from both her husband and Madame de Rochblave. Careful to make her voice casual, she replied, "I cannot imagine what the Rebels hope to gain if Jess Taga stops his raids on French and English settlements. What does he ask you to surrender?"

Madam cut in brightly, "The Hairbuyer, of course! Everyone knows that Detroit is buying the scalps of rebel settlers and their families. Did you not hear of it?"

Cameron removed his hand from Hansi's neck. "What do you say, madam? I have had these rumors investigated repeatedly. If you have any clear evidence, I should be extremely grateful for it. I was once forced to break one of my best officers on a charge that was never proved. Good God! We hear only rumors. I must have proof."

The lady was appalled by his outburst. "I . . . I only heard . . . one hears that there are scalp-buyers working for the British Army. I will certainly ask Governor de Rochblave to see what his spies can find. Some of the French trappers are in contact with this Captain Taga. Is it not possible that the colonials spread these stories to frighten settlers still loyal to the Crown?"

"Very possible," Cameron agreed grimly. "But whoever is responsible, I want to be told at once of any evidence that the French come by. May I count upon you ladies?"

Nothing could have pleased them more than to feel they might make a contribution to the frontier peace. By the time they had reassured him several times more, the women discovered that the hour was late and prepared to leave. Hansi breathed with relief that nothing more controversial had been discussed and hoped it would remain so. Then she and Shelby need not continue on the subject of Captain Jess Taga.

As Madame de Rochblave rose to leave, her eyes sparkled with sudden excitement. "Monsieur, we also hear of the danger from this Captain Taga. He behaves like a ruthless savage in his war against the British forces. And then we hear always the gossip about the men who buy the scalps of the settlers and their families."

"Well, madam?"

Hansi had a notion of what was coming. She waited nervously.

Madam continued, "What more obvious conclusion than they are one and the same? The savage Captain Taga. The savage Hairbuyer."

Cameron was taken aback. "Based upon what reason, madam? Why should he commit these vile acts against his own people?"

Thank God, thought Hansi. Her husband was too honorable a man to accept such a fantastic lie, even about his enemy.

"Why, monsieur? To achieve what is already achieved. To turn the entire frontier population against the British Army."

Hansi raised her hand and touched his arm. "You cannot believe that, darling."

While the ladies watched, he took her hand and raised her fingers to his lips, but his thoughts were clearly on Jess Taga. After a tense moment of silence, he agreed with his wife. "An appealing suggestion, I confess, but unlikely. As my wife reminds me, I also knew Jess Taga. He is not capable of such clever double-dealing."

One of the women openly stared at the Camerons, still sitting hand-in-hand. "One would not imagine you had been married so long, monsieur. Such devotion between you! Ah! If only certain other husbands could take you as a model!"

"Why not, Madame Dinard? Not every man is lucky enough to possess an enchanting female who adores him and indulges his every whim. Isn't it so, my love?"

"Yes, darling. Quite so." Hansi automatically agreed.

Madame Dinard sighed. "What a story their courtship must have made. Quite unlike the formality of most," she confided to her neighbor.

"Indeed yes," Hansi put in quickly, hoping to forestall Shelby's dramatic elaboration which she sensed was due at any second. "My father was an army scout. He is a loyalist and remains with Colonel Cameron's forces."

"At present on an exploring mission for me," Cameron explained. "There was never a man more loyal to his oath. I regard Nick Verin as my eyes and ears on the frontier."

To her husband Hansi put in, "That is understandable, sir. We consider the Cayuga-Mingo the finest scouts in the river forest. But then, I am prejudiced, perhaps."

The French ladies exchanged meaningful glances. "But is not Monsieur Verin a Frenchman?"

"What, madam? You have seen him in the town. Surely, his appearance, his deerskin blouse and trousers, his hair . . ."

Watching them, Hansi realized that they had seen many French trappers of similar appearance. It all seemed absurdly amusing to her. "My father's mother belonged to the tribe of Chief Logan. However, you will be happy to know that his father was French."

"And your . . . mother?"

Hansi smiled. "Dutch, alas."

Cameron drew his wife to him and propelled her toward the ladies. "You may see how fortunate I am to have won the affection of such a brave and forthright young lady."

"True, true, monsieur, madam." Madame de Rochblave murmured, curtsying to Hansi. The others followed her lead. No one said anything further until they had filed out of the long summer room, but as Cameron maneuvered her out to see them off along the little dirt street, she heard the long-familiar remark repeated in French throughout the group, "One can see he made her what she appears to be."

Shelby asked, "What were they whispering, my love? Their French was too rapid for me."

"They were saying you have made me a lady."

"And what does my little slave say?"

"Your humble slave says they knew us very well. She is grateful to her master."

"My dear love."

His relief at her reassuance was obvious. She felt the draining of tension in his body. They walked across the road, past narrow one-story houses with little private gardens, and as they had done on other days when Cameron found a free hour, they walked along the bank of the stream that flowed past Arbreville, emptying into the powerful Mississippi three miles southwest. Long ago the first white settlers had lined the banks of the stream with poplars imported from their native France. High overhead these trees now acted as windbreaks.

Hansi began to think over their conversation with the Frenchwomen and was troubled. "I hope papa will soon be returning. If he is found at Fort Sacklin, do you think they might . . . they wouldn't kill him!"

"God knows what they might do, if that Dinard woman's theory is right, and Taga is the Hairbuyer."

"You can't believe that nonsense. You yourself said Jess was incapable of such a thing."

Clearly he had been reconsidering. The idea repulsed her. Was it possible? No! The Jess Taga she knew would never be guilty of such fiendish crimes. But was the Captain Taga of today the same man she had once known and cared for?

"If you suspect him of such a thing, how can you invite him here to talk treaties and amnesties?"

"To gain time. I must have time if I am to take Fort Sacklin."

"It is preposterous. These hair buyers are not rebels."

Cameron said thoughtfully, "It seems preposterous. But then, I have never believed Major Hay was guilty! Yet I would have broken him. And he bears me no malice, darling."

Startled and apprehensive, she stopped in the path. "You have seen Major Hay?"

"At Fort Detroit. Hansi, I wish you would be more charitable toward old Geoffrey."

The years had not softened her bitter memories of Fort Blaine and her mother's death. "That dreadful man made a treaty with Chief Cornstalk to sacrifice us all. I shouldn't be in the least surprised if he were your precious Hairbuyer."

"Darling, don't talk like that. He was my most efficient officer. I haven't a single man here I can trust. I need him."

Panic and an old, festering hatred made her draw away from Cameron, though she immediately noticed

her action brought about a return of his nervous tension.
"He is to be stationed here?"

"I need someone I trust. I need Geoffrey Hay for
Sacklin when it is taken," he said quietly.

"I will never receive that man. He would have had
us all scalped."

He took a long, deep breath, looking pale and cold, but
unbending. "My love, you heard me say Jess Taga and
some of his men are to meet us here to discuss the
armistice. Taga will have good men he trusts. I must have
at least one man. And that man is Geoffrey Hay."

They had reached the crumbling, warped wooden
stakes that marked the north boundary of the old Arbreville fortress. She turned back toward their weathered gray
stone house. It pained her to know that her unbending
opposition to Hay caused her husband to suffer. Yet,
whenever she remembered Major Geoffrey Hay, she remembered that last Shawnee attack, and she could again
hear her mother's last stifled cry, as she caught the
Shawnee bullet.

Hansi had taken several steps before her husband
reached her, seizing her forearm in a harsh grip. His
voice was frozen, a stranger's voice. "Whatever our differ-
ences, we are not going to demonstrate them in public.
We will return arm in arm. Do you understand me?"

It seemed curious that he could inspire both fear and
pity in her at the same time. She let him escort her as he
chose. She knew that by nightfall he would "forgive" her
and consider the matter closed when he got his way, but it
was a major blow to her rapidly tarnishing image of
herself and her husband.

2

HOWEVER deep Hansi's hatred might lie, her loyalties were equally deep. Everything she and Nick had—including the fact that Nick was not now a hopeless drunkard—they owed to Shelby Cameron. She felt that she would never cease to feel gratitude, as well as affection for the man who gave her so much and needed her so much.

Within the week, while her fears grew for her father's present safety, she agreed to receive Major Hay. This turnabout came partly as an effort to punish herself for her new awareness of Jess Taga. The prospect of seeing him again terrified her. She was haunted by the possibility that he might talk Nick out of his devotion to Shelby, and she was afraid she might still feel something of his old attraction. Most terrifying of all was the fear that Shelby Cameron would guess the reason for her troubled sleep, and discover the enormous effort it took for her to remain his loving harem creature.

Whether Jess Taga was now a cold-blooded murderer or the same dear, friendly man she had known, he was constantly in her thoughts. So she reversed herself, to her husband's great satisfaction, although at great cost to her own self-respect. She made plans for the reception that would honor the British and French officers, including the hateful Major Geoffrey Hay.

Cameron had already sent scouts out to trace Nick Verin, but Hansi's doubts and fears for her father remained.

The generous loan of the governor's house to the Camerons thrilled Hansi. She got along familiarly with the Rochblave slaves, excepting a good-looking mulatto woman called Seline, who had been madam's personal maid. Madam generously insisted Seline remain to oblige her successor, but Hansi understood the woman would act as madam's spy in the household.

"It is a great pity about the return, Madame Cameron," Seline remarked, powdering Hansi's unwilling hair into a formal coiffure.

Hansi glanced at the woman's face in her hand mirror. "What return are you talking about, Seline?"

"Why, the scouts, madam. A great pity. Still . . . it may be that they have overlooked some little corner of the forest. There are so many trails. So many possibilities. It is unfortunate that the dreadful Captain Taga's men know them all better than our scouts do."

"If you are speaking of my father, he knows this forest better than any of Captain Taga's men. He was once their scout. But you know that, Seline, as you know so much else."

Seline's skillful fingers did not hesitate, as she concentrated upon Hansi's hair. "I believe the scouts sent out by *Monsieur le Colonel* have returned discouraged. The rumor is . . . but madam is not interested."

Resisting the impulse to smack her with the mirror, Hansi casually said, "All the same, you may as well tell me. That will relieve us both."

Seline spread her lips in a smile. "How well madam understands. As I was about to say, the rumor is that the colonel's personal scout, Nicholas Verin, has been taken by the rebels at Fort Sacklin and executed."

"Executed!"

"I believe the method used was hanging."

The woman's air of satisfaction restored Hansi's common sense. She set down the mirror with a sharp crack, but she refused to yield to the maid's provocation.

"We have no reason to believe my father has been hanged by the rebels."

Seline started to say something, thought better of it and stepped back to survey her work.

"Madam is satisfied?"

Hansi examined her head critically, forced to admire the woman's skill. She said as much and was relieved when Seline bobbed a curtsy and left. Shakily, Hansi sat down to think. Almost of their own volition, her hands curled into claws. *Please, papa, be safe. Dear God, keep him safe.*

The stillness of the early winter night was shattered by the voices of Cameron's men arriving early. If wine punch was to be the beverage of the evening, the soldiers intended to be well fortified before the arrival of the French guests. Hansi stood up, winced under her heavy coiffure, and testily walked across the room in her high-heeled, pointed-toe satin shoes, so popular among the *haut monde.*

After a few steps she had acquired an easy balance in spite of the elaborate extension of the satin and lace panniers over her leaf-green underdress. She stepped out into the narrow passageway that separated the two wings of the house. She heard her husband's voice in conversation in one of the long ballrooms, followed by the reply, in an easy, supercilious tone she had not heard since Fort Pitt. It was a voice she would remember forever, as she remembered the man she held responsible for the bloody attack on Fort Blaine.

She stiffened, recalling her promise to Shelby, and opened the ballroom doors. Cameron stood with his back to her, looking dashing in his dress uniform, the scarlet coat and white wig. Beyond him, facing her, was a powerful, heavy man equally resplendent in dress uniform, but she knew that face, the thick, lascivious lips, the small eyes peering at her sleepily.

"Good evening, ma'am. A pleasure to see you again, and looking so—prosperous."

Cameron swung around quickly, came to Hansi's side and kissed her cheek. "My love, Major Hay brings us some news. Tell her, Geoff."

"A pleasure, ma'am. Two of my scouts tell me they have sighted your father in the forest not more than an hour's march from this spot."

"Ah!" Cameron exclaimed with delight. "That brings the light to those beautiful eyes, my love. You see, I told you old Geoff would bring us luck."

The major pursed his moist lips, and smiled, a patronizing smile, which told Hansi how well he understood his commanding officer. She was happy enough at his news to overlook his intolerable manner. She returned her husband's embrace, which made the major remark sarcastically, "Still such an ideal marriage. It very nearly makes one believe in romance."

"You may believe in ours," Cameron assured him. "This enchanting child, after all the joy she has given me, still persists in regarding me as her savior, her rescuer from nameless horrors. If that is so, I can only say she is the fairest rose ever plucked from the dung heap."

Hansi swallowed this hurt—the unexpected comment on her former life—and inquired politely, "I trust you had an uneventful journey down from Fort Detroit, Major Hay."

"Naturally, ma'am. One of your old friends was my guide."

"Who might that be?" Cameron asked, pleased that conversation was smooth between these two old enemies.

"I rather imagine you know him as well, colonel. That excellent Shawnee scout, Yellow Painter. I believe he once knew your wife. However—" He shrugged.

Cameron's smile was set. "Fortunately, Hansi has long since thrown off that sort of background. Come darling, our guests are beginning to arrive."

They left the major to the wine bowl and moved toward the reception salon, once the governor's billiard room. The governor himself was one of the first to arrive, a composed man of middle years and considerable charm who obviously regarded the British incursion onto his ground as temporary. His wife was all friendliness and flutter. She made it a point to devote her attention to Cameron alone. The governor devoted himself to Hansi, obviously delighted to converse in his native French.

"It is regrettable, Madame Cameron, that your husband's army and our own have so often been at sword's point. We were relieved to find him so much the gentleman."

Surprised at the implication that he might have been otherwise, she said, "I have never known a man more honorable, more deserving of respect."

"As you say, madam. And for that reason we are persuaded he will find and punish the creatures engaged in buying the scalps of innocent settlers and their families. At first we thought these devils took their orders from Detroit and the British Army, but lately we hear rumors . . . in short, that the crimes may be laid at the feet of Captain Taga. What is your opinion?"

"Nothing could be more absurd," Hansi said sharply. "The Ohio and Kentucky settlers are his friends, his comrades."

Governor de Rochblave shrugged. "Yet how shrewd to arouse the frontier people against the Redcoats!"

"Such treachery is beyond Captain Taga's capability. If I were searching for the mastermind paying these Indians for settlers' scalps, I think it much more likely that—"

She broke off, suddenly catching sight of a man in the narrow passageway that separated the two crowded salons. She had looked up in time to glimpse only the moccasins, deerskin trousers, and a bare arm swinging a long rifle. Could it be her father? To the governor's astonishment she excused herself and abruptly made her way out of the room.

When she reached the passageway the scout was gone. But Hansi had not seen her father since mid-autumn when he had preceded the army's march down from Fort Detroit, and she could wait no longer. Picking up her skirts, she ran toward the small antechamber, to the astonishment of her guests, who could not believe the hoydenish behavior of the colonel's lady.

Pushing open the door, she interrupted a conference between Major Hay and a powerfully built Shawnee, whose shaven head glistened under the lit chandelier. The Indian gave Hansi a start when he turned and she beheld the flat, reptilian features of her old enemy, Yellow Painter. So the Puan look had been a lie. Even then he had been masquerading. He was always a Shawnee spy.

Recovering with an effort, she apologized to the major and started to leave.

The major's cutting voice stopped her. "An old acquaintance of yours, I believe, Mrs. Cameron."

"Yes," she said coldly. "I knew Yellow Painter when he wore Puan hair and spied on Fort Blaine."

Yellow Painter's lips curled back in a grimace that served as a weak smile. "For my Chief Cornstalk, the greatest warrior in the Ohio River Forest."

Hansi knew better than to further the bloody vendetta between them, but she could not resist the bitter reminder, "And so you betrayed the fort to your chief? The dead of Fort Blaine have you to thank—you and those in the fort who paid you."

"All in a good cause, ma'am," the major put in, unruffled by her implication. "As events have proved, there were those at Fort Blaine who were disloyal to the Crown. Now we are pleased to have all the tribes on our side."

"All the tribes you can afford to pay for their butcheries?"

She left the room wondering what new deviltry was brewing between the two men. She did not have long to consider it. By the time she returned to her guests she was thunderstruck to find Cameron introducing her father to Governor de Rochblave and his wife. She made her way to the center of the group and threw her arms around Nick's dusty, tired form and kissed his leathery cheek.

"Papa! we were so worried!"

Nick backed away from her, uneasily aware that his dignity had been impaired by this public display of emotion. "There was no danger," he answered her. "I know this land. You look well, my daughter. It is better to speak of these things alone."

Hansi cared very little about social opinion. She could not conceal her pride in Nick, who wore his dirty trousers and long overshirt with a special grace. His long, carelessly bound hair had begun to gray and he was older, not quite as agile as she remembered from her girlhood. But he drank less, and put great stock in Shelby Cameron's trust.

Cameron told Hansi proudly, "Nick has done a tremendous job. It may be the means of saving the entire frontier for the Crown. Come, Nick, the governor and his good lady will excuse you. We want to feed our best scout as he deserves."

For an instant Hansi wondered if this did not sound like a reward for a good watchdog—feed him. But she was also touched by her husband's praise of Nick. If she could not show her affection to Nick in public, she might at least demonstrate her gratitude to her husband. She put her hand in his.

He pressed her fingers gently, reminding her of her duty in a low voice. "You remain to play the hostess, my love. You do it so beautifully. The governor is very much taken with you."

"But I want to talk to papa. I haven't seen him for weeks . . . no, months."

"Now, Fire-Dawn," he said firmly, touching one of the curls which showered powder and revealed the true burning color beneath, "we all have our duty. I must be the first to speak with Nick."

Her father touched her shoulder, tentatively. "It is so,

daughter. There are things Colonel Cameron must know."

She looked from her father to her husband. "I understand. Major Hay is in there with Yellow Painter, one of Chief Cornstalk's spies when Fort Blaine fell. I don't want papa involved with those men."

"Well, well," Cameron pacified her, "we must see what is best. Yellow Painter is one of our scouts now. Hansi, take that French governor into your care. We need him."

"Ay, sir!"

He missed the irony in her voice and hurried away. Nick looked back at her once, loving warmth emanating from his eyes. He was proud of his new responsibilities. He was an important man in his own lowly field. He strode proudly behind Shelby Cameron in the direction of the room where Major Hay and Yellow Painter were deep in their own plans. Hansi thanked God—her husband's white god—for Nick's recovery from the despair of losing Eva.

Remembering all she owed her husband, she beamed all her charm upon Governor de Rochblave.

The Frenchman was not a fool, and while enjoying her company as he enjoyed that of every beautiful woman, he reminded her, "Colonel Cameron has enlisted a number of Frenchmen under the British flag, but this is not our war. I am informed by courier that French soldiers are promised to the rebels to fight under Washington."

"But the rebels have been everywhere defeated, monsieur. On Long Island, in New York, in the southern colonies, in Canada. And there is that wretched army snowed into Pennsylvania for the winter. They are not likely to provide a threat from Valley Forage."

"Valley Forge, madame. But it was scarcely a defeat in Massachusetts. Your troops may have won their battles in Boston, but they have since abandoned the area. Your lines are too far extended, the army too far from its bases. In your own country over the sea, this war is singularly unpopular."

"It is not my country, monsieur," she countered evenly, displeased that he equated her with her husband's army.

"You forget, my dear," Madame de Rochblave reminded her husband, "Colonel Cameron's lady is the daughter of that handsome Indian."

The Governor nodded. "Quite true. This forest country really belongs to neither the British nor the colonies, but to your father's people, madame. Yet, I must confess, I doubt the Indians can hold it."

"My father is faithful to his commander."

The governor said crisply, "Honor can be suicidal."

She made her excuses and went to mingle with her other guests, but she was as deeply troubled over the governor's words as by the presence of Major Hay and Yellow Painter in her house.

The festivities continued throughout the winter evening until almost an hour before dawn. Hansi was anxious to hear Nick's adventures and hoped Cameron would permit a cozy chat with her father before taking her to bed. It was disconcerting when the two men arrived in her dressing room. She hoped that Cameron would not hover over them while they talked.

At first satisfied when he stood staring out at the first blue rim of dawn, she soon realized that Cameron stood there expressly to overhear the talk between them. She could learn nothing of importance about Nick's trip to Fort Sacklin. She instinctively felt that he was troubled about something he had learned, but she could not imagine why it should be a secret—unless it was some military plan, and she knew better than to pursue that subject.

As for Nick, he kept trying to discover what her life was like. Had she been busy? How did she like her French friends?

"I don't know, papa. I don't feel French. And I don't feel like one of the squaws in Chief Cornstalk's camp." She lowered her voice, hoping her conversation would sound like an indistinguishable murmur to Cameron across the room. "Papa, I don't know what I am."

Without looking around, Cameron said firmly, "You are English, darling. I made you English."

Nick studied her and said, "You are happy?"

"Of course. Everyone is kind. Did you reach Fort Sacklin? Who is commanding there?"

"Lieutenant Helm."

Remembering how well her father had liked the Long Knife lieutenant, she was startled. "Did he recognize you? Papa! They could have charged you as a spy."

Cameron cut in, "Nick risked his life for us. He might well have been taken and hanged by your old friends."

"The Long Knives would never hang me."

Hansi glanced at her husband while she gripped Nick's hands. Panic swept over her.

"You mustn't risk so much, papa. They know you by sight. Let the army send someone else."

Hansi was not surprised when Cameron came over and dropped a protective hand on Nick's shoulder.

"Hansi, you must not make a coward of our finest scout." Nick stirred and he added, "Not that you could, my love. I am frank enough to say there isn't one soldier or officer with Nick's courage and ability."

Entering into Cameron's military affairs for the first time in their marriage, Hansi spoke cautiously, "Papa is still only a scout. He is better and braver and more clever than your men, and yet he cannot be one of them."

The two men stared at her. Maddeningly, they seemed to agree that what she regarded a serious injustice was as it should be. "Perhaps you can assure her of what she knows all too well. Tell her, Nick," Cameron said, finally.

Nick's expression was unmoved, but she thought his eyes told her a great deal. In their depths was a plea for understanding. "Daughter, you hurt yourself. You know Redcoats do not willingly serve with men of the tribes."

"But, papa, you have done so much for these idiotic young Redcoats."

He waved her words away at the first sign of Cameron's rising anger. "Daughter, think. There are those who hate men of my blood even more than the Redcoats. That is the truth. The Redcoats accept me as what I am. A scout. Think on it."

Hansi settled back, feeling as if she might crumble. No

one knew better than she the bitter, implacable hatred between Jess Taga's Long Knife units and the frontier Indians. They needed Indians, but only as the British needed them—to scout and to spy.

"And I am your daughter, papa."

For an instant she hated Cameron as he contradicted her softly, "You are no longer an Indian. You are Shelby Cameron's wife. You might even ask Jess Taga's views, my love. He will be arriving here in a few days. . . . Now, let us end this useless talk. It is dawn. Time we were in bed."

3

THE entire household slept late the next day, full of
Negus, Rum Fustian and Sherry Flip. Except Colonel
Cameron, who never drank. Hansi woke before noon and
drank her morning tea, a habit acquired from her
husband. She asked Seline if Nick had been to see the
colonel.

"Very early, ma'am. Something about the lower French
towns on the Great River. He is to find out how much
support Kaskaskia and Cahokia will give to the British."

Hansi bolted upright. "What? Is he being sent away
again?"

"At once, they say."

Hansi flung back the bedcovers abruptly and pushed
away the tray. "I must dress immediately."

With a speed that appeared unseemly to the maid,
Hansi deftly dressed in her shift and an elaborate green
day gown with a fresh white fichu, and hurried down the
stairs through the silent house. It certainly seemed that
her husband was trying to keep her father from her. She
had no notion why. She walked abruptly into Cameron's

office. He was sitting with his elbows on a map spread out over the surface of his enormous mahogany desk. Hansi wondered what campaign involved him so intensely, then realized he was not looking at the map at all. He seemed to be staring into space.

"Shelby!"

He did not stir. For an instant she wondered if he had heard her. Then he looked up, his austere expression relaxing a trifle, and he rose politely. "Yes?"

It was one of the few times he had not referred to her with an endearment. But then she seldom used his first name, and never in such a sharp tone. Sometimes she suspected his affection was automatic, but it was one of the many painful questions of her marriage she never could entirely resolve.

"Where is papa?"

He closed his eyes, looking terribly tired, opened them and held out a hand, beckoning her to stand closer to him. "You were up very late, my love. What brings you down here at this hour?"

"Why shouldn't I be up and about? You are. My father is. Why are you sending him away before I can talk to him?"

He drew her around the table toward him, his answer to all her complaints. She was aware of a great pity for him and wasn't sure why this splendid, superior man often aroused in her feelings he would despise in any other man.

"Because Nick is extremely valuable to me. I cannot trust anyone else as I trust him. We are about to embark on the most crucial operation since I came to the frontier. No time must be lost. Does that answer your question? Do not frown like that. I can't bear to see wrinkles in that lovely brow."

She was not moved by his flattery, but by the knowledge that his new military actions greatly troubled him. Although anxious for her father, she was also able to appreciate her husband's need for her. Finding herself encased in his insistent embrace, she kissed him on the crown of his head and caressed his face, aware suddenly that there were more gray strands in his dark hair than she remembered. "I'm sorry, darling," she said softly, "I didn't mean to disturb you. I know how busy you are."

He looked at her. "What would my life be without my devoted little slave? But some day, when you are very old, and very elegant, will you then leave me for some young dashing rival?"

She tried to cheer him into better spirits. "Now, how could I leave the finest, most honorable man I've ever known? I know you wouldn't hurt papa. You saved his life when you took him into your service."

All the same, she wished he would share just a little about Nick's assignment. How dangerous was it? What was he doing, Something Nick disliked. She had guessed that the night before. Had his task something to do with Fort Sacklin's commander, Kentuck Helm, whom he liked and admired from the old days? And, by extension, Jess Taga?

She looked over Cameron's shoulder, trying to read the map. . . . To the east lay nothing but endless forest, rivers and swamps, and at their heart, on the Sacklin River, Fort Sacklin.

"You are not going to try to take Fort Sacklin before the spring, are you?"

He let the map roll up under his palms and stared up at her. "Why not?"

"But those lands are completely buried by snow and ice in the winter. When the snow melts, they call them the 'drowned lands.' "

He was watching her carefully. "Lieutenant Helm is Taga's representative," he said in a measured voire. "Are you so interested because you know that to conquer Fort Sacklin means conquering Jess Taga?"

But can you conquer him, she thought, and was immediately ashamed of the thought. "No. But I know this countryside," she continued. "Unless you march immediately, you will face drastic problems. You will be delayed by the Amnesty Conference, and afterward, if the conference succeeds, your plans will have been for nothing."

To her surprise, his features brightened and he smiled at her as one smiles at a naïve child. She was still puzzled when he kissed her and firmly guided her to the door. In the antechamber, to her astonishment, she passed Major Hay, and the French trapper-guide, Daniel Greathouse, striding in to meet with her husband. She would always blame Hay and Greathouse for the attempt they had made to sell out the settlers and militia of Fort Blaine.

She found her father preparing for a long overland march. He had been offered one of the army mounts but scorned such inefficient methods of forest travel.

Nick shocked his daughter by swinging around with one hand on his hunting knife as he heard her footsteps.

"Daughter!"

Hansi found it even worse that he did not relax when he saw her. He forgot the knife but his body remained stiff and tense as he drew her into his tiny room, smiling tentatively. "They told you I leave now?"

"It is all so strange, papa. You've only just returned. Shelby says you are going to the other French towns. Why couldn't he send someone else?"

"Colonel Shelby says he trusts me."

"But of course he trusts you. Who would not? Papa, what else is it?"

He brightened. "It may be I will meet Captain Jess at Kaskaskia and come back with him to the conference. My friend Kentucky Helm at Fort Sacklin said Captain Jess is still my friend, even though I am with the Redcoats. It will be good if we meet."

"You feel you owe something to Kentuck Helm, don't you, papa?"

"I was discovered at Sacklin. I might have been hanged for a spy. Kentuck let me go. Colonel Cameron knows this. He knows how I feel. When he speaks of winning Sacklin next spring, he does not wish me to listen. That is the reason he sends me to Kaskaskia. It is natural."

She touched his shoulder. Ever since Eva Verin's death it had been difficult to bring out his true and deep emotions. He had returned to the reserved ways of his tribe, or perhaps he was afraid of rejection by the outside world. He had been so badly rejected by his wife.

"I hope you will always be friends with Jess and Kentuck, papa. If that's all you are worried about, you have no trouble at all."

She watched him, hopeful of a change in his spirits. The closest to a change, however, was the warmth in his handclasp as he covered her hand with his.

"Daughter, there is one thing I have not said before. It is time to say it. A man has good and bad signs in his life. You were always my good sign."

For an instant she was afraid she would disgrace him by crying. She hugged him instead, and made him promise to take no chances on his journey. He accepted this as he accepted her embrace—a trifle stiffly—but she understood.

"Colonel Cameron trusts me as he trusts his officers. He thinks other men are honest as he is. Also, he is afraid he cannot rule without them. That is weakness."

"No, papa. Not weak."

He looked at her. She avoided his eyes, and silently patted his shirt sleeve. She picked up his shotbag and powder horn.

"These are so old, papa. You should have new ones."

"My woman made the shotbag for me. She made all this fringe. You talk foolishness."

She smiled and said no more. When he left the monastic little room she followed him. *Like his squaw,* she thought. But it made a difference when the brave who walked ahead was a loved one.

Outside the wind whipped up a cold, wintry rain. Everyone was scurrying for cover. When Hansi expressed her regret that his journey should begin so unpleasantly, Nick assured her, "It is better so. They cannot march in this weather."

Before she could question him further, Nick turned to salute Cameron, who stood watching from his study and then moved out of sight.

To Hansi, Nick said quietly, "He trusts me. But also others who are bad. He may listen to you. You can save him or destroy him. Never trust those about him."

Major Hay, Yellow Painter, and Daniel Greathouse flashed before her mind. "I will take care, papa. And you."

"Of what will you take care, my love?" Colonel Cameron asked pleasantly, stepping into the street to join them.

"We were saying our good-byes. Papa is leaving. We should thank him for rushing off only a few hours after he returned. Don't you think so, Shelby?"

"How cold you sound, darling. I have never liked the sound of my name on your lips." With his wife safely encompassed in the circle of his arm, he held out the other hand to Nick, who took it slowly.

"My dear fellow, no one knows better than I how much I owe to you. Nick, you are the rare breed—a truly honest man." He smiled at Nick's uneasiness. Hansi, who felt that such praise was long overdue, was happily content as the men exchanged handshakes and Cameron wished his scout a successful journey.

"Now it is my turn to say take care," Cameron added. "Remember, many of the tribes around the French towns may be rebel sympathizers."

"And keep warm," Hansi reminded.

Nick grinned. "I've got a bottle of Spanish rum in my shotbag." Then he looked long at Hansi, as if to frame the picture of her he carried in his mind's eye. Hefting his rifle over his shoulder, he started off, never glancing back. Hansi watched until his stride broke to a jog-trot and Cameron gently steered her indoors. She obeyed without enthusiasm.

The rest of the afternoon, while she worked with the other women to prepare the quarters for Captain Taga and his men, she kept worrying about the bad weather and her father. And Jess. Would they meet? How wonderful if they met and became friends again!

Shelby Cameron remained in his office very late that

night. Hansi awoke several times, worried, uneasy, yet not at all certain why. Violent winds and rain continued to beat against the shutters and Hansi kept picturing her father, no longer a young man, jog-trotting against the cold rain in the darkness. She almost welcomed the thought of that rum bottle he carried with him. Unable to sleep, she got up and walked about the chilly room, unable to be still. Surely something was wrong downstairs. She wondered if she missed her husband or, more truthfully, if she was puzzled over the reason for his preoccupation throughout that day and evening.

She listened and thought she heard muffled voices somewhere outside the building. The front shutters were closed, too difficult to open at this hour. She took her warmest dressing sacque, put it on over her nightgown, and went out into the damp hall. The sounds were much louder now, outside the north end of the building.

Hansi opened the door to a darkened music room overlooking the north. One floor below the window she saw the narrow, pebbled walk that opened into the main trace leading northward.

The road seemed eerily alive with movement. A company of Redcoats, carefully holding their accoutrement to avoid the metallic jingle, marched northward through the rain. She was still trying to make sense of the scene when she heard voices directly below. She began to tremble uncontrollably—more from fear than the cold—as she recognized Major Geoffrey Hay's arrogant, thick voice.

"Depend upon it, sir. Ten days. No more. We've twice their force. Greathouse will guide us there."

"Time is everything," said Shelby Cameron. "Within a month the ground will be impossible for any force, including Taga's."

"Taga? We've scotched that viper with this move. Half his strength is at Sacklin and we'll attend to that fast enough. Farewell, sir."

"Good luck."

"Count upon it, sir."

Whatever they were scheming, Hansi decided, they could not possibly be headed south to destroy Nick Verin.

Her husband would never countenance such an act! But it had occurred to her momentarily that Major Hay might count the murder of her father an added pleasure if he happened to come across him alone.

She had no idea how many men had been in the fore-front of that march, but she guessed more than a full company had departed in the black night. It did not seem possible they were headed for Fort Sacklin, which lay due east, and, at all events, such a conquest at the very time the enemy was invited to a peace conference would be the highest breach of honor.

Would it be even greater dishonor for her to betray her husband and warn Jess Taga when he arrived? She had never felt so helpless in all her life.

A few steps away Major Hay turned back. "My com-pliments to the lovely slave girl, colonel."

Whatever Cameron replied in his low voice, Hansi could not hear it. She felt sick with revulsion against her hus-band, not for having confided the intimate secrets of their marriage bed to her enemy, but against herself for having yielded to Shelby Cameron's desperate fantasies.

4

I am a coward, Hansi told herself that morning as she dressed, ignoring her breakfast tea tray. She knew if she lingered her husband would be up to join her for tea and a few moments of love. The tradition began early in their marriage—a time of her morning humiliation, which made him ecstatically happy. Afterward, he delighted in tutoring her in the ways of the genteel.

She had never refused him. Whatever her feelings, she owed him so much. But the last week, haunted by the realization that her private degradation was known to Major Hay, she had begun to dread her husband's demands. Would he relate every detail of their intimate life to others? Doubtless, he did it to hide that strange insecurity of his, she tried to tell herself. Yet, there was more to her change of feelings than revulsion. Since Major Hay's secret expedition set out, she began to increasingly mistrust her husband's military honor.

Had Nick tried to warn her?

She knew she had overrated Cameron, assuming his only imperfections were his sexual fantasies. But that had been forgiven because he was invariably fair, a soldier of the highest sense of duty and loyalty, incapable of dishonor.

And he had been so good to Nick! Again, she found herself making excuses for him.

Seline was holding out Hansi's heavy weather cloak for the long walk she intended to take when Cameron arrived. He appeared calm and handsomely self-possessed. Seline bobbed her curtsy and bustled past him. For some unaccountable reason Seline had never liked him, Hansi thought.

Cameron crossed the room, removed the cloak from Hansi's hands and insisted upon wrapping her up. "Since you are determined to leave me, my love, the least I can do is see you are protected."

"Leave you, sir? It is only that I am longing to take my exercise before the conference begins. You know how busy we shall be later, what with dinners, teas and balls." She attempted a smile, and hoped her voice sounded natural and firm.

His hands lingered on the collar of her cloak, softly caressing her neck. "And how happy my little slave will be to pour chocolate for the famous Captain Taga!"

She shivered under his touch, looked up at him. His gentle expression had not changed. His remark seemed to be harmless. She said, tartly, "I wish you would not think of me as your slave. I am your wife."

"So that's it?"

She could feel his hands relax. She had not guessed he was so tense.

He went on, "Is that why you have been behaving so badly this past week?" His laugh was youthful, contagious. He touched his lips to the nape of her neck. "Why should you not wish me to speak of you as you are, my love?" He pulled her toward the long mirror. "Consider. I created that enchanting creature you see before you. Do you actually believe you are the same female I found at Fort Blaine? . . . That bedraggled little flower I plucked out of the mud? Don't you see, darling? I molded you, with infinite care. Any man would envy me the prize I hold between my hands."

I wish I were still that girl at Fort Blaine, she thought to herself miserably. Jess was right. Jess knew her. . . . Aloud, she asked, "Was that why you told Hay what I am to you?"

"He told you!" He stepped away from her, releasing her. "Darling, I am proud of you. I wish I might shout to all the world what I—"

"Own?"

Nothing of her own pain and anger seemed to reach him. There was no mistaking his relief. "So that was what all this has been about. I had begun to think you were repulsed by me, or that you no longer loved me—a thousand horrors! And now I find it was a mere matter of words!"

"Merely that. May I go now?"

"Certainly, my love. Incidentally, Captain Taga and his cutthroats are due late in the day. We plan to receive them here in the two salons, the Rochblaves, you, a few officers of the French regiment, and myself." He seemed to be waiting for her reaction, and finding none, continued in the same good humor, "I hope you will wear your very best, and absolutely dazzle the fellow. You recall he wasn't optimistic about our marriage and we want to let him know just how wrong he was."

"I remember. I'll be back shortly. Good-day, my dear." She kissed his cheek obediently and went out.

Outside, against the cold winds, Hansi's mind raced over the half-pieces of information she knew about Hay's expedition, trying to decide her next step. The town had buzzed with rumors after Hay and his men slipped out in the night. The story went out that they had been sent to put down an uprising among the Piankashaws, who had been issued red axes and who were collecting scalps for sale to the Hairbuyer.

The new wave of talk about hair buying infuriated the

British, especially Colonel Cameron, who took it as a slur on the good name of his men. The French continued to play a waiting game, unwilling to support the British cause until the identity of the Hairbuyer had been proven.

Hansi could not resolve the questions that flooded her mind. Hay had specifically said Fort Sacklin, nothing about Piankashaws or scalping. Could that mean that Kentuck Helm was the Hairbuyer? Did Hay intend to follow the trail to him after the Indian raid? Terrible thought, she realized quickly, remembering Kentuck's dancing eyes. But there was definitely a military connection between the two stories. She longed to talk to Jess, to warn him. She knew he would explain things truthfully to her. Would that betray her husband's cause? No use pretending to herself . . . she knew the answer was yes. . . .

Seline came running down the ice-crusted path in wooden clogs to warn her, "They have been seen! The rebel captain and six men. A dozen other rebels are marching to join him from Cahokia. You think maybe they plan to capture the Redcoats in Arbreville?"

"Not with only eighteen men," Hansi quickly answered, running home beside Seline.

She fully intended to follow her husband's instructions, but when she reached their bedchamber and found all her clothing for the reception laid out as if to remind her of her duty, she was furious. "Good God! What now? Am I not even permitted to choose my own dresses?"

The young slave girl who assisted Seline was shocked at her mistress' crude behavior and glanced at Seline, who shrugged and rolled her eyes upward. Hansi had seen this before among her servants. It seemed as if, in spite of all Shelby Cameron's efforts, Hansi was still far from the lady he thought he had created.

Somewhat subdued by the maids' reaction, Hansi behaved as even her husband could have wished, reflecting all the while that Jess Taga would despise the frippery pattern doll about to emerge from the yards of green satin and taffeta, poufs, rosettes and lace, almost all below the waist. Above the waist, as any but a blind man could see, was very little more than Hansi's own golden flesh, her neat global breasts very much in evidence, thanks to the teasing use of elegant gauze.

"And now the emerald," Seline ordered her assistant, having taken an inventory of her mistress' appearance.

Even the glory of her husband's family emerald cross hung around her throat on a silver chain annoyed her. She did not want to look like a property created by Shelby Cameron and paraded before Jess.

"And the hair. The curling tongs and the powdering box," Seline commanded.

Hansi put her hands up. "No! I want *it* at least to be natural."

The two women openly gaped at her, as though she were mad. Seline began with gentle persuasion. "The colonel wishes it, ma'am. All the ladies will be properly coiffed."

"Then I shall be different. Give me the brush."

While they stared, openmouthed at her defiance, Hansi brushed her thick red lengths of hair until they glistened. She wanted to be the old Fire-Dawn, except that now her hair was cleaner than when Jess Taga had seen her last. She was determined that he should not think she had grown above herself. She took the small emerald earbobs from the maid's hands. She could not deny that the flash of green in her flame-red hair was flattering.

All the same, when Cameron came to fetch her she was shaking, nervous and unsure.

"Come, my love. Not shy, are you?" her husband asked as they went along the upper hall to the great staircase. "You will completely eclipse those wretched French crows." He shook her arm jokingly. "They have never troubled you before. Only this morning Rochblave complimented me on possessing the most beautiful woman on the frontier."

"It must be my . . . headache."

He was solicitous as always when any ailment, large or small, troubled her. "My love! I am sorry to hear it.

I'll ask Madame de Rochblave if she has any of those pastilles ladies use."

She could not bear his fussing. It only made her feel more guilty. "No, no. It is nearly gone. Don't trouble, darling."

"Well," he said smugly, "that is something! I think this is the first kindness you have bestowed upon me in a week."

Conscience stricken, she moved closer to him, feeling his body respond. They walked down the stairs together. At the landing she saw the governor, his lady, the Dinards and several British and French officers, all of them staring up the stairs. Hansi flushed at their attention, wondering for the thousandth time how she found herself in stuffy rooms with people she would never understand, when all the time she knew in her heart that her home was a cabin in the forest, smelling of pine and laurel and spring flowers and winter warmth about a snapping log fire. And the kind of hard work she had known as a girl. . . . *What am I doing here? Who am I? I never belonged here. This is the life mama wanted for me, but I am my father's daughter and as much a stranger here as he is. Oh, Manitou, hear me . . . What have I done with my life? . . .*

"Madame Cameron, Monsieur le Colonel, what a handsome picture the two of you made coming down the stairs!" Governor Rochblave complimented them.

It was almost dusk, and clusters of candles had been lighted everywhere. These, and the heat from several hearths gave the long double salon a dazzling look in spite of the drab winter weather outside. Nervously, Hansi accepted a glass of champagne, and drained it in a few gulps. One of Cameron's aides came in from the street and reported to Cameron, "He is in the town, sir. Didn't stop to get into correct uniform or anything. Still in those damned stinking skins, sir."

Cameron smiled. "Those skins *are* his uniform. But don't tremble, my dear fellow. He won't eat you. He and

I were once"—he glanced at Hansi—"allies, so let him come, skins and all."

There was a stir around the open double doors at the far end of the salon. Hansi became aware of the betraying pulsebeat in her throat and covered it with her free hand. Behind her, a French footman refilled the glass in her other hand. She was too anxious to notice. She hardly knew what to expect, the sometimes angry, sometimes teasing and flirtatious Jess Taga of her girlhood, or the savage Captain Taga, suspected of countless frontier brutalities.

Three men appeared in the doorway, but even at the opposite end of the long room no one doubted which was Jess Taga. He had only to take his first step forward, which had all the easy grace and power of a great forest cat. His long hair, Hansi thought, appeared very much the way it had looked at their last angry encounter.

As he moved down the length of the room, women murmured excitedly, their minds obviously on matters other than political. Hansi finished her champagne automatically, staring down the line. She now saw that his face was older. Jess' lean, hard look reminded her, unexpectedly, of her father's high-boned face. He looked as ruthless as the popular image of him. His eyes seemed to seek her out. They widened slightly as he saw her in the receiving group. This was her first indication that his feeling for her, whether love or hate, singled her out from all others present.

She held out her hand carefully, thinking how different this was from the old style of greeting between them, when he would lift her off the ground, swing her around and teasingly pretend he had in mind to rape her on the spot.

"Captain Taga," Cameron said in his genial way, "it must be more than two years since we last served together."

Jess looked at him coldly, ignoring everyone else. "Two years, three months and three days . . ."

Cameron remarked dryly, "You were ever a man for details."

". . . and ten hours, I believe."

A buzzing spread through the nearest line of guests. Hansi could not help glancing at her husband. She fancied he looked pale.

As Jess bowed over Hansi's hand, not too amiably staring her out of countenance, Cameron said, "My love, you remember Captain Jess Taga."

Hansi cleared her throat but her voice sounded thin to her own ears. "Oh, yes, very well indeed. Congratulations, sir, on your interest in the cause of peace. We do not forget that your army and my husband's army once fought side by side." What a pompous speech! But belatedly she discovered it was worse than pompous.

A glint of amusement slightly softened Jess Taga's hard features as, at the same time, Hansi realized her gaffe. The French present knew too well against whom the English and the colonials had fought. There was a furious inhaling of breath, especially among the women, at the humiliating reminder. But Governor Rochblave had ample experience in diplomacy and remarked loudly to Jess, "My dear captain, if we French had allied ourselves to your brilliant Long Knives I am persuaded our Redcoat friends might not have won Quebec from us."

Jess acknowledged the compliment and Cameron's introductions to all the dignitaries present. It seemed to Hansi's sensitive imagination that Jess was more than necessarily gallant to the French wives, who glowed under his casual attentions.

She did not want to pain her husband, who was busy with introductions and polite talk, so she made an effort to play the hostess in the expected manner.

One of Jess Taga's aides was an attractive, flirtatious young gentleman from tidewater Virginia, a lieutenant named Mead Fairfax. He told Hansi at once, "By the Eternal, ma'am, I never expected to see anything half as pretty as you so far from Virginia."

She laughed. The champagne began to work its magic and her problems seemed less immediate. The lieutenant refused champagne, asked for Blue Ruin, and confided, "I didn't think I'd have your company this long, ma'am, you being Old Jess' object and all."

"What? Upon my word!"

"Not but what it was all respectable," the young soldier added in haste. "We'd never a doubt of that. Only it's a long-standing joke that Jess pricks up his ears whenever Colonel Cameron's name is tossed about. We'd no notion why, 'til Captain Abernathy said Old Jess had had ideas of marrying you . . . that is, he'd ideas above his station, maybe."

"Above his station! Do you know anything of me?"

From the way he blinked and said, hurriedly, "Nothing, ma'am," she guessed he did know her background. He had hoped, perhaps, that he could boast to the other Long Knives about Nick and Eva Verin and their wretched daughter who had been expertly molded into a lady.

Inspired by the champagne, she laughed once more. "My father is Nick Verin, Cayuga-Mingo Indian scout for the British Army and the finest man I know. But I am quite sure Jess Taga never felt inferior to the Verins."

"Indeed, ma'am, no . . . that is . . ." He grinned self-consciously. "It's only one of the things they whisper about among the Long Knives, Jess being an old friend of yours. Forgive me, ma'am, but we didn't think you'd be . . . like you are."

"Newly rich . . . the colonel's lady . . . full of elegant pretenses? Is that how Captain Taga describes me?"

"Never a word like that from Captain Jess, ma'am, never. He's had his women. He's that popular with the females, you'd not credit it. But whenever Colonel Cameron's talked of, he acts odd. We all thought . . . knowing you'd stood his friend at Fort Blaine—"

"Say no more. I understand, sir. He was my father's friend. There you have the truth."

With Lieutenant Fairfax close at hand she moved among the guests at the reception. She found it amusing, though not surprising, that so many of the French ladies present were delighted to meet the handsome young Long Knife. Many of them spoke only French and as Fairfax spoke none, Hansi translated between them.

By the time they reached the hall, music had started in the second salon. When Lieutenant Fairfax expressed an interest in the French frontier reel being played, the pert, slightly anxious daughters of two French officers were more than delighted to show him the correct steps until their mothers drew them away in horror. Hansi explained to the stunned lieutenant that the young French girls were heavily chaperoned. "Only the prospect of marraige will make the slightest intimacy possible, sir."

"And you, ma'am? Will you take pity and show me the way of it?"

Refusing, she managed a small laugh. She was relieved when she saw her husband talking with Jess and the governor, and moved to join them.

Her husband was just saying, "I suggest, as a beginning, captain, that you give us the names of the men responsible for issuing red axes to the Piankashaw Nation." He glanced at the governor as he spoke, and Hansi suspected the demand was made in order to curry favor and sympathy with the French present.

Lieutenant Fairfax murmured to Hansi in amazement, "Your pardon, ma'am, but the colonel's talking rubbish. We've no red axes. We're no Hairbuyers. We leave that to the Redcoats."

Meanwhile, Jess was replying, "You always did have a sense of humor, colonel. I'll take your suggestion in that light."

Then Madame Rochblave, spotting Hansi and the lieutenant nearby, addressed Jess archly. "You and Madame Cameron are old friends, are you not? After— what was it?—two years and ten hours, I am persuaded you must have a great deal to say to one another."

Jess deliberately avoided looking at Hansi. His voice was clipped, to the point. "You are mistaken, madam. Colonel Cameron's wife and I have nothing to say to each other on any matter. . . . I haven't met that young lady, Madame Dinard's daughter. Will you be good enough to present me?"

The next moment he left the little group with Madame Rochblave fluttering on his arm. The governor watched this with interest and remarked to Cameron, "It would appear that we husbands have more to fear from the terrible captain than do the settlers." As Cameron still watched the departing captain, Rochblave added in the same easy, half-ironic way, "I should not have thought it likely that he was the Hairbuyer. Nor would it serve his side in your war. However, I haven't your intimate knowledge of the man."

"I have not said he was the Hairbuyer," Cameron replied sharply, "but he may very well know who it is. And it would be greatly to his advantage if it were thought that my army was guilty."

"Yes," the governor agreed. "For one thing, he would win the support of the French along the Mississippi."

Remembering that British companies were said to be currently tracking down the Hairbuyer through his Indian allies, Hansi asked, "What would the British gain by paying for the scalps of settlers and their families?"

Rochblave smiled. "Such acts certainly limit the building of further settlements by the colonials, who are all American sympathizers. Am I right, colonel?"

"You would be," Cameron replied crisply, "if my army were guilty. Come, my love, we must not neglect our other guests."

Hansi managed to put a distance between herself and Jess for the rest of the reception, but it was inevitable they meet at parting. Her head had begun to throb, and she wanted the gala to end as quickly as possible, resenting her social obligations.

Officers passed, bowing over her hand. Then Lieutenant Fairfax brought her fingers to his lips with a soulful sigh. She forced herself to respond warmly. Immediately afterward her hand was taken in a painful grip. As she winced and looked up, she found herself perilously close to Jess Taga's mouth. Her lips quivered nervously and she raised her eyes, meeting his gaze fixed upon her with a blazing light—whether hatred or love, it was hard to guess. It took her by surprise and she felt naked, shaken by the greatest emotion of her life.

He raised his head, said with cutting indifference, "Good to renew old acquaintance, ma'am. Some good may come of this conference after all."

Then he was gone. Another officer took his place. She did not dare to look after him.

Later, as she walked up the staircase to their quarters with her husband he broke their silence to remark, "Well, my love, our old friend the captain acts like a spurned lover. You did not tell me you had once refused him."

"Nor did I."

"You did not refuse him?"

"He did not ask me."

Evidently wanting to be hurt, he kept opening the wound. "But if he had?"

"I have a headache, Shelby. I cannot imagine anything that interests me less at this minute than your quarrels with Jess Taga. Please don't pursue the matter."

She was relieved when he obeyed her. He did not mention Jess again that night. But long after, in the dark of their bed, he stared, sleepless, at the ceiling. Hansi wondered if he felt as she did—that the ghost of an old love shared their bed.

5

THE next few days saw so little accomplished between the British and American members of the conference that Hansi puzzled over the reasons for holding it at all. Lieutenant Fairfax explained the American side, but could not explain what induced Colonel Cameron to call for the amnesty.

"It's good for us, ma'am," the young Virginian said as he and Mademoiselle Dinard, with Hansi as chaperone, walked past the frozen bowling green bordering the walls of the old French fortress. The two gates facing the town stood wide open as they had been for years. Even the arrival of the English army had not sent the French rushing to the dubious safety of the fort's walls.

The lieutenant added, "We're getting a look at Arbreville—finding its defenses. We've an idea of the size of the Redcoat forces stationed here. Jess—that is, Captain Taga—enjoys walking about your old fortress here. Seeing the way the French defended it in the war twenty years gone by. Between you and me, ma'am, Jess says a lady of six could take Arbreville today." As she stiffened, he went on hastily, "Not that Jess would dream of it, with the peace parley and all."

"Naturally," she put in. She looked at him. "Then why do you warn me?"

He shrugged. "We've the chance to make friends with Rochblave, especially now that the French king sent officers to support our cause. All we need is to turn this Frenchy to favor us."

Mademoiselle Dinard said then, "But yes, monsieur. The Redcoat soldiers hold us French by force of arms. The governor might consider that you rebels—"

"Patriots, ma'am. Or Americans, if you please."

Mademoiselle agreed excitedly, "Governor de Rochblave may think you Long Knives are rescuers from the tyranny of the British Army."

But Lieutenant Fairfax frowned up into the icy white sky. "It does beat all, what the Redcoats want out of the conference, or why they called for it. Just to waste time."

Pretty, dark-eyed Mademoiselle Dinard laughed.

Nevertheless, Hansi was uneasy. It was not like Shelby Cameron to waste time deliberately.

It had begun to snow. They hurried their steps. A great clatter and clanging, punctuated by shouts, came from the front of the house. Mademoiselle Dinard screamed, "They are quarreling! Oh, monsieur! Madam! They are going to war here in the house! They will kill each other."

Hansi began running through the hall toward the double salons at the front of the house, but was slightly reassured by the lieutenant's chuckle.

"Don't be alarmed, ma'am. Sounds to me like a bit of practice. Friendly duels. They're not at each other's throats yet."

He was right. In one of the long salons, with the carpets rolled back as if for dancing, two Americans and two Redcoats were laying about with naked dress swords, already having raised welts, nicks and not a few scratches. They were being cheered on by a half-dozen Frenchmen. Shocked and disgusted, Hansi backed out into the hall.

"They will ruin the salon," Mademoiselle Dinard

whined. "Already they have cut away a dozen candles and scarred the floor."

"These Frenchies," the lieutenant whispered to Hansi, "always the essentials. Candles and floor—that's what concerns her."

"I daresay she is right. I am going to fetch my husband."

Hansi had taken Mademoiselle Dinard's arm and was ushering her out when Jess Taga suddenly appeared in the hall. At his first sight of Hansi it seemed as if his expression might soften, but the now-familiar hardened lines of his face came into evidence. When she touched his sleeve he looked at her with contempt until she spoke.

"Please stop them, Jess. If one of them is killed, or badly hurt, there will be an end to all hopes of amnesty."

He put her aside more gently than she expected, crossed into the salon. Now worried about his safety, she followed him to the doorway. She should have known better. He walked directly toward the first pair of thin, unsubstantial flashing blades, not as deadly as the Virginians' own long knives but painful enough to stop a sensible man. Jess took out his skinning knife and struck hard with the flat of it against the two swords exactly at the instant of their crossing. The blow sent shivers along the blades and throught he arms of the two adversaries.

The Englishman swore but drew back, lowering his point. The American dropped his sword, which clattered on the floors. Humiliated and red-faced, he stooped to pick it up. Jess had already moved on to ruin the next bout, amid catcalls from the British and French, and protests from his own men.

Hansi did not feel easy until he had halted the last bout. He had not accomplished this feat unscathed, for which his own men seemed to take gleeful credit. When he returned through the crowd he was clapped on the back and hailed with friendly calls of "You'll carry the scars of this day's work, captain."

By the time he reached Hansi she saw that a crisscross of bloody scratches over his knuckles and the back of his hand had begun to bleed, and a cut on his cheek, as well. Even the sleeve of his long shirt had been slashed.

"I'll fetch basilicum powder and bandages," Hansi said. She knew he would turn impatiently away, dismissing such trivial matters in disgust. To her surprise and relief, he hesitated, and gave Lieutenant Fairfax a look, with a slight indication of his head in Mademoiselle Dinard's direction. The lieutenant took the young woman by the hand. After a last glance back at the Long Knife commander, the French girl went off with him.

Jess watched them go, then turned to Hansi. For the first time since their parting long ago he genuinely smiled at her. "Where do you intend to perform this act of mercy, infant?"

The single name by which he conjured up long-buried memories of their old relationship made the tears sting behind her eyes. She blinked them away. "Let us go out to the kitchen or the stillroom. There will be some powder there."

He caught her reaction. She knew she should not be happy to see him moved by her tears, but she was. It was sinful. It was wrong to be so happy. All the same, she felt excitement run through her body. . . . He still cared.

He walked beside her. She had almost forgotten how it was to move at his side, to try and keep up with his stride. The earthy masculine assurance of him filled her with longing. Nick once possessed a little of that quality, which his wife had nearly destroyed, but Nick was regaining it at last. No woman could ever destroy it in Jess Taga!

As they went into the stillroom beyond the kitchen, where two women were preparing the afternoon dinner, it occurred to Hansi that she might now confide to Jess what she knew about Hay's attack on the Piankashaw village and perhaps on Fort Sacklin as well. But this would be a treachery beneath contempt. She would be betraying her husband. . . .

"What are you thinking about?" Jess asked, watching her closely.

"I was wondering where I last saw the basilicum powder. Ah! Here it is. On the upper shelf." She stretched to get the box.

He reached over her and took down the box. A streak of blood from his hand scraped across her cheek. He gently rubbed it away with his thumb. She suffered the exquisite pleasure of that touch without revealing the depth of her feelings.

"Here. This cloth will do."

"No bandages." He grinned. "They interfere with my aim."

As she wiped away the stains and dropped powder upon the wound, she said, "You would do well to make peace now. Then we can all be friends again. They say one of your armies is sealed up this winter in Pennsylvania, another in the Carolinas, and your recruits are all three-month men running home to their farms."

"Come now. We've only just become friends again. Don't let us quarrel over politics. Besides, those armies on the Coast are not my men. They are not Long Knives. . . . Fire-Dawn, why didn't you wait for me?" As she stopped with her fingers on his hand, bewildered by the rapidity of his question, he added, "You know I loved you."

By a giant effort she kept her fingers from shaking. "You never said so. Am I a reader of minds, like the medicine men of my tribe?"

"You did know. I saw it in your face. Someone made you frightened of me. That's the truth of it. Was it Cameron?"

"No. Never." She nearly blurted out the truth. It seemed only right to protect her husband in this small thing, even if she betrayed her mother's warnings against "men like Captain Taga."

"Are you happy?"

"There you are. It's stopped bleeding."

"Damn you!" Showering her with powder from the injured hand, he caught her shoulders and shook her. She cried out before she was silenced by his mouth, rough upon hers, forcing her to respond. She had never known such fiery hunger in herself. She melted, as he drew her closer still, all her long-stifled love for him finally released.

Footsteps in the passage outside brought them back to the present. Still glowing from the passion of their brief union, they separated as the black cook stuck her head around the stillroom door.

"You called, ma'am?"

Hansi slipped out of Jess Taga's arms, recovering her common sense a little late in the day. "No, thank you," she called. "I slipped. The captain—that is—you acted very quickly, captain."

He stepped back and away from her, saluted with jaunty sarcasm. "Not so, madam. I acted too late, I'm afraid. For the second time, I've acted too late."

Although he had made way for Hansi, she found herself unable to move. Her thoughts were chaotic. She knew she must not let herself be swayed by him, his nearness, his gaze that held her. . . .

The memory of her vows to the priest at Fort Pitt pursued her. In marrying Shelby Cameron and swearing she loved him, she had committed an unconscious sin. In her philosophy, sins must be atoned. Or else God—or Manitou—would punish her even more by striking down all that she loved. She could not compound that first great sin and destroy her husband's happiness just because she found but two years too late that Jess Taga was her kind of man. Jess was still watching her when she passed him and went toward the antechamber of her husband's small military office. She did not dare to look back.

The British aide admitted her at once. She found Cameron closeted with Governor Rochblave. She had hurried too quickly and did not have a ready excuse for interrupting their discussion. Flushed and embarrassed, she begged their pardon and confessed, "I have forgotten what I wanted to say."

Both men reseated themselves. Her husband found her words charmingly feminine and took her hand. He would have pulled her down upon his knee but she refused to be cuddled like a doll. Instead, she stood beside her husband while he drew her to him with an arm too close under her breasts for comfort. She knew he liked to demonstrate his possession of her and she tried now, with her guilty conscience, to respond willingly. It was impossible under Monsieur de Rochblave's eyes.

She ventured, "I think I wanted to ask how the conference has gone. Are you any closer to an amnesty on the frontier raids?"

Cameron shook his head. "I had hoped for more reason and common sense among our old Long Knife friends. It seemed to me that humanitarian considerations should argue in favor of a frontier peace, since this year has been disastrous for the American continental armies. But I am afraid Captain Taga doesn't agree. He brings forward so many matters that are extraneous."

"The scalp-selling Indians, for example," put in Rochblave. "Each side seems to consider that the white men who send out the red axes and agree to redeem fresh scalps belong to the other army." He smiled. "It needs only that someone should prove the hair buyers take their orders from a French officer in Kaskaskia or Cahokia or even here in Arbreville.

She knew he must be joking, but his mention of the other French towns was her cue to the subject of Nick Verin. "In which case, my father may discover something. He is in Cahokia now."

Cameron broke in, "We'll see, my love. One more parley session after Governor Rochblave's banquet today may do it."

He looked much too calm, she thought, too sure that the next throw of the dice was his own. As for the governor, to Hansi's observation he had become very friendly with Jess Taga during these past days.

The town's leading citizens had looked forward to the Frenchman's dinner for the Amnesty Conference since announcement of the parley first went out. The British officers shared their enthusiasm, being familiar with the superb dinners served in the creaking old barn that now served as Rochblave's formal entertaining chambers inside the walls of the disused French fortress. Jess Taga's men were divided in their enthusiasm; the genteel Virginians anxious to enjoy the celebrated cuisine, the Kentucky settlers' sons insisting that they had no interest in wearing clean shirts, and sitting mumchance while the Frenchies babbled in their heathen tongue.

All the same, that afternoon, in spite of a heavy snowstorm, Hansi saw nearly a hundred persons drive or walk through the wintry weather to the barracks room inside the fort's open gates. They all ate and drank everything set before them at the long baronial table that Rochblave had managed to rescue before it was claimed for Colonel Cameron's quarters. The bare walls had been decorated with French banners and evergreens from the forest that made the ugly room into a bower of pleasant, leafy scents.

Hansi was uneasy. As the chief guest, Captain Jess Taga was expected to be seated with the first lady of the banquet. She had supposed this would be Madame Rochblave, but for some reason known only to Rochblave's devious mind, she found herself next to him, while Madame Rochblave sat beside Cameron. Hansi was somewhat relieved to find that Cameron had other matters on his mind and seldom looked her way. She therefore owed it to him to remain even more circumspect than usual in her behavior.

Jess Taga had no such compunctions. When wine was to be poured for her, he was first to oblige. When the wild turkey and its uniquely flavored sauce were served, it was Jess who cut the meat from the bone for her, making curious little remarks about everyone present that made her laugh in spite of her resolve not to attract attenion.

"What a delightful old bird!" Speaking of a roasted chicken. "It does put me in mind of Mistress Abernathy when she wore her gown tight-laced." And in a lower voice, "Why do you suppose I am minded of a wily fox with pointed ears every time I feel our French host's eyes upon me?"

Between efforts to stifle her own giggles, she managed to say, "You are really *too* bad!" but he poured them each another glass of the wine and went right on making jokes.

Once he looked at her directly as he picked up her lace-edged napkin from the carefully cleaned puncheon floor, and in that moment said flatly, "This is good-bye. I've done with dreaming and hoping. I'm not a dreaming man."

As he gave her the napkin and their hands met, she asked in a desperate plea for understanding, "Did you give your oath to your country?"

His eyebrows raised. "Certainly."

"Well then, I gave mine to him. Until he breaks it, I cannot."

In a harsh, low voice she scarcely recognized, he said, "And of course, he will never do that. He is a man of honor."

She could only nod. The subject, and especially his manner, was too painful to pursue. She looked away, only to discover Governor Rochblave watching her. He looked as though he understood everything they had said to each other and was enjoying it. After a little thought, she could see why. He had watched his territory taken from him in the politest way by armed forces. Another armed force was seeking his support. If he could keep those two enemies at loggerheads, he might still win.

Her gaze shifted from the Frenchman to Cameron and she realized with relief that his attention had moved to the double doors halfway down the room. Beneath the rattle of dishes, glasses and silver she heard the old, warped doors as they were opened by a footman in livery. Apparently he was delivering a verbal message to Lieutenant Fairfax, who excused himself to his dinner partner, Mademoiselle Dinard, then to his host, Rochblave, and left the room.

Jess had not noticed. He was studying his wineglass as if, in those dregs, he could find the riddle of the universe. Cameron, however, watched every move made by the departing lieutenant and the footman. Hansi had a chilling notion that he knew exactly what this interruption signified.

The lieutenant returned, his open face now drawn and tense. Without a word of apology to his host he hurried around the long table toward Jess Taga. Fairfax leaned over between Hansi and Jess to mutter something to his commander. Hansi heard the single word "Sacklin" and guessed the whole of it.

She looked down the length of the table and had no doubt her husband was completely prepared for this news. Jess Taga stood up at the table. The sound of his chair crashing backward onto the floor jolted the room to attention. Several delicate little screams went up as Captain Taga's voice, sharp as an ax, shook them all as he addressed Cameron at the far end of the table. "Is this true? Has Fort Sacklin been attacked by your forces?"

Cameron made no pretense of misunderstanding. His voice was conspicuously quiet and controlled. "I learned of the victory myself this morning. Fort Sacklin has fallen to His Majesty's forces under Major Geoffrey Hay."

There were gasps, exclamations of treachery, and Governor Rochblave's plea, "Messieurs! Consider the ladies present."

Hansi saw that his amusement was barely concealed. She did not for a moment suppose his pleasure was dictated by devotion to the British government's cause. He simply felt that it would be to the advantage of his country's position if the two enemies remained at each other's throats. Then, too, Sacklin had formerly been a French possession. For him, this scene was full of delicious irony.

Already the Long Knives had drawn back from the table, eyeing each other and then their leader, wondering what to do. Their hands felt vainly for the knives they had deposited in an antechamber before sitting down at the table with their female partners. All present knew that with Jess Taga's forces divided and spread along the Mississippi trace, he would have no hope of immediately recapturing Fort Sacklin. But the longer they had to wait, the greater the weather problems until after the spring thaw.

"And all this while we are discussing peace! So much for the honor of a British officer!" Jess put such contempt into the condemnation that several red-coated officers rose to their feet. Cameron waved aside their rumbles of anger. Though he flushed at the insult, he said in his quiet way, "I regret the subterfuge, but I cannot forget that all of you fighting against us once swore allegiance to king and country. Which of us then is the less honorable?"

Jess dismissed this with a sharp chopping gesture. "Not a tribe in the Ohio forests would be capable of such treachery during a peace conference. We leave that for the British gentlemen."

Pandemonium threatened, but Cameron's voice cut through it all. "Silence, gentlemen! Captain Taga has the right with him in this matter. But I can only paraphrase what your own officers said at the battles of Breed's and Bunker Hill, in Boston. *You may retain the victory of honor, but we retain the fort.*"

Cameron's calm demeanor had its effect on his men. They exchanged looks that bespoke a certain shame at the dishonorable end to the Amnesty Conference, but amusement at the trick played by their commander twinkled in their eyes. The Long Knives were still talking among themselves, offering to "slit the bastard's gizzard," but Captain Taga looked down at Hansi.

He said to her, "You knew of this?"

"No! I could not be sure. Jess, I would never . . ."

He smiled, not a pleasant smile, nor with the slightest trace of the warmth she cherished. "You would never— but you did, of course. You kept me charmingly occupied while your honorable husband pulled off his little coup."

She heard herself protest hoarsely, "I couldn't be sure. I didn't know!" But he had already turned to leave.

Cameron's calm quiet voice stopped him. "I ask one favor, sir."

Captain Taga laughed. "Are you in a position to ask favors of us? You do not lack for boldness, colonel."

"How did you learn so quickly that we had captured Fort Sacklin? The scout who informed me this morning was exceedingly fast."

Jess was no longer listening. He went on, but Lieutenant Fairfax, who could not forget his native good manners, explained stiffly, "By an accident you could not have foreseen. A detachment of Long Knives marching up from Cahokia came upon a dying redskin who warned them."

Governor Rochblave forestalled Cameron's next question. "May one presume to ask, monsieur, are we now to expect a tribal war as well as all else?"

Lieutenant Fairfax shrugged. "The redskin was a scout. Possibly one of yours. An arrow in the back did him in."

Cameron called out suddenly, "The arrow came from what tribe?"

"A Piankashaw, I should think. I believe they said the arrow had their markings. They are not fond of your scouts, colonel."

"Is my scout still alive? What did he say?"

Jess Taga cut in, "Come along."

The lieutenant started after him, but turned again to add, "He asked for Captain Taga and then said simply, 'Tell him the meeting is a trick. They have marched to take Sacklin.' "

Hansi was spinning. She heard Cameron ask, as he moved down the table in her direction, "Where is my scout? Is he still alive?"

There was a buzzing in her head. She understood only snatches of what she heard.

"He died several hours ago," Fairfax said. "They brought the body here. He's your property, I imagine, colonel, since he carried dispatches for you from Cahokia and Kaskaskia."

Someone screamed. And again—cutting, frightful sounds of anguish that spread panic through the long room. Unaware that the screams were her own, Hansi looked around blindly. Cameron was at her side, swooping her up in his arms. It was Jess she saw across the room.

He was staring at her with growing horror. She saw his lips move and knew he asked her, "Nick?"

She heard herself shriek, "No! No!"

But of course she knew it was.

6

AFTERWARD she never remembered the long walk through the snow to the stables in the town. People fluttered around her, saying she should wear clogs in the cold night, reminding her that her cloak was thin. Irritating voices that meant nothing. Cameron walked by her side, murmuring loathsome clichés. "You must think of it as a heroic death. . . . In the line of duty. . . . He would have chosen to go that way. . . ."

She was moving between piles of hay inside the stable toward the glow of a single storm lantern. She saw Jess Taga's powerful figure striding rapidly ahead of her. He reached the little group around the light. Several of his Long Knife soldiers knelt by a blanket covering the body on the ground.

"Are you sure you want to go on, my love?" Cameron asked solicitously.

She ignored him. Jess had turned back a corner of the blanket. He studied the quiet, frozen face and looked at Hansi. She thrust off Cameron's arm, moved quickly until she reached Jess. She spoke for the first time since Jess condemned her at the dinner. "Are we even now, Jess? You think I betrayed you? And your scouts murdered him." He flinched and she was glad. Her legs gave away and she dropped to her knees. She had a blurred view of Nick's face, unnaturally pale and rigid in the lantern light but otherwise looking as if he slept.

In a moment he must open his eyes. . . .

The snowfall outside muffled all sound. Hansi remained on her knees, watching her father's face. The world around her was full of strangers whispering, and among them was Shelby Cameron. He took her tenderly by the shoulders.

"You are freezing, my beloved. You must not remain here."

She looked around. None of the Long Knives remained, not even Jess Taga. Was it possible to hate Jess for this?

Cameron started to lift her to her feet.

"No."

"Darling, you can do nothing for poor Nick now."

She pushed him away. Two red-jacketed soldiers waited nervously, anxious to be rid of her. She ignored them. Nick's cheek was like cold rock. He felt nothing.

She was alone.

Cameron led her away as if she were blind or helpless. He kept murmuring empty phrases, begging her to lean upon him, to look to him to replace Nick in her heart.

"If you could only cry, darling, this would pass. It must pass. You have the rest of your life to live. And I am here. Remember always, I am here."

During the icy, snowbound night that followed she found it strange that she cried so little. Cameron awoke to find her sitting up in bed, staring at the closed shutters. He tried to console her with talk of Nick's popularity and usefulness in the army. He mentioned that Nick should be buried as a soldier. She did not care for these hollow honors. Nick was gone, that was all that mattered, murdered.

"He was not a man of religion. His burial doesn't matter. Papa won't be there."

"Let me try and help you, my love." The break in his voice caught her unawares. "Don't shut me out."

She looked at him, wondering that he could feel her pain so deeply. Or was it something in his own suffering that sympathized with hers? Gradually, he drew her down into his arms, and to satisfy him she lay there unmoving, but through the night she kept remembering . . .

A stand of high grass bordered the military burial ground Cameron had chosen for Nick. It was gray against the white sky and looked dead, but she knew that in the first days of spring the grass would be back again, omnipresent, eternal. No one could say that grass was really dead. Nick was like the grass. She felt his presence amid the stark tree limbs and the icy-tipped gray thickets.

"Oh, papa . . . papa . . ." she moaned.

She could not cry. Awake and asleep she ached with a constant dull pain deep within her. It was not only the pain of her loss of her father, there was also the horrible knowledge that Jess Taga was indirectly responsible for his murder.

When the services were completed, Governor Rochblave called Cameron away to discuss plans for assuming command at Fort Sacklin.

At the same moment, the stout little French priest, Father Laage, approached Hansi. "Madame, may I beg you to walk with me to the far end of the burial ground? Just there, by that stand of laurel and sycamore—behind it is the trail to Kaskaskia."

She could only imagine he wanted to talk to her of religious matters. The idea annoyed her. She was in that state of deep bitterness where no gentle consolation could reach her. But she went, because she did not wish to show him disrespect. He meant well.

Arbreville's citizens, gathered along the trail, began to

separate and return to town, but one among them remained. Jess Taga's Long Knives had long since marched
out, but Jess had waited to attend Nick's burial. He was
dressed for the long trek to Kaskaskia. Hansi had no
doubt the French had befriended him and would go soon,
openly, to join his side.

Even at a distance, Hansi recognized his powerful
stance. He wore padded deerskin leggings, useful in the
icy weather. Over his buckskin shirt was a blanket with
a hole in it, like those Nick used as both a heavy cloak
on the march and a blanket at night. Crossed bandoliers
holding powder horn and shotbag hung across his broad
chest. A skinning knife and a tomahawk sat in his belt,
and he held his long rifle. His familiar old black hat was
tilted low over one eye.

With an hysterical desire to laugh, she thought, *He
looks like a pirate.* But he also looked like every man she
ever loved. He was Nick's kind. Her kind. How had she
ever believed she could become a proper lady, living in a
great house, practicing everlasting pretense?

For a moment she felt she could cry. She smiled at
the priest. It was all too late now.

As they approached Jess Taga, Father Laage saw them
staring, each with a private memory of bitterness. He
spoke quickly. "Madam, Monsieur le Capitaine asks me
to convey sorrow over the loss of your splendid parent.
Monsieur asks me—"

Jess interrupted abruptly, without any warmth. "I'd as
soon have killed Old Kentuck with my bare hands as to
get Nick murdered. . . . You know that."

She struggled to avoid his eyes. Jess was with the
enemy that had killed Nick. She said, "I understand. Even
if one of your people murdered him, you couldn't have
known about it." Then, without intending to, she burst
out, "Oh, Jess, why must we be enemies?"

"You made it so. I did not," he said flatly.

She felt as if all hope of peace between them was
gone forever. "Father Laage," she said, turning away,
"my husband will be expecting me."

Before she could get away, Jess called out, "One thing

more, *Mrs. Cameron!*" There was no mistaking the whiplash in his voice. "Those red axes are getting mighty close to you. Open your eyes!" While she stared at him, dumbfounded, he stared at Nick's grave and the hard earth still piled up beside it. He said nothing more but turned and strode away.

Cameron was waiting for her with the governor. He was too proud to mention the Long Knife enemy, but Rochblave, ever ready to irritate tender spots, remarked, "One must admire Captain Taga for offering his condolences, considering the circumstances."

"His men killed my father," Hansi said coldly.

They went inside to his office, where Cameron began removing warlike objects from the pile beside his desk. "I imagine you will wish to keep Nick's property," he said.

She nodded. He placed the long rifle across her blackgloved hands, his own hands lingering on hers as he murmured, "You are being very brave, darling. You are a good soldier, like Nick."

She smiled faintly. "Thank you. You could not say anything that would please me more."

Then he brought out Nick's tomahawk, his knife and shotbag, which she caressed with finger and thumb, remembering how much it had meant to Nick. The thought of Nick brought her back to the unanswered questions his death had raised.

"The talk in town is that Hay discovered to whom the tribes have been selling scalps," she said cautiously.

Cameron answered easily, "As you say, dearest, mere gossip. We must catch the tribes in the act and, thus far, we have failed. At the moment the capture of Fort Sacklin is the most important thing."

Individual settlers were not important—that seemed evident, she thought, but she said, "Yes, I understand. But can Hay hold Sacklin? Jess Taga looked very determined."

Cameron laughed at her naïveté. "Taga can't possibly get over the drowned lands before spring. His troops are scattered. What has he? No. We've nothing to fear there.

In the spring when he is able to move his mob of cut-throats, we will be ready for him there."

No matter. She told herself she did not care what Jess did. She hugged her father's weapons to her body as if to absorb all the small memories of him, which kept slipping away. It occurred to her that after Cameron's understanding and sympathy, she should express her appreciation.

"Darling, take care," she said in a soft voice.

"Trust me, my love. Yellow Painter and Geoffrey have been my right and left hands since time out of mind."

She knew that. "Shelby, you must not trust them! They will end by bringing you down."

He laughed at her nonsensical views. "You are going to bring up that idiotic hair-buying talk. I don't want to hurt you, my little Fire-Dawn, but it's time you admitted the truth. Nick knew it. We discussed it. The Hairbuyer is Captain Taga. Or if not Taga, then Helm. He is to be brought here en route to Fort Detroit, by Daniel Great-house and some other of Hay's men. There he will be tried for his crime—treason against the Crown."

"I cannot believe it. Papa and I both liked Kentuck. I knew him well."

"So Nick said. But he was suspicious. And I know Geoffrey Hay." He added gently, "Now, my little slave must leave me to my business, which is the running of this war."

"I'm sorry, darling." She kissed his cheek and left, clutching Nick's belongings. Her husband's loyalty to Hay was dangerous and even stupid, but it was the part of him she most admired, and sometimes loved.

One evening in late January, with the night sky threatening rain, Hansi came in from a walk to the burial grounds as a Shawnee scout passed into the long hall toward Cameron's headquarters. She immediately knew that loping stride and the fierce, proud, shaven head. Yellow Painter.

Governor Rochblave's unexpected voice startled her in

the dark. Where had he come from? How had he approached her so quickly and silently? "Madam? Are you curious about that redskin's dealings with the colonel?"

She swung around, annoyed. "Your Excellency means something by that, I trust?"

"Madam? I seldom mean anything. I amuse myself. It amuses me now to see if I can make you eavesdrop on your husband. Such a very wifely occupation."

"Not mine, monsieur," she snapped, moving on.

He did not seem offended, only amused in his cynical way. "I might have liked your father. In the end, common sense made him betray your husband's cause. I have always been an advocate of common snese. Why do you think your father betrayed his oath of loyalty to the Crown?"

Cameron had never reproached her father for his dying betrayal. He had let it be assumed that Nick uttered the warning to the Long Knife detachment in his death throes. No one had ever mentioned "betrayal." What did Cameron really think? And why had Nick Verin destroyed a lifetime of loyalty in one final minute's betrayal. *Why?* Was there more to that betrayal than anyone yet knew?

"I cannot discuss my father with you, monsieur."

He shrugged gracefully. "I have often found the little powdering closet between the salon and Colonel Cameron's office most instructive. But I fear I am boring you. Good day, madam."

To her immense relief he left her to her own chaotic thoughts. Among them was an image of the elegant, sophisticated governor hidden in a powdering closet, his ear pressed to the wall between it and Shelby Cameron's office. To the astonishment of a British aide in the main hall, she began to laugh aloud as she went toward the private apartment above stairs.

Yet, what could her husband and Yellow Painter be saying to each other? She had reached the landing when she stopped and considered. She was sure Yellow Painter had something to do with the hair buying. Long ago at

Fort Blaine she had heard the Shawnee and Daniel Great-house speak of hair buying to frighten the settlers out of the rich Kentucky valleys and the Ohio lands across the river. She knew her husband's anxiety for a military victory on the entire frontier. Was it strong enough for him to ignore an investigation for fear of uncovering the guilt of his subordinates?

He must not trust Yellow Painter. Surely, the danger to Cameron's career deserved another effort on her part. She took one step back down the stairs. Then another. She decided to tell him about Rochblave's spying. She retraced her steps to the ground floor and was relieved to find that the young British aide had gone.

The little antechamber was cold and dark, illuminated only by the light from the partially open door of the colonel's office. Hansi made her way into the ante-chamber. The conversation she could hear sounded harm-less.

Cameron was protesting, "But to leave tonight? This soon . . . you cannot expect it."

"Excellency, you said you had all you need. All we can carry on horseback." That would be Yellow Painter talking. "One day, even ten hours, and you may not get a horse through the drowned lands. It must be tonight."

"Major Hay knows what to do. No buying of scalps while the Long Knife lieutenant remains at the fort. Tell them there will be no more red axes given, no scalps purchased at Sacklin. It is a loathsome business at best and it has failed miserably to stop those damned rebel settlers."

Hansi wondered if she had heard correctly. She wanted to turn away. The honorable Shelby Cameron the Hair-buyer? It could not be.

"Excellency, it was to keep the half-blood scout from warning the Long Knives, that you had me kill him. Now, you wish to protect a Long Knife like Kentuck Helm? A man who is second only to Taga himself?"

"I don't want to discuss it further. You think it was easy to have Nick Verin murdered? He was my friend."

"He would have betrayed you."

"And you bungled even that. He very nearly did betray us. He was not dead when you left him."

Hansi groped for the wall, pressed her cheek against the cold wood and tried to concentrate on keeping her balance. For the first time in her life she felt that she wanted to die. There was nothing around her but endless darkness with a streak of light like a sword blade cutting through the middle of the room. Was she going completely crazy? Voices speaking of her father's murder as a necessity? One of them her husband's.

"Excellency, Daniel Greathouse and two of my tribe are bringing Helm through Arbreville on their way to Fort Detroit. It is too far without this halt for supplies. He can be . . . executed here."

"No. At Fort Detroit."

"It is better to do it here, Excellency. He must die. It is necessary. I know this."

"You know everything, it seems. But you cannot fool my wife. She totally mistrusts you."

"The little bitch caused me trouble from the—"

A hand slapped the desk so loudly Hansi was jolted from her stupefied condition. "If you ever again insult Mrs. Cameron, you are a dead man!"

"Ay, Excellency. But the daughter is like the father. And he betrayed you."

"He would not have done so, had you not bungled. You are fortunate the poor devil could say no more when they found him."

"He wished to warn the Long Knife about Helm's danger. He wished to betray you. His death is a good thing."

"To murder a friend is never a good thing. It was necessary. That is all. . . ."

Hansi thought hazily, *Will the next step be my death?* She began a stealthy retreat, one step at a time. There was silence in her husband's office, as if Cameron were considering his reply to Yellow Painter's suggestion.

Her first hint that her presence was known came when

a shadow crossed the light streaming from the colonel's office. She swung around, too late to fool the big Shawnee who stood in the doorway of the office staring at her, his cruel eyes glittering in the half-dark.

7

BEFORE Hansi could gain control of herself Yellow Painter sneered, "You come to see the colonel?"

"Who is it?" Cameron called from the inner room. A chair scraped the floor as it was pushed back suddenly. The question was repeated, on a more anxious note. "Who is it?"

Hansi pulled herself together. Would they actually murder her if they guessed what she had heard? Yellow Painter—certainly. But her husband, a man who genuinely loved her?

"It's Hansi. You are very late, Shelby."

Cameron pushed the door open wide, came out into the anteroom. He looked unusually pale. But she had no doubt her own looks betrayed her strain. Did they also betray her terror?

"My love," he greeted her as he crossed the room toward her. He teased her gently. "Are you in such a hurry to have me come to you?" He tilted Hansi's face up and kissed her. "You are shaking."

"It is only the rain. I was thinking of . . . Papa's grave."

He hugged her stiff, resisting body. "You mustn't think about that, darling." She raised her head as her husband and the Shawnee exchanged glances. After what she had heard, there was no mistake in the understanding she saw between Nick's two murderers. And yet this man could hold her tenderly in his arms, as if to shield her against harm and hurt.

Yellow Painter said stolidly, "I have forgotten. There was a map. I will show you how Greathouse is bringing Helm to this place. I must show you. Alone."

Frowning, Cameron asked, "What is this? I need no maps."

There was a step in the hallway outside. First the muffled, low voice of Governor Rochblave, and then a British aide, filtered inside. "But, sir, Mistress Cameron is in her own apartment, not with the colonel."

Hansi seized this chance to escape. She called out, "I am with my husband, monsieur. I had forgotten you wished to see me." She freed herself from Cameron's reluctant hold. He looked hurt at her obvious rejection, and she found it incredible that he could love her and yet do what he had.

Rochblave looked in at them from the hall doorway. He was all politeness and apologies but carefully ignored Yellow Painter.

"Monsieur, may I borrow your exquisite lady for a little time? A matter of five—ten minutes. The oldest female in town, a Madame de Corfe, was promised a brief visit by Madame Cameron. Madam has been kind to her, and the old lady wishes to make her a small gift, a crucifix."

Cameron refused, politely.

"The map," Yellow Painter cut in. To Hansi's sensitive ears, there was more to his words than the examination of a map. He wanted to speak with Cameron in private and he particularly did not want Hansi present.

The Frenchman persisted, "In all likelihood, the old lady will be dead by morning. If you please, madam."

Torn between Rochblave's highhandedness and Yellow Painter's persistence, Cameron let his wife go. "Come

back soon, darling," he called. "Remember, this weather is
going to make rivers of all the trails east."

Rochblave took her arm. Something in the pressure of
his other hand on her wrist warned her that this was more
than a mere charity call. She promised Cameron without
looking around, "Very soon, Shelby," and went out into
the night with the governor.

The governor broke Hansi's turmoil of silence. "May I
assume from your manner, madam, that you have overheard something you were not meant to hear?"

For the moment Hansi ignored his probing. "Where are
we going, monsieur? As you know, I have never met this
Madame de Corfe."

"Madame, to save useless discussion, let me confess. I
saw that you would not deign to use the powdering closet.
You preferred the more dangerous antechamber. Being
less brave, I chose the closet, so I am aware of what you
overheard."

"You heard?"

"I have discussed the matter with one man since I first
suspected that your husband was the Hairbuyer. That
would be just prior to the amnesty parley."

"You discussed it with a man. What man?"

"One who is anxious for your welfare. Ah. Here we
are."

He scratched on a door, some sort of signal, and a small,
stoutish Frenchwoman ushered them inside a cottage.
There she saw only Jess Taga standing with his back to a
roaring fire in the parlor. He looked up as they came in
but did not move toward them. Nonetheless, in spite of
the rough, granite set to his features, his eyes betrayed
him. He was exceedingly glad to see her.

"You came," he said abruptly, "so you must have
learned the truth." It was not the greeting of a friend, but
then, Jess Taga's relations with Hansi had frequently been
violent and quarrelsome. "Governor, leave us alone."
Still forbidding, he waited an instant with his hands

clasped behind him before adding "if you please," as if the words had been wrung out of him.

Rochblave grinned. "I trust, after what you and I have heard tonight, madam, that you will feel safe with this old friend."

"Yes, monsieur." All the same, the ghastly thing she had heard from her husband's own lips had left her so shaken she was terrified of almost everyone.

When they were alone, Jess stepped forward, dropped her weather cape onto the ancient rushes covering the floor, and stood looking at her as she shivered within his firm grip.

"God knows you can't be frightened of me," he protested.

"No . . . it's—"

"Infant, don't cry. Whatever you do, don't cry."

In his comforting arms she poured out her misery. "Oh, Jess, he killed papa. He did. He murdered him."

Jess was silent. She realized he had not known the worst details of Nick's death. In his special, gentle way, so incongruous with his rough surface, he soothed her. "You are safe now with me. You are never going back to him." He seated her beside the fire and knelt before her. His forefinger wiped away her tears. "Sweetheart, I made one mistake when I let him take you from Fort Pitt. I loved you then. I'm not a changeful man."

She could not quiet her rambling thoughts. "He needn't have ordered Yellow Painter to kill papa. Why did he do it?"

In a voice more calm than he felt, he said, "Because Cameron has to be sure. He leaves nothing to chance."

She raised her head. The murky aspects of her life with Shelby Cameron began to be illuminated. She said thoughtfully, "That is why he loves me. He needed someone inferior, someone he could raise from the mud. He told me so, only I didn't understand. You see, I am his conscience."

Jess laughed scornfully. He had no such feelings of guilt and inferiority and openly considered her his equal, as he made plain now. "Infant, when you aren't blubbering like a baby, you are the equal of anyone alive. And prettier than most." He cupped his hands under her hair and studied her face. "There's my girl. You've got your color back. Are you able to ride tonight?"

"Yes." To get away from the horror she had learned tonight, and with Jess! But there was the enormous danger to Jess. "No!"

"What? Yes and no?"

She began to recover her sense. "No, Jess. Consider. How many men have you at hand tonight?"

"Myself. Isn't that enough for you?"

She tried to smile at his joke. "You don't understand, Jess. My husband still has half his force here in Arbreville. He will never let us get one league from town. And something worse. Yellow Painter may talk him into executing Kentuck Helm. They are bringing him here."

"What! Damn them! I've got to take this place before Kentuck gets here!"

She knew he was asking himself "How?"

"If I leave now," she explained. "Shelby may have him executed out of vengeance. But if I remain—just until you can muster up troops—"

"No! I won't let you stay with him."

She loved his concern for her, but reminded him, "Only for a week. A fortnight at most. Then, perhaps Kentuck can escape from here. I think we can count on the governor's help. Then I'll come to you."

He considered this and found it sensible, but worries nagged at him. "I swore you and I were not going to be separated again. If our friend the Hairbuyer guesses what you're about!"

"He must not!" She looked over her shoulder.

Jess shook her playfully. "See here, Hansi, you are not some ornament that belongs to Cameron. You are not his property."

How well he understood the truth! It would be a sin to leave her husband, but the greatest sin had been her marriage to him in the first place.

Remembering her husband's obsessive need for her love, her enslavement to his strange desires, she pitied him. It was hard to hate a man who loved her, yet it was that same man who said, *I did not wish to kill Nick Verin, but it was necessary.*

"I wanted to destroy him when I first heard him tell about papa's death," she blurted out suddenly to Jess. "I wanted him to suffer."

"I know, sweetheart. Don't worry. You'll have your vengeance."

"What will happen to Shelby Cameron?"

"The Hairbuyer will be sent to Williamsburg in chains, to stand trial for his crimes." She winced and he added, "That is how it must be."

"But how can you capture him? You've so few men. Half of them captured at Sacklin. Surely, you don't intend to attack Arbreville with what is left of the Long Knives!"

He said nothing. She knew better than to pursue a military matter. Besides, she was fairly sure he intended to rely on the support of the French. She hoped he was right to put his faith in Governor Rochblave.

She got up, dreading the painful and hypocritical few days to come intimately devoted to the man who had been her husband and master! The man who murdered her father and scores of others! And all that time, she had no doubt, he had truly loved her. *What a strange, twisted, pitiful man,* she thought. And how little she had understood him. . . .

Jess was reluctant to let her return, but Governor Rochblave added his common sense advice to Hansi's, with a personal note of concern.

"I do not wish our new French allegiance to be known until we are able to place ourselves in your little army."

"*Little* is the word," Jess said grimly.

It was agreed that Rochblave agents would carry messages between Hansi and Jess.

In saying good-bye Jess took her hands and kissed them, and she flushed with warmth and reassurance. But there was still a shadow between them. She kept seeing her husband's face in her mind's eye, and feeling his touch upon her aroused and waiting flesh. It would take time to turn her memories against him. She might despise him but pity had not yet been quenched for the one reason that she knew that Shelby Cameron loved her sincerely, in spite of what he had done.

Rochblave hurried them.

As she lost the last warm touch of Jess Taga's hand and walked out with the governor, the latter offered her a modest crucifix of carved wooden beads.

"From Madame de Corfe," he explained and she forced a smile.

In spite of the late hour, red-coated soldiers began to gather about the house. Did they know the identity of the Hairbuyer? And had they smiled slyly when they followed Nich Verin's coffin to the graveyard?

"Remember, madam, what we are to do," Rochblave reminded her as she left him on the step.

She nodded, unable to speak, and started into the house, as her husband called to her from the antechamber of his office. She turned, assuming an ease she was far from feeling.

"What? Are you still where I left you?"

"Come and show me your gift from the old lady." He came out into the hall, drew her to him and touched her brows with his lips. "How cold and wet you are, my love! And you are late. It is time you were dry. More comfortable. Come."

All her fine presence of ease and devotion vanished in panic.

"I can't! The . . . the rain is so depressing."

"Rain never troubled you before," he chided her softly, with his cheek against hers. She knew he was trying to warm her into life. "In fact, you like bad weather. Darling, don't you love me, when you know how much I need you?"

"I'll be warm presently." She looked up in a kind of hopeful panic. "Very soon, I promise you."

"You promise. Well?" He laughed shortly, without

humor. "You see, Yellow Painter. My wife promises. We'll drink a stirrup cup, as my father used to say."

"Of course." She breathed more easily.

He escorted her into his office. The Shawnee followed silently and stood in the doorway watching the whole procedure in disgust.

Cameron poured French brandy into the bottom of two pewter cups, and offered his wife one.

"Wish us well in our war, darling, and at the same time let this warm you."

"Yes. Good luck to the most honorable man I know." His cheeks reddened. In pleasure or secret shame she wondered as she sipped the thick, burning liquid.

He raised the pewter cup to his lips. "And to my wife, faithful and true!" He glanced out at the dark night which seemed to crowd in at the unshuttered window. "Darling, drink."

Trying not to show her revulsion at the thick sweetness of the brandy, she finished it, and was rewarded with his kiss.

"Now, my love, I'll see you off to bed and assure myself you are comfortable." She made no answer and he sighed.

With his arm around her they walked across the hall to the staircase.

She could not understand what was happening to her. It was almost impossible to keep her balance. *How odd!* she thought . . . *I must be drunk . . . but so soon!*

She fumbled for the door, found her hand caught in Yellow Painter's cruel grasp.

"Take care, damn you! Let me have her." That was Cameron's voice she heard before she was swept up into oblivion.

8

THERE were moments when Hansi was certain that
shadowy faces were laughing at her. How ghastly to find
herself drunk! She had never known such a frightful
humiliation before. Her memories of Nick's drinking had
always protected her. Yet, there she was in her bed. . .
or was she in her own bed?

She distinctly heard Seline say, with a giggle, "So the
mighty Redcoat got there too late and found no Captain
Taga waiting to be seized. Got away free, I tell you! And
a good job of it. These fine Redcoats, bah! Look at this
one. Drunk as a lord."

. . . *But I am not drunk . . . I am not!* She wanted
to shout it but couldn't get the words out. Helpless, she
went back to sleep with one comforting thought: Jess had
gotten away.

She had odd dreams. Traveling. Rocked and thrown
about, in a carriage. And then sleep again as dawn
appeared over the horizon.

She awoke to find herself in what she assumed were the
commander's quarters in the old Arbreville fortress. So

there were war threats from some direction, else why would she have been removed to the fort, and why would the parade grounds be so busy?

She sat straight up in bed, then groaned at her frightful headache. Obviously, while she was out with Rochblave the night before, Cameron and Yellow Painter had decided to take no chances on her knowing the truth about the Hairbuyer. Or had they followed her—Yellow Painter being the obvious spy? Why not simply murder her? Ah, Cameron's tender heart, she thought ironically. He could send men out to scalp scores of settlers, but he was reckless in trying to protect the woman he loved. Certainly, Yellow Painter must have favored killing her outright as a nuisance and an old enemy.

And how right you are, Yellow Painter, she thought, with gritted teeth. *You and I, at least, understand each other. Shelby Cameron is not our kind.* It had taken her over two years to discover that.

She got out of bed in her nightgown with the lilac ribbons at neck and wrists carefully tied in bows. That would be Cameron's hand. Wincing as her every movement sent pounding throbs through her head, she made her way over the thin, threadbare carpet to the door. It was locked. Quite clearly, she was a prisoner.

She considered her situation. Her head, thumping and clanging away, gave her an idea. She took a long, deep breath and borrowed courage from the memory of Jess Taga. Jess must have guessed what had happened when Cameron went to capture him and failed. Where was Jess now? Would he start immediately to recruit new companies of Long Knives? Rochblave must have warned him of Cameron's coming. There was no one else who knew.

A clatter and loud screeching of gates turned her attention to the window. She saw the French make way without enthusiasm as over a dozen men entered the fort—six British soldiers, two Shawnees, and, in their midst, heavily manacled, were six Long Knife soldiers, including Jess Taga's closest comrade, Lieutenant Kentuck Helm. They were all roughly treated, but Kentuck seemed to be singled out, cuffed around by a heavy, bearded

French trapper all in buckskins, with a fur hat. Daniel Greathouse. Perennially grinning, he looked very much as Hansi remembered him long ago at Fort Blaine.

While she watched, wondering how her old friends could be freed, and remembering that Kentuck had saved Nick Verin's life at Fort Sacklin, she saw her husband walk across the grounds to meet the little group. He saluted Kentuck, who raised manacled hands to his forehead in answer.

They all disappeared then. Kentuck was taken into the region of the kitchen and stillrooms beyond the commander's quarters. An odd place in which to hold Kentuck prisoner. The others apparently were to be housed in the old barracks. But when she considered the placing of Kentuck separately, it seemed clever. There were stillrooms that were locked and cold, an excellent temporary substitute for one who might prove to be especially difficult.

And am I to be a prisoner as well? Hansi asked herself, as she tried her own door again, listened carefully, but heard nothing. She knocked once more and this time thought she made out the sound of booted steps approaching.

She heard the door unlock. Shelby Cameron came into the room, looking strained and worried. She suspected he was uncertain of himself and of his reception. But he smiled, that gentle, well-bred smile of a man who would never dream in dealing in blood. "My love, you are on your feet. You should be in bed. Let me make you more comfortable."

She forced herself not to retreat but to welcome his arms. He picked her up, chiding her for having moved about in her bare feet. "You have been very ill, you know. You had a bad night. We must take care of you."

Hansi swallowed and played the game he had chosen. "I have such a dreadful headache. You've no notion! Everything is so confused."

"What do you remember, darling?"

"Nothing, I'm afraid. At all events, it's vague. I went to see an old woman."

"Did you see anyone else?"

She looked up innocently. "Only the governor. There were several doors, one that closed abruptly when I came in. Why?"

He seemed reassured that she had not met Jess. "That is precisely why I brought you with me to the fort, my love. Brain fever is not a thing to play with."

"Brain fever!"

He set her down carefully among the tumbled bed-clothes. "That is the opinion of Parkins, the company surgeon. It seems to have been coming upon you for some time. It attacked you on a sudden last night and, when I foolishly gave you that brandy to drink, you fell unconscious. Then you began to rave. Hairbuyers and Jess Taga and other hobgoblins. Had you no sensation of unreality earlier in the evening? No horrors you imagined? Scenes and conversations that did not seem real? We are fortunate in your case. You suffered only a few hours. You seem to be recovering nicely now."

She wondered cynically what he considered the proper treatment for this curious and imaginary brain disease. He fluffed up the pillow behind her head. "Often I am told, the disease turns its victims against those the victim loves best. All sorts of fantasies are paraded before his mind."

"Her mind," she corrected him flatly. How could he believe she was such a fool! Then she remembered the danger of letting him guess her true felings. "Such fancies! Oh, Shelby, I can't even remember . . . so muddled . . . just horrors. But tell me why we have moved to the fort."

"We are threatened, my love. Last night we very nearly captured Jess Taga, who was spying on the town. Painter saw him leaving. He escaped, but we have reason to believe he is recruiting followers to attack Arbreville itself. Rochblave believes we are safer in the fort."

She hoped she had not revealed any of her own shock that he had guessed Jess Taga's plans. She murmured, "Can we hold out here?"

He patted her hand. "Hostages are the answer."

"What do you mean?"

He was proud of his scheme. "Lieutenant Helm and several others will be held by us as hostages. We had intended to send them on to Detroit for trial but their arrival here this afternoon was a great piece of luck. If matters become tense, we will simply use Helm and the others as hostages. While the bargaining proceeds, Rochblave will be bringing up his French company from Kaskaskia to our defense. That will buy us time for reinforcements to arrive from Detroit. I have already sent out runners and a French guide."

She feigned shock at what appeared to be the Frenchman's duplicity, and silently prayed it was Cameron and not Jess who remained his dupe.

Cameron's spirits seemed to rise by leaps and bounds as his wife fell in so exactly with his expressed views. Seeing this, and desperately anxious to obtain her freedom through that locked door, she suggested, "It appears to be near on my dinnertime, I am that hungry! What is the hour of the general mess?"

"I waited, so that I might have the company of my little slave. Parkins seemed to think you might come out of your sleep by afternoon, as you have done. How pretty you look, in spite of your wretched illness! Indeed, Parkins thought you were dead when I brought you into the fort."

"When was that?"

"We arrived before dawn."

She figured rapidly. It would take Jess at least twenty-four hours to reach his men, several hours to organize the march, and certainly another day to unite the Long Knives camped along the Mississippi. It was unlikely they would arrive for several days. And if Rochblave had betrayed Jess . . .

Cameron ran his finger along her brows. "Why so thoughtful, darling? I will dine here with you, but you know, my little slave has been a very sick girl, so you mustn't expect to have more than a bowl of good broth and perhaps a glass of watered wine."

"But I wish to dine with your officers. To show them I am quite well. I want to walk about the grounds."

"But my love .'. ."

In days past she would have scorned to wheedle and entice a man who loved her, but she thought of Nick and exuded all her charm. "Dearest, I hate it alone here. I want to watch you with your officers. You are so impressive. I feel as though I had been away from you for an age. I am not acquainted with anyone here except poor Lieutenant Helm. You say he has just been brought in?" Cameron frowned. Hansi added with a sigh, "And I daresay, you are right. He must be punished just because you captured him."

His manner changed slightly. "That should not be your concern, darling. The man swore allegiance to King George and then broke his vow. He is a traitor."

"But you cannot regard an enemy in battle as a traitor!"

"You forget. This is not a foreign country. This is our country, and he betrayed it. If we do not punish him, the Shawnees will claim him. You know how bitterly the Long Knives and the Shawnees hate each other. By this one stroke we might achieve all the trust from the Shawnees that we have tried to gain for so long."

He was watching her reaction. There was no mistake in that. He tested her. She only hoped he did not seriously plan to give over Kentuck Helm to Yellow Painter and those other enemies. The Shawnee death was a horror too unbearable to think of. More than ever, she knew Kentuck would have to be saved. He was certain to be killed by either the British or the Shawnees. She clenched her fists under the coverlet and forced a smile, wan and pathetic.

"You know best about war, my dear. It is not a woman's province. . . . But I could not stand the thought of their torturing the poor man."

"Certainly not." He was clearly relieved that she did not plan to interfere. "I believe they make their prisoners slaves, and knowing Lieutenant Helm, I have no doubt he will soon escape."

It was a specious lie, not worthy of the clever Hairbuyer. But she accepted it—or appeared to. Torture and the stake were not things she could discuss with him without betraying her own determination to outwit him.

A bit archly she asked him, "Are you quite sure Kentuck won't dig his way out of his prison, or wherever he is held? They say he is tricky."

"Hardly. There are too many of his enemies in the fort. And those French, who might have helped him, are outside the fort, in the village. They are only allowed inside the fort during the day, for trading purposes and to entertain the . . ."

She looked at him innocently. He reddened, smiled, and said, "At all events, the only French liable to be near the pantry stillrooms are females. And they are all involved with my own men."

He had told her what she wanted to know, confirming what she had already guessed. It was so easy it almost frightened her. Kentuck Helm was held in one of the kitchen stillrooms, rather than in the barracks prison.

"Now, I must dress," she reminded him. "I can't wait to attend your officers' mess. It will be the first time in too long."

"I can refuse you nothing, sweetheart, when I think how nearly I lost you. You were a very sick girl last night. I'll send a woman to help you dress. But you must promise me that if you feel at all faint, you will return to bed."

"Ay, sir."

"That's my good little slave." He patted her hand again and went out to send in a powerful Shawnee woman who spoke no English and would not answer any of Hansi's questions in her own tongue.

Hansi was still somewhat shaken, in spite of all her determination, when Colonel Cameron escorted her into the officers' mess hall, the scene of Rochblave's ill-fated banquet. Nor was she reassured by the sight of so many unsavory men, like Daniel Greathouse, seated among the British officers.

Though she tried to ignore the trapper after introductions were made all around, she was aware during a young officer's analysis of her "brain fever" that nothing she said or did escaped the ex-trapper's eyes. His thick lower lip was wet with wine. He let the lip dangle while he looked her over. "Madame Cameron with brain fever? Who would believe it, messieurs? It must have been a lesser ailment." He addressed the others. "Madam has pretty eyes. And pretty ears—so beware, gentlemen!"

While Hansi sat staring at her plate in a paralysis of fear, Greathouse laughed at his own joke.

"You do not amuse anyone," Cameron told him coldly. "Find some subject other than my wife."

She was relieved. She wondered how much Greathouse knew about her "brain fever." She made very little contribution to the dinner conversation but no one seemed surprised. Her recent illness was excuse enough. She managed to regain enough of her nerve and common sense to praise the grilled buffalo steaks and the apples, preserved from the past season. This praise gave her the chance to add words of praise for the army chef who had prepared the dinner. "I shall certainly wish to inspect that hearth of his and find out how he prepares his meats," she remarked lightly. Then, seeing Greathouse look up from picking his teeth, she added, "Is it permitted to walk the walls here? I should think the view would be a sensation." She addressed Cameron. "Madame Rochblave is forever rambling on about her water colors of the scene around Arbreville, but the fort itself is historic. I should like to see it."

As she had hoped, this took their minds off her remark about the kitchen, though she could read the suspicion in the trapper's face.

Cameron was right about Hansi's diet. She soon found that chewing the flavorsome buffalo steak only brought back her headache, and in her present state of nerves, nothing served her so well as hot tea, a beverage normally served after the midday dinner.

When the officers had dispersed to their late duties the colonel was called upon to settle a dispute between a sentry on the wall who claimed he had seen a large painter prowling the bank across the river, and another sentry who insisted it was a hungry bear. Daniel Greathouse offered to escort the colonel's lady back to her quarters. Alarmed, Hansi protested that she would wait for her husband, but Cameron laughed at her offer.

"Darling, I assure you our poor friend is quite harmless. Dan, why don't you show Mrs. Cameron around the fort before dark. There is no reason why you should remain a prisoner in your room, my love."

"No, indeed," she exclaimed, more brightly than she felt. "And I so wanted to see the walls, and the view."

And to get to the walls, she knew, they must pass through the mess kitchen. She hoped it would sound natural if she suggested various different places of interest to hide her actual goal. She wanted to see how many guards were placed around Kentuck, and what the greatest problems in his escape would be.

At a nod from Cameron the trapper offered his arm with a strutting pose. She placed her fingertips on his sleeve but could not bring herself to move closer. Whatever the evil in Shelby Cameron, she would always feel that Daniel Greathouse and Yellow Painter fed the worst side of him.

And the trapper felt her loathing, though she tried to make a pretense of amiable indifference. She knew she would have to be exceedingly careful. He missed nothing. Therefore, as they passed what had formerly been a stillroom-pantry, she made no mention of it. Greathouse obliged by explaining it.

"There the good Redcoats have the kitchen house. The kitchen with the stillroom and pantries beside it, all within the corner of the stockade wall." He was watching her.

"Excellent," she agreed. "Perhaps later the cook will tell me his method of searing the meat. With some herbs, I fancy, or perhaps a jelly."

"Shall we stop now?"

She shrugged. "I thought this fort was not defensible."

"The colonel relies upon his hostages, madam. There

are more important hostages than the Long Knives. Or perhaps I should say—there *is* one more important hostage."

She was not at all sure what he meant. It was certain to be unpleasant. So she changed the subject. "How many of the tribes are allowed inside the fort! I had no notion."

"Only those friendly to the colonel. The Shawnees demand that we turn over the Long Knife, Lieutenant Helm, to them." He peered coquettishly into her face and she turned away.

"I thought a trial was customary under British law."

"Precisely. He was found guilty just before mess."

"What a pity! All the same, I think the army would be shocked if you turned Kentuck over to the Shawnee Nation."

"Very true. In confidence, I may tell you. They may be used as hostages, but there is no hope for their lives."

She flinched but, with an effort, made no further protest. There was even less time than she had thought.

Shall we visit the kitchen?" he pursued the subject. "The stillroom and pantries?" Obviously, he wanted to make her betray herself.

She pointed to the southwest blockhouse they were passing. "I see my husband has had sturdy ladders put up. This fort was in sad disrepair until yesterday."

By this time she felt that he must realize he was not going to trick her into a betrayal. He ended by returning her to the colonel's quarters, and she understood that she had passed the test when Cameron came in to share hot tea and to assure her of his pride in her. He did not quite confess the test but said, "It is not every man who can boast the love of a loyal and lovely wife. I am lucky. So very lucky. Are you happy?"

She nodded. She had not believed she could feel like a Judas in betraying him. But so it was. He hesitated a moment before leaving. The plaintive quality in his voice squeezed her heart with pity.

"Tell me you are happy, Fire-Dawn. You did not answer me."

"Of course. I am happy."

He waited, looking at her. What else had he hoped for? What other assurance? After a long and uncomfortable pause, he went out.

From her window she watched until he disappeared across the parade ground. Then she went to the cupboard where his extra uniform jackets hung. None was there now. Had he feared leaving them near her? Or was this a coincidence? There was her weather cape, still slightly soiled. She took it out, threw another cloak over her shoulders and then the all-concealing cape on the outside.

She knew she dared not remove Cameron's greatcoat from its place in the cupboard. It would be missed at once. She thrust the coat against the back of the cupboard and, hearing a heavy thump, discovered one of the pistols he often carried. It was loaded. She dropped it into the large pocket of her weather cloak. When she stepped out of the passage onto the parade ground she was thankful for the faintness of the starlight. Even the lanterns set around the square gave little light. Staying in the darkest areas, she moved to the kitchen and slipped inside. Just beyond the kitchen, through the open doorway, she could see a young soldier standing guard in front of the stillroom-pantry where Kentuck was held prisoner.

Nervous and shaking, she put her plan into action. Going to the big, blackened fireplace, she took the large pot off its hook over the dying fire and, concealing herself behind the door, threw the pot the full length of the kitchen against the wall of the next room.

The terrific din roused the guard who came trotting into the kitchen with his rifle across his arm. Hopelessly confused, he swung around, then trotted to the opposite end of the room. The black pot had rolled to a stop in a corner and apparently he believed the noise came from the room beyond. He opened the door, got his rifle at the ready, and entered the room used for routs and dancing.

Meanwhile, Hansi swung around the door into the stillroom, hurried to the locked pantry. She whispered "Kentuck!" He was at the barred window.

"Great Jehosephat! The infant!"

She wasted no words, stuffed the cloak and pistol between the bars, and moved silently back to the kitchen. The young soldier was still banging around in the ballroom. She could hardly believe her luck when she reached the parade ground door.

She slipped out into the darkness and suddenly found her wrist seized and twisted in a grip that made her cry out with pain. The hand was that of Yellow Painter.

"Caught the witch in the act, Excellency."

But infinitely worse was the knowledge conveyed by the voice of the trapper Greathouse, in his triumphant boast, "It's as I said, colonel. You can't trust these half-bloods, even if you make love to 'em."

9

IN their own quarters Cameron and Hansi stared at each other, really seeing each other for the first time since her capture.

She broke the painful silence. "Why, Shelby? You were a gentleman. A loyal and honorable soldier. Why have you done such a horrible thing?"

"You interfered with military justice. Helm is guilty of betraying his allegiance to the king. And much worse. He and the other Long Knives have raided our Indian allies. Committed crimes of war fully equal to ours."

He still did not understand. "I'm not talking about myself. I committed a crime against the British command at Arbreville. I knew the danger when I tried to free Kentuck. Shelby . . . how could a man like *you* become the Hairbuyer?"

He looked down at his hands. The knuckles were very white. He freed his hands, put them behind him. "I hoped you would believe the brain fever tale and imagine that what you heard had been a part of your illness. Greathouse and Yellow Painter thought I was a fool, but I hoped—desperately hoped—you would accept my explanation. It was the only way to save you, and you have destroyed that tonight."

"Shelby, for over two years I've known you as intimately as any human being can know another. The man I knew could never have been the Hairbuyer."

"I don't expect you to understand." But he seemed anxious to make an attempt. "You see, we knew, long ago at Fort Blaine, that settlers were pouring into the Ohio and Kentucky valleys, causing more and more trouble with our Indian allies. It was only a matter of time until there would not be an Indian left in the Ohio Forest who supported us."

"But how could you begin to do this horrible thing?"

He avoided her too-searching eyes. "It began with one small Indian raid upon a settlement. A settlement, I might remind you, that had driven a tribe out of its ancient home. These Indians showed Major Hay the scalps, told of their success, pointed out that their act would frighten others out of coming into that country. We had our own soldiers in those regions of the forest, keeping the peace. And at my advice, they paid the raider for the scalps. . . . That was the beginning."

"The beginning. And how long after? How many others?" she asked incrudulously. "Shelby! Have you never had trouble sleeping nights?"

She thought for an instant that he would touch her, and she drew back instinctively. He stiffened, said in his icy, official voice, "Since the war started, this has been our only answer to the raids on our forts by the Long Knives and the other half-savages like Jess Taga." He hesitated. "Now, I confess, it seems to have failed. The French here on the frontier are turning to the Americans because of it. . . . How can I make you understand how it was, why it seemed necessary?" He turned on her so unexpectedly she held onto the bedpost to give herslf strength.

"I thought when I took you out of the mud—did everything for you, loved and cared for you, made you a lady—I thought that when you heard you might remember these things and forgive me." The emotion he had so carefully frozen out of his voice seemed to be overpowering him, and she did not want to see him warm and passionate in his own defense. She wanted to go on hating him.

"Hendrickje, you owe me everything, and you pay me with this betrayal. You are your father's daughter. I took a whining drunken redskin and made him a respected scout. And he betrayed me."

"You murdered him!"

"Nick was a traitor!" he shouted. And then, a trifle more gently, "Would you have preferred that we hang him? If I had my own choice of death, I would rather die in the field, as he did."

She held tight to the bedpost and managed to ask dryly, "And will you hang me?"

"I don't know what will become of you. I cannot save you from your own folly. You know that, don't you?"

She took a deep breath. "Why should I expect mercy from the Hairbuyer?"

His face contorted as if the effort to restrain his anger proved too great. "I loved you, Fire-Dawn."

"I keep thinking of the scalps of those women, and of the children, brought to you for payment."

He struck her with the flat of his hand. Her head hit the bedpost, but she felt nothing. She blinked and tasted blood from a thin scratch at the side of her mouth. She licked it off. She knew she had driven him to this final degradation.

He stared at her and then at his hand. He looked as gray as ashes. But before he or Hansi could retreat from this stand a loud snapping sound aroused him. He went to the window, pushed it open and leaned out. The parade ground was alive with running men. He stopped one of them.

"What ails everyone?"

"Sentry thought he made out a band of hostiles, sir, but it was only some local Frenchies returning with their traps, sir."

Cameron turned, passed Hansi without looking at her

and went out, locking the door. She hurried to the door
and heard him call, "Sentry. Remain here. The woman is
not to leave this room."

"The woman, sir?"

He did not explain further. He was gone.

Hansi leaned against the door, her head whirling. She
asked herself if there was any hope. Greathouse and
Yellow Painter would certainly see that she did not survive
to repeat her treachery. But almost as painful was the
scene that had marked the end of her marriage to Shelby
Cameron.

Her knees were trembling again. It was freezing cold
but she did not feel it. She went back to the bed and sat
there an endless time, holding her aching head until she
finally went to sleep.

It was after sunrise. She heard loud shouts, military
orders being bellowed, and running men. Then came a
noise like branches being broken for firewood at some
distance. Rifle fire.

She swung off the bed and rushed to the window. The
icy river winds swept across the parade ground and in
through the bars of the window. But the weather meant
nothing to her. She had scarcely reached the window
when she heard another, more distant "slap," and was
shocked to see one of the west wall sentries weave back
and forth, his rifle dropping from nerveless hands. Then
he plunged backward to the hard, frozen parade ground
below.

Cameron called for a doubling of the strength on the
forest wall facing the south, from which direction the
enemy would come. A mistake, Hansi thought, for in
some cases it left the wall above Arbreville itself un-
defended. But then, Cameron could not know that the
French might join the Americans.

Jess and the Long Knives had arrived. How had Jess
done this incredible thing? There could now be no question
but that the French were on Jess Taga's side. Would the
town follow the governor's lead? Hansi's fingers tightened

on the bars. She longed to be out there, to open those gates into the town—to do something!

A figure scrambled over one of the gates. More followed. She held her breath. Two men in buckskins, one wearing a brimmed black hat, the other in a fur cap, had leaped to the parade ground.

Under her window she heard a soldier cry out, "The French! They have gone over to the rebels." She watched in growing horror as two Shawnees dragged the fort's French baker across the parade ground. Yellow Painter appeared behind the Shawnees. Hansi saw his ax rise. Then it was brought down with bone-crushing force upon the Frenchman's head.

The Shawnees uttered chilling cries of triumph. Yellow Painter stuck his ax, still dripping, into his belt and took out his scalp knife, the blade catching the brightness of the morning sun. With the utmost skill he loosened the scalp of the still-squirming Frenchman and held the long gray hair aloft.

Yellow Painter's victorious yell drowned the shriek of the dying man. The powerful Shawnee kicked his prey out of his path and sent his tribesmen to search for other Frenchmen caught inside the gates by their duties or by accident.

In her panic Hansi moved back until she could see but not be seen. She knew quite well that Yellow Painter would not lose this opportunity to be rid of her, an enemy who was not only a traitor but of French blood to boot.

A tremendous onslaught upon the frail gates was answered by rifle fire from the walls. She saw the fort's old French cannon wheeled out across the ground to meet those who would first pour through the gates. Cries of joy from the walls warned her of the defenders' success. She saw her husband's tall, red-coated figure on the wall and wondered, with dread, what she would feel if Cameron were to die at Jess Taga's hands. But the reverse possibility was much more terrible.

Two men had been hit as they climbed the ladder of the blockhouse on the river side. One of the soldiers

clung to the ladder. The other clawed, lost his footing and
went flailing the air to the ground, where he was still.
Cameron reached over the ladder, dragged up the remaining wounded man. A British officer was racing to
command the defense of the main gates where a battering
ram had begun a deafening wood-cracking barrage from
the town side.

The parade ground was already littered with wounded
and a few who were already dead. Now, Hansi saw a
female among the still bodies. Not one of the British or
French wives. To judge from her bright blue head cloth
and many-colored skirts, she was one of the local French
girls who entertained the soldiers inside the fort. She had
been caught as she ran and had fallen forward, in an
ungraceful sprawl she never would have been guilty of in
life. At least, she had not died at the hands of Yellow
Painter who was now approaching Greathouse.

The trapper had been helping to place the cannon
while soldiers, inexperienced in handling this obsolete and
foreign war machine, fumbled to load it. Greathouse and
Yellow Painter stepped away from the cannoneers and
spoke together. Whatever the discussion, Yellow Painter
was pressing for some action when Cameron on the wall
shouted a message to those on the ground. The message
was repeated through a speaking trumpet: "They want to
parley. Three Long Knives with a white flag."

Greathouse and Yellow Painter broke apart. The trader
made a gesture of agreement and the Shawnee ran off
toward the officers' quarters that had been crowded in
beneath the east wall and beside the commander's quarters. Hansi whirled around, frantically looking for a
weapon. If the Shawnee moved on down through the
officers' quarters he would soon reach Hansi.

She tried the door. Still locked. Desperate now, she
looked over at the barred window embrasure. If she
screamed for help at that window would anyone hear? Or
care?

A rat in a trap.

Her husband had given the order to open the small trace

gate for the three Americans to enter under their white flag. Meanwhile, Hansi heard voices speaking in the Shawnee tongue near her window.

"He is the second to the Long Knife chief. They will risk anything to save him."

"Not enough. There is another. The half-blood woman." She recognized that voice. It was Yellow Painter.

She ran to the door and shook it, putting all her strength into the effort. Then she kicked at the door, calling, "Sentry! Help me. Sentry!"

For a minute or two there was no sound. Then she heard the crack of floorboards under shuffling feet. She had no doubt they were the light moccasins of Yellow Painter and his Shawnees. She started back to the window and called out to the passing soldiers. Amid the uproar of voices, running feet and rolling wheels, her voice was lost. She was still there when the intruders shook the door with their combined weight. A second, a third time and the door burst open.

Across the room Hansi and Yellow Painter faced each other. Yellow Painter's teeth flashed in the morning light. "Fire-Dawn, you were promised to me by Chief Cornstalk long ago if the Shawnees took Fort Blaine. It was better for you if you had come to me then."

He moved silently over the carpet. Since there was no place to run, Hansi allowed herself to be hustled out of the room like a gallows-bird between two warders, with Yellow Painter going ahead, but though her limbs were stiff and icy, her wits began to work. If Jess Taga's men arrived inside the fort under flag of truce, her life and Kentuck's would be bargained for and very probably saved. But then the price occurred to her. The price of surrender was too great. And who would trust the word of men like Greathouse and Yellow Painter? Could they even trust Shelby Cameron who had already broken the Amnesty Conference and whose word was now worthless?

When she reached the parade ground with her captors, Hansi was pushed first one way and then the other by running soldiers. She welcomed the chance this gave her f escape and broke free, but Yellow Painter got his two ands around her waist and lifted her back into the midst f his comrades. Kentuck Helm was being dragged out of is prison by a rope tied to the cords that bound his ands. His wrinkled face looked swollen, marked with loody scratches and dark bruises, yet he managed to grin at her, lending her a little of his courage.

"He's here, lass. Old Jess'll get us out," he promised er before one of the Shawnees cuffed him across the mouth. He was like all the Long Knives who, though often older than Captain Taga, thought of him as their leader and savior, their indomitable "Old Jess."

Cameron had gone back up on the wall to watch the approach of the Long Knives bearing the truce flag. In the center was Captain Jess Taga, looking as dark and as fierce as Yellow Painter. He had not yet seen Hansi and Kentuck. Nor had Cameron.

Meanwhile, Cameron called down under the flag of truce, "May one ask how you arrived here so rapidly, captain?"

"Thanks to some help from my friend, the governor. He found out who you really are. He didn't like what he heard. Your hostages knew I would come. They knew nothing would keep me away. You should have known as well."

"And did you sprout wings and fly, sir?"

Jess laughed. "We've had the help of every French trapper on the Mississippi. I've had them handy since the night you disgraced our little parley. They know all the shortcuts, the best crossings. And they've been gathering my Long Knives for this march."

"Congratulations. But what do you offer to surrender?" Cameron asked as he descended the steps toward Jess and his men.

Neither Cameron nor Jess had yet glanced at the center of the parade ground. There stood the Shawnees, Daniel Greathouse, and their chief prizes, Kentuck Helm and Hansi Cameron.

Jess waited until Cameron had nearly reached him

before answering coolly, "Your Excellency mistakes ou
humanitarian effort. It is you who are invited to surrender
The French have joined our forces. The next step mus
be your surrender. Look over at the powder magazine."

Cameron barely did so, managing to preserve his own
dignity in a moment of potential ruin.

"I yield to your choice of words, sir. I have no in
tention of surrendering, but since you offer the oppor
tunity for discussion, what are your terms?"

"First, that you deliver up to the army of the Conti
nental Congress the towns of Arbreville, Kaskaskia and
Cahokia, as they are at present, with all stores and
ammunition. Second, that this garrison deliver themselves
as prisoners of war and march out with their arms
Thirdly—"

"You never did lack for impudence," put in Cameron
with his frosty smile.

"Thirdly, the garrison is to be delivered up this day at
noon."

One of the men who accompanied him, a Frenchman,
whispered to him. Jess grinned. "I am reminded of the
fourth condition, that the garrison settle accounts with all
traders of the city of Arbreville and its inhabitants
within three days. Fifth, and of first importance, that all
prisoners held by His Majesty's forces be turned over to
us at once, unharmed."

Cameron's dark eyebrows raised. "Are you finished?"

"Very nearly." Jess spoke softly now, but he was
heard by all those standing around the parade ground.
"Criminals of war will be turned over to this army for
transportation to Virginia, where they will be tried."

Hansi flinched at the blow this must be to her proud
husband whose dishonor would be known throughout the
civilized world. Cameron moistened his colorless lips.

"What criminals of war do you refer to, sir?"

"I name Major Hay, commander of Fort Sacklin, and
the Shawnee scout known as Yellow Painter to be two of
the principals. The third, the trapper known as Daniel
Greathouse. The fourth is the officer known to his Indian
allies as The Hairbuyer. You, sir."

Cameron had been prepared but it was plain to Hansi that most of the garrison and many of the French witnessing this scene were hearing the truth for the first time. Governor Rochblave, watching from a distance, was one of those who knew, and Hansi caught his faint smile. Cameron's name spread through the ranks and along the stockade walls and he looked up, well aware of the revulsion in every face. He was like a gladiator in the arena condemned by the mob. His cheeks flamed and his hand went to his sword, but the gesture was only instinctive, Hansi knew. Or perhaps he was done with the fight and thought only of making an end to this horror.

Jess said quietly, "If you will surrender your sword, sir—"

He was interrupted by Daniel Greathouse who called to Jess, "You do not ask *our* terms, captain. Lay down your arms. Surrender yourself to the colonel as a traitor to His Majesty's government."

At his challenge both Cameron and Jess turned and for the first time saw Hansi and Kentuck and their captors.

Yellow Painter, holding Hansi against his body with one arm, brought the other up under her chin with his scalping blade pressing hard against her throat. The blade still carried the stench of the French baker's drying blood. Another Shawnee shoved the point of his knife against the back of Kentuck's neck.

Indignation made many of the British mutter in protest but Kentuck could speak for himself. "Pay no mind to me, lads. Make your own deals."

Hansi tried to be as brave but the knife blade was too tight. She could not swallow, much less speak. Her tongue was like a dry stone. She saw the blaze of anger in Jess Taga's eyes and something else. He was afraid for her. He swung around to reach the Shawnee, but Yellow Painter put more pressure on the knife. Hansi felt the blood pounding in her head. Jess halted almost within reach of Yellow Painter.

Cameron kept moving, striding slowly toward Greathouse, as if in thought. The trader missed the melancholy

promise of death in the commander's dark eyes, and
boasted, "You'll listen to me next time, I think, sir. Take
the Long Knife prisoner while we've the chance."

Cameron glanced at Jess. Whatever passed in that exchange of looks between enemies, they had made their
plan, in a concerted effort. To the trapper, Cameron said
very quietly, "Your weapon."

Greathouse was taken by surprise. "Sir! We've got the
rebs where we want them. You will not destroy us all for
that damned little half-breed traitor. No. By God, you'll
not!"

"Give me your pistol. I order you!"

Attracted by the argument, Yellow Painter and the
Shawnees turned their heads to watch. It was the instant
both Jess and Cameron had counted on. Jess leaped for
Yellow Painter's head, cracked his two fists across the
Shawnee's skull just over the ear. The Shawnee's knife
dropped from his fingers as he wavered, his head wobbling
on his neck, and then fell.

Close by, between Cameron and Greathouse, the pistol
had gone off with a puff and a small explosion. At the
same time Kentuck's bound hands flailed out fiercely at
the two remaining Shawnees. Redcoats, Long Knives and
French poured out across the parade ground, stopping the
Shawnees. Hansi sank to her knees. Jess drew her to him,
comforting her gently.

"You are safe now, sweetheart. It's all over."

It was as if they had returned to the days at Fort
Blaine, before she dreamed of that far-off, handsome
stranger she had never really known. Jess kissed her.
"Better now? Feeling ready for another battle?"

She looked up with the beginnings of a smile.

"Ah," he said, "much better. We'll be fighting again in
no time."

She laughed and then winced as the sound tore at her
sore throat. She saw Governor Rochblave standing by,
calmly filing his fingernails. Having helped to throw out

is uninvited Redcoat guests, he now did the sensible
hing. He observed as others cleaned up the bloody mess
f the battle.

Lieutenant Fairfax passed them with his battered
risoner, Daniel Greathouse, still grinning. Jess looked
round, then down, more slowly, at Hansi. Much too late
he began to realize the significance of the trapper's being
live and walking.

"Jess! That shot I heard when you leaped at Yellow
Painter. Was it the trapper's pistol?"

Kentuck leaned over them. "Colonel's been askin' for
you, lass. Even men like that got feelings, I reckon."

With Jess' help Hansi got to her feet. She heard her voice
ask hoarsely, "Is it bad?" She did not wait for an answer.

Cameron lay where he had fallen. The dark blood had
spread over the breast of his uniform jacket and seemed
to gush out in ever wider circles. His eyes were closed.
He breathed with difficulty. A British officer had rolled
his own jacket beneath the dying man's head.

"Mistress Cameron, the colonel called your name."

Still badly shaken, Hansi grasped Jess Taga's hand
tightly before she sank down in the rapidly thawing mud
beside her husband's body.

"I'm here, Shelby."

He raised his hand toward her face but lost strength
and she took his fingers in her free hand.

He opened his eyes but she had the feeling that he did
not see her. He tried to speak. She lowered her head,
spoke his name again. He whispered, "I did not mean . . ."

Had he realized at last the horror of his crimes? But
when he tried again, it was on quite a different matter.
"I did not mean to strike you. You know that, didn't
you?"

"I know."

His eyes closed tiredly. Hansi looked up at Jess and
the soldiers gathered around. "Is he in pain?"

Jess shook his head. She bent over Cameron, kissed
his lips. They were cold to her touch. Jess knelt beside her,

touched Cameron's wrist and then his throat, beneath the collar.

"He is gone, Hansi."

She had thought she was too exhausted to cry, but the simple words caught her unawares.

When Jess lifted her from Cameron's side she could not explain, but he seemed to understand without words.

"What will happen now?" she asked, trying to change the direction of her thoughts.

Jess said, "We've won the frontier. Now let the toy soldiers win the Coast. Boys, send up our viper flag." And up went the Virginia Long Knives' pennant of the coiled rattler with its warning DON'T TREAD ON ME.

Hansi smiled at Jess' confidence but after his fantastically swift march over the forest frontier in record time she did not believe anything was beyond him. She looked around for the first time, seeing the activity everywhere as the bodies of dead and wounded were removed and the British Army prepared to evacuate the fort. Kentuck Helm and the Long Knives returned to inspect their former posts and the French civilians talked of balancing monetary accounts with the outgoing Redcoats.

Hansi studied the window of the room in which she had been held prisoner. She was too tired, too full of anguish at the sight of so much death to appreciate her own near escape, but after two years of a life that should never have been hers, nothing comforted her and made her as happy as the sight of Jess beside her, issuing orders, doing incredible things with ease, and reaching out to her now and then, just to be certain she was there.

"We're off for Sacklin when we've settled in a strong force here," he announced.

She laughed at his bravado. "One or two. Even a half dozen men might make it. But not an army. You know it would be impossible this time of year."

"Of course. And the hair buying major knows it. That is why he won't be expecting us. Surprise. That's how it's done, infant."

She shook her head, smiling wryly over his enthusiasm,

ut her knowledge of Jess Taga presently told her that he
ight very well succeed in doing the impossible.

I wish papa could have known we are together again,
he thought, and then, invigorated as always by the sight
f the bright morning sky, she whispered, "Perhaps he
oes."

Romantic Fiction

If you like novels of passion and daring adventure that take you to the very heart of human drama, these are the books for you.

☐ AFTER—Anderson	Q2279	1.50
☐ THE DANCE OF LOVE—Dodson	23110-0	1.75
☐ A GIFT OF ONYX—Kettle	23206-9	1.50
☐ TARA'S HEALING—Giles	23012-0	1.50
☐ THE DEFIANT DESIRE—Klem	13741-4	1.75
☐ LOVE'S TRIUMPHANT HEART—Ashton	13771-6	1.75
☐ MAJORCA—Dodson	13740-6	1.75

Buy them at your local bookstores or use this handy coupon for ordering: